Also by Mary Burns

Suburbs of the Arctic Circle
Shinny's Girls and Other Stories
Centre/Center
The Private Eye: Observing Snow Geese
Flashing Yellow
You Again

To Brian and Ann

THE REASON FOR TIME

Mary

Mary Burns

 ALLIUM PRESS OF CHICAGO

Allium Press of Chicago
Forest Park, IL
www.alliumpress.com

This is a work of fiction. Descriptions and portrayals of real people, events, organizations, or establishments are intended to provide background for the story and are used fictitiously. Other characters and situations are drawn from the author's imagination and are not intended to be real.

Book/cover design by E. C. Victorson

Front cover image:
Portrait of a young woman
photographer: Mathew J. Steffens
from the collection of Thomas Yanul (1940–2014)

Author photo by Rachael King Johnson

ISBN: 978-0-9967558-1-8

Library of Congress Cataloging-in-Publication Data

Names: Burns, Mary, 1944 author.
Title: The reason for time / Mary Burns.
Description: Forest Park, IL : Allium Press of Chicago, [2016]
Identifiers: LCCN 2016002001 (print) | LCCN 2016008555 (ebook) | ISBN
   9780996755818 (pbk.) | ISBN 9780996755825 (pub)
Subjects: LCSH: Irish Americans--Chicago--Fiction. | Chicago
   (Ill.)--History--20th century--Fiction. | Nineteen tens--Fiction. | United
   States--History--1919-1933--Fiction. | GSAFD: Historical fiction.
Classification: LCC PR9199.3.B7923 R43 2016 (print) | LCC PR9199.3.B7923
   (ebook) | DDC 813/.54--dc23
LC record available at http://lccn.loc.gov/2016002001

For the previous Marys

A secret is a grave/But who sees me?
I am my own hiding place.

Gaston Bachelard/Joë Bousquet

WORKING GIRLS

The working girls in the morning are going to work—
   long lines of them afoot amid the downtown stores
   and factories, thousands with little brick-shaped
   lunches wrapped in newspapers under their arms.
Each morning as I move through this river of young-
   woman life I feel a wonder about where it is all
   going, so many with a peach bloom of young years
   on them and laughter of red lips and memories in
   their eyes of dances the night before and plays and
   walks.
Green and gray streams run side by side in a river and
   so here are always the others, those who have been
   over the way, the women who know each one the
   end of life's gamble for her, the meaning and the
   clew, the how and the why of the dances and the
   arms that passed around their waists and the fingers
   that played in their hair.
Faces go by written over: "I know it all, I know where
   the bloom and the laughter go and I have memories,"
   and the feet of these move slower and they
   have wisdom where the others have beauty.
So the green and the gray move in the early morning
   on the downtown streets.

—Carl Sandburg, *Chicago Poems*

Author's Note

The Reason for Time is told in the voice of a young woman who lived through ten tumultuous days in Chicago, in July 1919. Words she uses reflect the language of her time, and what we now consider to be ethnic slurs are in no way intended to be disrespectful.

MONDAY, JULY 21, 1919

THE DIRIGIBLE FELL that fast gusts of pushed out air rustled my skirt around my ankles, and wasn't I across Jackson Boulevard by then, not knowing whether to tilt back my head to look or duck for cover? First the spreading shadow, then the odd shout sprung up from here and there, bunching into a roar when that big silver egg dropped flaming from the sky right onto the Illinois Trust and Savings Bank. And one of the parachutes meant for escape? Didn't that fall flaming too, a candle soon snuffed on the ground barely a block beyond. Others floated through the billows so thick you couldn't see what was attached to them, but you hoped it was someone made it out alive. "Look!" But where to aim your eyes first? *The Wingfoot Express.* Looked so impressive on the ground, it had, over there at the Grant Park field, but knowing how flimsy it turned out to be had me wondering what fools'd wanted to go along for what the papers called a joy ride. No joy for them that day, maybe never again.

The screaming started with the plunging made it more terrifying. A great boiling soup of sound, roar of fire, shattering glass, clanging bells, keening voices, clattering metal. Then an unholy minute, sure not even as long as a minute after the explosion, when them gas tanks fueled the airship went up and I might a been deaf. It was that still I thought I'd been killed, like all them in the bank and the fellows crashed into it. But I was not about to die then, no, not killed, only bleeding, and just a dab of blood it was on my neck, like something'd bit me. Window glass spitting way across Jackson Boulevard, could a been, and no one caring or even remarking that slight injury or me at all in the crush, as half the bodies in the Loop shoved forward, despite the police hollering at us all to make way for the big-wheeled fire trucks rolling in. The brave ones spilled off the trucks and aimed their ladders up the side of that stricken building, poked their fat hoses into the busted out windows to douse the inferno inside. Above the usual stink of smoke and horse droppings, the throat-catching billows of oily gas and also a singeing, like hair being marcelled in a hot iron.

We could only imagine the terrors. And who were all them yelling in there? The girl with the stained fingers took the envelope my boss Mr. R gave me to deliver, being too proud to go begging himself? Me admiring the lace collar on her shirtwaist, nice and narrow like a delicate frame around the throat of her maybe one of them hollering for help?

First the shock, then the curiosity and the crowd livened with the sort of thrill comes with fright, same as when the *Mauretania* steamed into New York harbor, everyone rushing the decks, and me and my sister Margaret—just girls—getting near lost in the excitement as I might well have become lost on Jackson Boulevard the Monday that July. I am small, I have always been small, and I early learned to make my way how best I could. Still, being closer to the ground than most, I never saw much of the goin's-on at the Illinois Trust and Savings. The man directly in front of me in his summer jacket, sweat bubbling above his starched collar, and all them in straw boaters or fedoras conspired to block my view. A pair of overalled colored boys too, maybe sixteen and just stepped off the northbound train, could a been, exclaiming in their funny voices, "Lawdy me," just like in the minstrel acts. Then laughing as if they found each other comical. From somewhere in the throng a newsie hollered,

AIRSHIP CRASHES! BIG SLAUGHTER!

His voice too tweaked by wherever his family'd dragged him from. Bold as brass they tended to be, the newsies. No papers could be printed instant as that.

Just minutes before, I'd waited for that lace-collared correspondent'd come through the wire cage from the grand rotunda with all its marble, and the light shining down through the glass above, throwing patterns over rows of desks with their identical lamps lit, though it was full afternoon. Lamps burning under shades the shape of flowers, prettier than we had at our place. The wire cage around the girls working on their letters and adding the day's receipts. How'd they got out? Or had they? God have mercy on their souls.

What a time, too, it being near five o'clock and people streaming out the office buildings. More and more people crowding into the street, all of them after joining we many already there and seeking what protection we could beneath the shoulders of the big bank buildings. Fair to perishing as the heat of the day pooled into that hour, yet jostling together all the same, claimed by the event, opinions motley as the crowd. How could I leave? The rest thinking the same, no doubt, for we milled around and rumors spread faster than the influenza took Packy the year before. Hundreds dead inside, including the bank president, who was to receive Éamon de Valera that day and wasn't he from our home place, Margaret's and mine, of Ennis, de Valera? And didn't he want money to take back for the new republic? Then came the report that it was not de Valera at all but Mr. Armour himself who'd been inside with the bank president.

"Counting his money!"

"Fried like his bacon!"

"God rest his soul, poor man."

"What soul? No heart. No soul!"

The crowd talking to itself, searching for reasons. Flying too low over the Loop, the *Wingfoot*'d been, and this to please the photographer who paid the dearest price for his ambition was one theory you could get for free. Another blamed the crew for smoking cigarettes inside the blimp. Like a regular conversation and all, except flattened beneath the haze of the sun and we straw-hatted mortals packed onto Jackson Boulevard like pigs and cattle jammed into the Union Stock Yards to the south. Horns blaring from a few trapped motorcars and just let a horse try to enter. Reporters from all the papers, and photographers with their big cameras popping as they forced in to record the scene.

We wouldn't know the facts of what was unfolding before us until we saw the morning editions, the sober stories chronicling the perished, how many'd died, and who. The very afternoon, the tallest, the closest, one of the ruffians bullied to the front may have seen it all, but the only dead body I glimpsed was slung over the shoulder of a fireman stepping down a ladder propped up against the bricks. One of the flyers, just a heap by then, could a been a suit of clothes coming down, rung by rung, on the shoulder of that courageous fellow.

A rumor whistled through about how the wrecked airship'd landed right on the vault and those at the front were grabbing wads of bills flew out with the window glass. That started more pushing and shoving and I nearly lost my hat, my sister Margaret's hat, truth be told, had the wider brim I'd wanted for later, when my chum Gladys and me'd planned a stroll in the park. Gladys worked for the Cosmo Buttermilk Soap Company in our same building, the grand building she told me about after sickness forced me to quit the catalogue company where we'd met. Gladys usually did all the talking, me being the quiet type, and no doubt'd wanted to spool out another chapter in the romance she imagined with Charles Francis Brown—the artist had a studio on the seventeenth floor of our Marquette.

On account of the commotion that afternoon, we never did get our stroll. Gladys'd run up to seventeen seeking comfort from Charles Francis, though she claimed she wanted only a view out his window, faced south and west, from where she could see the terrible goin's-on, never imagining that one of the heads under the hats belonged to me, Maeve Curragh. I had to pry off the lid to protect it, but when I found space enough to lift my arms and dig the hatpins out I could see the rim'd already bent in a way not intended. In the circumstances, Margaret would understand, and while she could not fix everything needed fixing, turned out, a hat'd never stumped her.

~

The papers? They did it somehow, managed to get a story in the last edition.

LEAPS FROM BALLOON ABLAZE!

Headlines standing like inch-high sayers of doom. Newsies shouting it and dressing up the story, praising the heroic firemen and they were heroes.

RICH AND POOR ALIKE PERISH!

yelled those dirty-eared boys had the imaginations, for they couldn't a known yet who'd died. People flocking round at the car stop to grab a sheet still wet with printer's ink, scraps from the morning editions and candy wrappers tamped beneath every kind of shoe. Reports blaring from front pages made a paper wall along the lineup.

WILSON IS ILL

KNIT WORKERS STRIKE FOR HIGHER PAY

HOUSE GIVES THE NOD TO HOME LIQUOR STORES

And there in the upper left box, under *The Very Latest News*, a paragraph telling how the dirigible'd been flying from Comiskey Park to the Loop all day, and hadn't we seen it pass ourselves, from our office on the ninth floor of the Marquette? Heard the motors humming, glimpsed the shadow it made on the tall buildings, and flocked to the windows for the sight. Not much of a story so soon, but enough to report how the airship'd fallen burning and people after drifting through the sky in parachutes. "A gigantic flame shot skyward." This time I knew more than the papers because I'd seen it all, yet didn't it seem more real when you saw it printed? Right there in black and white, and not just me reading it, no. All the big shots mattered to the city'd read the same. Really everyone.

When I squeezed onto the Madison car the conductor watched my nickel drop into the box and asked me what I'd been up to with my hat tilted so, an ostrich feather straying from the crown and my hair nearly undone. But he didn't say it neat like, talking directly to me and waiting an answer. Not that one with the peak pointed down his forehead like his wavy hair's a line of geese he's leading somewhere, the cap pushed up from his face flushed pink on account of the heat flowing in through the windows and from the temperature of passengers filled the facing forward seats, the benches, the standing room. No, not that one. He was regular on the Madison line, this one, a winker and a talker name of Desmond Malloy. I'd been pushed near up to a man saw him one evening and said in voice so loud you couldn't help but hear, "Is it you then, Desmond Malloy? The conductor himself? And how's your old da, lad?" He wasn't a lad no more, the conductor, and said as much to the fella. They continued their blather over my head, about the da and his bum leg had to be taken off, and wasn't it a sorrow for the mother and wasn't he lucky then to have four strapping sons to help their folks, and had he heard the latest from City Hall?

The man got off same stop I did and I stepped down after him, but if Mr. Desmond Malloy took any notice of me, he showed no sign of it until the evening of the day of the *Wingfoot Express*. I'd watched him, though. A handsome fella, and kind, too, to help his da, but what got me first was the droll nature of the man. He had a patter same as Uncle Josh in the vaudeville and he laughed at his own jokes same as Uncle Josh, too, using us, the riders as his subject, teasing, and it lightened the journey sometimes felt long at the end of the day and rough when the car jolted to a stop on account of a horse and buggy blocking the rails, or someone running across.

"Don't be shy, you with your feathers all ruffled. And her eyes sparkin' like she's got a new fella," he said to the other passengers, most who didn't hear, others who maybe smiled, because wasn't he going on again, this conductor came to seem our own, often here at the end of the day on the Madison line. Not till he peered down did it became clear he was talking to me.

"Would that be the truth of it, miss?"

In the crammed-to-the-windows car, my face—not the roses and cream some girls had, but fair enough still to blush—broke out in little patches of perspiration commenced to funnel right down to the corners of my mouth, and my instinct was to flick my tongue out to catch the drops since I hadn't the elbow room to dig for the handkerchief in my pocketbook. Sniffing, I said only if he'd seen what I saw, all the destruction and who knows how many killed, his eyes would be sparking too.

"What's that, miss?" he asked, leaning close, face tipped over mine. "The crash and all the destruction? You were there, then? You saw it all? The dirigible of death?"

"Hadn't I just been inside the bank myself?"

It came out as a whisper caused him to lean even closer, his breath a bouquet of tobacco and chewing gum.

"You've had the fright of your life now, haven't you darlin'?" he said. "And you are darlin', but you must have a name." Before I had the chance to tell him I did indeed have a name and it was no business of his, he pulled himself straight up, raised his voice, called out, "Halsted Street. Next stop, Halsted!"

Thousands of workers at the Yards'd walked out on Friday, but they'd walked back in today and those didn't live near could change at this corner for the Halsted line would get them to the Yards. Bodies crushed toward the door, separating the conductor, Desmond Malloy, and me. I watched the shoulders of his dark blue uniform bobbing among, and mostly above, the rest and when I got to the door myself there he stood with a rolled-up *Trib*.

"Have you seen the mornin' news, dear?"

Dear, was it now? And him aiming the paper towards my crooked elbow, poking it into the V it made along my sweaty side, me dipping my head in thanks and, with one hand on my hat, stepping onto the cobblestones slashed by the steel rails. And then, topping it all, didn't he wave at me? I laughed, despite the sad story I had to tell them all at Bridey's that night on West Monroe, up the block where most everyone had yet to learn about the terrible goin's-on downtown.

Oh, yes, I was all the rage, holding court at the back. The rickety assemblage Bridey called a porch, one of them landings on stairs angled down like the pleats of an opened squeeze box, like all the other stairs on that block and all the other blocks, so's you could nail up a clothesline on a house faced one street and connect to a house faced another street altogether. We got used to the sight of the neighbors' union suits, the dishtowels, and bed sheets decorating the alleys. Looking up, you could imagine a stage, really, like the makeshift shows they put on at the athletic clubs and at St. Patrick's Hall.

But that night Bridey's porch made the stage and me the star attraction, puffed up by the attention they were after paying me, the lingering fright, too. Margaret collected pennies from Lucille and Frances—girls also boarding with Bridey—and Mrs. Smith, Bridey's elderly relative from somewhere, not Ireland, put in her share. The two fellas had rooms on the floor below climbed up from where they'd been sitting to catch some air. Bridey sent her addled son, John, down the road to fetch a pail of beer. It turned into a party with me the guest of honor describing the whoosh of air and the crash, the minute fell silent, the fire in the sky, and the great lumpy pillows of smoke smothered the sun. Only then did I remember the piece of glass'd flown out and hit me in the neck and put my hand there, irritating the new-formed scab, and didn't fresh blood bubble up and raise a stir, everyone thrilled like they'd been there themselves.

"Did ye see any of the dead then, Maeve?"

Bridey Clancy's the one rented the top floor of a three-flat and made her living from we handed over the weightier half of our weekly pay to sleep in one of her hall rooms—three to start, but then the one she'd managed to divide somehow so's she could cram in another lodger and still have quarters to advertise as "private" on the sign in the parlor window. We had the smallest, Margaret and me. The two of us shared a bed no bigger than the straw pallet where we'd snuggled as children, yet it seemed smaller, Bridey's bed, for while neither of us was big, we had grown into women. Margaret near nineteen and engaged to be married, me the year older.

"God rest their souls," said Bridey, but her warty eyelids never fell over the staring washed-blue out of respect or nothing. Dark had mercifully taken over, and though the simpery drafts off the lake rarely reached us with any strength to speak of, we did get a whiff, at least, with its reminder of the afternoon downtown. Bridey, she lifted the bottom of her apron and mopped away whatever it was clung to that long black hair she couldn't see to pluck out, then, in her declining years. For Bridey it would be a slow decline, though I heard tell of her death only years after the fact of it.

"Just the poor fellow they carried down. But I told you that, sure."

"Do you know how many so? Was it hundreds?"

Bridey liked to imagine the worst, as if knowing would make her feel better about her husband got rolled into one of them machines at the steel plant. Could a been that, or something deeper in her character. If we didn't empty our wage packets, on the Saturday she wanted our rent, she predicted a dark road ahead for us, Margaret and me. We'd be condemned to one of them houses with a shaky reputation. We would turn into the type of girl picked up soldiers and such at Dreamland, or loitered at the athletic clubhouses where the rough and fast fellas peeled their eyes for girls who didn't know better. Yes, there were many places—and Bridey'd cited all of them—where a body could drift into a situation would start tears in her mother's eyes. Girls!

Yet she knew we'd last seen our mother near to eight years back, her hugging us and kissing us and knotting her fingers in my tangles, pulling my head back and studying my face as she did when some notion took hold. Searching me as if I were a stranger she'd found by surprise, or the field beyond, and making me promise to look after my sister, and not to forget her or him—our mammy or our da—or Fiona, who'd died since we left, or little Nuala, or our Gran, or Uncle Thomas. All we were leaving behind. She let go my hair to reach in her apron pocket and pull out a boiled sweet for each of us. Then she turned her head and pointed her chin out as if looking off at that field again or some fascinating sight, for wasn't it the best thing that two of her daughters had the vocation? And wouldn't the nuns find more for us to eat than our crippled da?

Girls! After what we'd seen?

We sat outside until the singing started, Margaret and me, though the others went in before, first Bridey, for all she hated to miss anything. There was only so much to tell and I'd told it, and she needed her bed. "How in heaven's name will I ever get any rest, with the image of them poor burning people filling my head?" she asked, accusing me like. Though hadn't it been her wanting the gory details?

"Do you think it was burnin' skin you smelled so?"

"I wouldn't doubt it, then, Mrs. Clancy. That smell, like scorchin' the hair off a pig. But we'll learn what's what when we see the mornin' editions."

"You bring one back with you and then we'll be up to snuff and there might be pictures."

They all knew me to be mad for the papers and hadn't Desmond Malloy guessed it, too? Touching the inside of my elbow with that one rolled up, his teeth gleaming as he smiled big. I picked up the *Daily News* most evenings, first searching on the car for one left, only spending my two cents when I had no luck. If Margaret'd stepped out with her Harry, I took it to Thompson's or one of the other neighborhood lunchrooms and had myself a good read with my supper. Still, I accepted the *Trib* from Desmond Malloy and not just because it was himself offering it. In our life we'd a been fools to refuse what we could get for free, even if it meant saving only a couple a pennies. I did not wonder to myself right off what it might cost me and isn't it a marvel how we don't know. How the time we're in is like the narrow part in an hourglass, where sands from the past gather only to separate and land in different places in the time to come. Or so we thought until that wild-haired scientist fellow—same one stares at me now, from the picture on the wall across from where I lie, on this bed bound to be my last—while that fellow showed how the past can drift into the future and the future dribble into the past, and plenty of sand stalls right there in the middle of the hourglass, like that week in Chicago when everything happened at once.

I certainly took the paper. Why not?

The singing and the fighting combined, your fiddle and your drum, the regular orchestra along this stretch as the men stumbled back from the saloons. Common as the clackety-clack, the screeching of the last cars, the clop of horse hooves, the wailing of babies, angry words dashed out windows, and sometimes hollering, too, before the street settled. Still, we didn't want to go in, Margaret and me, for we'd been through the world and all since sucking on those sweets our mammy gave us, and this new thing caused us to marvel at how near Death stands. That batch taken so spectacular, like the big city itself, full of noise, bluster. People from every corner of the earth, skin in every color skin can be, the rhythms of the talk, the words themselves unfamiliar as the mouths spoke them.

Too, with the rest of them gone, I could tell Margaret about the car man gave me the paper. Desmond Malloy. Desmond with that hairline arrowed down over his forehead, eyes green as the moss that furred the stones in the old friary on Mill Street, in the home place, and eyebrows shaped like the friary's arches, that same tumbledown building where we Ennis children played, the daring most of us. Margaret didn't recall the friary as clearly as me, though she'd tagged along and I'd helped her scramble over the stone sill to join the others in the weeds inside.

"A paper, though, Maeve, not the crown jewels. They're terrible flirts, them car men."

Margaret scanned the alley where some animal—could a been a rat, for the rats were big as piglets—scratched for garbage, snuffled and whimpered a little, so maybe a dog not a rat.

"It's the land of the shillelagh and my heart goes back there daily, to the girl I left behind me when we kissed and said… Goodbye…" If not as many Micks here as in Bridgeport and some of the other neighborhoods in the city, them that were let you know it. Yet 'twas no John McCormack crooning down there, and she drifted, Meggsie did, the beginning of a doze. Soon a bottle crashed against the house and someone yelled down for quiet. "Working people need their sleep," said the shouter. That woke her up and she let me steer her in, and she paddled at the basin while I lay on our bed staring at the roses ghosting out from the dark wallpaper, remembering those days when the odd finger of sun fell on the mossy stones of the old Ennis friary. They appeared that soft you wanted to lay your cheek on them.

TUESDAY, JULY 22, 1919

I HAD TO TELL her, didn't I? Not only did the woman need to know Margaret and me could pay each week for our room, Bridey Clancy had the curiosity of someone didn't get out much, but parsed the world through the boarders she pried open with her questions.

"The Chicago Magic Company? I won't have no spells or nothin' under my roof, miss."

I wanted to turn up my lips in the way I'd seen Mr. R do when a customer stepped into the shop and, his voice gone all sandy, Mr. R revealed what he called the grand mystery of illusion—*It's all in the power to make people believe.* Only to tease, sure, but Bridey kept her place clean and provided us with leftover slivers of soap and a gas plate in the room, and gave over a square of her ice box for our provisions. We'd needed a place for us both once Margaret turned in her cap and her apron, and Packy's mother—the lady would a been my mother-in-law, Mrs. Dwyer she was—knew a good woman had a clean house on the Near West Side, didn't charge too much. There we were then, through everything, until Bridey Clancy pointed us to the door.

"Oh no," I said to Bridey that first day. I told her Mr. R made me swear an oath of secrecy, her not knowing about my history with vows, them promised devotion in exchange for passage. "You have to be a member of the magician's society to learn such things, Mrs. Clancy. I'm just the girl movin' orders along in the back."

Still, she never stopped peering at me curiously, suspicious, imagining more to me than you'd think a small body could hold. "I knew it," she said in the end. "Didn't I know all along." But not that day. When Margaret and I went out the Tuesday morning, Bridey only stood at the landing.

"Don't forget the papers so, Maeve," she reminded me, and I promised her that I never would. Not that day especially.

AIRSHIP AFIRE CRASHES
THROUGH LOOP BANK ROOF

BLIMP BURNS, KILLS 12
THOUSANDS SEE CREW LEAP IN PARACHUTES

MARTIAL LAW FOR RIOT IN CAPITAL?
5 DEAD, SCORES INJURED

You could stand near the stacks, read the headlines as the papers flew up into the hands of readers while the curly haired little wop newsboy—looked small to be doing the job he did, still in short pants, and with a cap above his swarthy face—while he chanted in a sing-song loud as one of them stars on stage.

MOTHER SOBS OVER MESSENGER BOY
BURNED TO A CRISP!

And the boy kitty-corner made a duet of it,

BATHIN' BEAUTIES GET THE NOD! PITCHERS!

Today none of that was enough, and I couldn't wait to see if I found a paper on the car. I handed my coins over to the little Italian and took the morning *Trib*.

The smoke came as if self impelled, driving all before it, a perpetual explosion. It was inexhaustible; one stared, waiting to see it stop, but still the great streams rolled out. They spread in vast clouds overhead, writhing, curling, then uniting in one giant river, they streamed away down the sky, stretching a black pall as far as the eye could reach.

That's how it was, sure, the paper had it right enough, smoke writhing and curling in a giant river pushed by the wind from the lake. Those hadn't seen the tragedy must've smelled it. But those had seen it turned out to be wrong in their reports of the victims, for it was not the bank president, nor Mr. Armour, nor the Paddy from Clare neither, but just ordinary souls lost in that awful wreck. Another full-inch-tall headline under the date—July 22, 1919—and the names of the dead like to spilling over a black-bordered box. Thirteen in all and two of them boys, messenger boys, one of them just fourteen.

Well, hadn't I been younger still when I took Margaret by the hand and the two of us set off with the nuns for America? Both of us put to work you'd think more than a child ought to do. The eternal scrubbing of the pine-board floors, the soapy tubs for washing clothes and bed linen, looking after children, some the dark-skinned ones scared us so at first because we'd never seen skin stayed dark after a good scrub. We had bushels to learn. Never stopped that, the learning.

I came to love the babies, many of them grew the nappy hair, its feel of fresh-dug turf, and the eyes big and merry unless they were wailing out of loneliness or hunger, for those hadn't been abandoned to the care of the Sisters of Perpetual Grace lived there because their mammy was sick and they had no da. Didn't the little ones make me think of home and the sister we'd left, Nuala? Who'd just stood on her own for the first time and walked a few steps, and hadn't she then tried to follow us out the wicket gate?

Fourteen he was, the youngest of them the airship finished. And if it wasn't bad enough the messenger lad'd had to quit school, he'd been killed on his second week at work! What about his family sent him out for it? Now they'd be missing what he brought in, what would become of them in their sadness and misery?

I opened my pocketbook, thinking to gnaw a bit of the bread I packed with my boiled egg for lunch—food taking the place of a comforting arm around me—and there's a candy I missed, or Margaret put there to surprise me before we said goodbye at the corner. A caramel, too, soft, as if the Blessed V'd ignored the things we'd done to get here and was smiling down, saying, *Here you are, Maeve, don't feel bad.* The Holy Mother taking the place of what my own mother would a done in the same circumstance.

"Here she comes!"

As if we were, all of us waiting there, too deaf and couldn't hear the rumbling wheels ourselves, see the front end of the car swaying like a hound's nose sniffing right, then left. The burning eye at the front glaring through the thin milk light of the summer morning.

Car already full this close to the Loop, but I could hook my arm around a pole and hold the paper out and the greasy ink would not soil my shirtwaist.

DEATH IN HOSPITAL SWELLS BLIMP TOLL

The last to die, the thirteenth, a photographer. *Herald Examiner* man name of Norton, and him after asking if the equipment he'd tried to bring out with him'd suffered much from the fall. If his pictures'd survived. Well, they never did, nor him neither. Another story about how aircraft would no longer be allowed to fly through the Loop, no matter who wanted to photograph it, and how Mayor Thompson would ask the Congress and them for laws. The reporters got to use their best language, scribbling about the horror and how crowds were after jamming the bank for a look at the destruction, and the bank manager saying there'd been no money lost, as'd been rumored, and only a small fraction of the bank's business area damaged and even that not beyond repair.

Then a big advertising space the bank'd taken to announce it'd be open for business as usual, with a promise the Goodyear company would make it right for the thirteen dead and all the injured. We never did learn what they got, the victims, if anything.

I steadied my arms best I could so's the letters wouldn't dance and dizzy me as I read, glancing out now and then to see the sun pink the sky way over there by the lake. It was going to be hot as blazes again, maybe hotter than yesterday. The air already boggy, no wind.

~

Cooler in our place, at least the front shop with its polished dark-oak shelves of curiosities—the satin capes, the wands, the glossy top hats, and purple wizard caps with silver stars sewed on them. Decks of cards for sale and magic boxes with secret compartments and special coins to use for tricks, glass cases for the best illusions. Old posters showed Mr. R striking various splendid poses, and, in a frame only painted gold but appearing actual, Houdini himself, his eyebrows bent over tortured eyes, as if on this occasion he might be foiled by the handcuffs binding his crossed arms at the wrists. Every morning I turned the patterned brass knob beneath the frosted glass with its arc of letters said *The Chicago Magic Company*, entered the shop and greeted pretty Florence—always there before me and standing at the counter—that picture of the Great Houdini started me thinking of the fixes Margaret and me'd been in and got out of, same as the man himself.

To keep his place the biggest magic concern in the center of the country, Mr. R was always scheming, thinking. He wanted to expand the enterprise, add a bureau specially for touring magicians wanted to try out their newest tricks. It's why he'd sent me to the bank the day before, with a letter he said would outline his vision. He no doubt wanted a loan of money to fit out the place, too, or why describe his plan to a bank? But he never said. Typical of him to be so formal when he had a telephone in the office, could have called for an appointment. But, no, he liked to keep his schemes close to his vest and do things the old-fashioned way, Mr. R, and hadn't my errand put me right in the middle of a true historical event?

In the space behind the shop at the front, closed-in cubes housed Mr. R, and Mr. M—the Rainbow Paper Company proprietor shared our place, though we never saw him much. An opened up room had a row of desks for me, Eveline, Ruth, and the big raised table where George, our artist fella, scratched out the drawings for the catalogues, the tricks, or effects so-called, and the paper party favors Mr. M hawked in a publication of his own. George didn't work every day, but when he did come he bent over his tilted board near the window looked out over South Dearborn Street. Then there was Billy, the stock boy, who did come every day but only for the couple of hours it took him to package up what'd been ordered and load the packages into a big bag for the postman, and to tell us the latest joke he'd picked up. Billy hoped to take to the stage himself one day and he practiced on we girls at the back whenever he had the chance.

'Twas a grand building to enter each morning with them Indian heads carved in bronze above the elevator doors around the foyer, the bright blue mosaic set out in pictures made of thousands of stamp-sized tiles, the story of Jolliet discovering Chicago, and Père Marquette trying to make Catholics out of the Indians. Eight months into it I liked to choose my elevator, the one under Black Hawk, or Hairy Bear, the names alone spinning my mind into wild fantasies. But the day I entered first—shy-like, the beauty of the place dwarfing me same as the tall buildings outside—I followed the gloved hand of the colored man, Clyde, waved me through the ridged marble pillars towards an open cage without even noticing which head hung over the one I stepped into. Hadn't I felt I was getting away with something?

Yet it was Gladys told me about the job, and Gladys a girl just like me meant anybody could work there, and so I rode up to the ninth floor where Mr. R himself presided over the counter at the time. He wanted two girls, one to handle the front so as to leave him free for other business, his studying and practicing, his jawing, his cigar smoking, but he could tell right off I didn't have the zing to chat with the parlor magicians and the vaudeville types visited the shop. As he studied my face, divining me, the heat spread over my cheeks same as lard on the bread the sisters would take out of the mission's big oven at swallow's cough, before the sun crawled up the sky and all the little ones woke hungry.

A sorcerer himself, Mr. R dressed natty in clean cuffs and collar each day, his black hair slicked a quarter to one side, the rest to the other, like an open book more than half-read, his mustache an even brush above lips thin as Bridey's soap. George used Mr. R as a model for many of the drawings in the catalogue. He managed a good likeness, too, save for the eyes, the small blue-black points drilled into me that first day. Drilled but didn't penetrate, for he said, "I take you for the trustworthy type."

He never invited me to sit down or nothing, but said why he needed more staff was because he aimed to attract all the magicians, the conjurors, and spiritualists passing through the city. Countless numbers of them had to be because every show in all the many theaters offered an act of the kind, from the simple ones where things appeared and disappeared—some fellow in a tuxedo plucking a real rabbit, twitching and twittering with fright, out of one of them hats like displayed on the shiny dark shelves—to the most mysterious. Mr. R held forth, describing dreams that turned out to be harder to realize than rabbits. For wasn't he after the biggest fish, even Blackstone and Thurston, and the young card man Vernon, even the Orientals. Imagined a cozy room, he did, where he'd set out a bottle and a humidor and his newest invention and, under the spell of the camaraderie he'd created, Mr. R would learn the secrets he craved and all them others could demonstrate their new acts. Sounded a grand dream to me, and didn't my heart speed thinking maybe Anna Eva would visit, too, though she was getting on then and you didn't find her touring to Chicago often.

I'd seen her myself, at the vaudeville, with Gladys, us sitting up top the balcony of the Majestic—but closer would have been too much then, it being my first show. There I sat in my best shirtwaist and a hat so big the man behind asked me to hold it in my lap. Anna Eva came on late, the surprise guest, when I wondered how there could be any more. Already a chimp'd circled the stage on roller skates, a girl'd danced with a chair between her teeth. There'd been a ragtime song and dance by a man in blackface. A couple of fellas wearing tall hats and sporting mustaches stretched out beyond their cheeks, with boots'd clomped across the boards, got in some kind of pretend-tussle. The audience'd stamped their feet and some'd whistled when one of the cowboys chased the other off.

When the music changed to something eerie, caused shivers, Gladys squeezed my arm. The grand velvet curtain—always red they were—lifted in gathers and there she was, Anna Eva herself, though I didn't know her name just then. Anna Eva standing, her fair head bowed until the curtain, hoisted high as it would go, let clouds of vapor escape from even higher. Seemed like she stood in the sky. Cheers greeted her appearance and her lips curled in that sweet smile I came to dream of later. Dressed all in white she was, silk, lace-trimmed, and the man introduced her—a young man in a tuxedo and hair with the shine of patent leather, such as I was to see on Mr. R—that fellow shouted out, "Ladies and gentlemen, I am privileged to introduce the fabled woman of mystery, the very same that stumped the Great Houdini, the incomparable Anna Eva Fay who will perform her famous cabinet mystery!" Mystery he called it, not trick. We saw her tied into the cabinet, heard a banjo playing, tambourine rattling, saw them same objects fly out, then her, standing untied. A marvel, really, and it made us all laugh with amazement, most of us, them not doubters. How did she do it? we wondered, and since then I have found out. But the real magic came with the mind reading I was to see later, just the summer before that Tuesday in Chicago when Mr. R hired me to work for him at the magic company.

The trustworthy type, he said. Anna Eva herself could not have been as convincing as me that day. Makes me think I did have the gift Mammy saw in Ennis. Comes from having been born before dawn. A present from her could a been, and why her regard lingered on me the moment of our leaving. Yes, I have considered that, how I foresaw the opportunities I would discover at Mr. R's place, even if it was only a job I wanted then. Yet, if I could truly see what others could not, it had to be a knack came and went. Or maybe 'tis a body resists what she knows because feelings drive harder than reason. The bold in me moving ahead, hadn't it always been so? Worthy of trust? Me looking for employment and all, I only let my head tilt to the side and smiled and so came to be situated at a desk in the back, sorting the cash from the money orders, sending out the tricks, the illusions, so-called. Illusions when all we really had back there was a mess of paper.

July heat climbed through the morning as I slit open envelopes, divided a few coins and bills from the money orders and stamps customers were supposed to send and mostly did. It's the rare bird ignored the advice at the front on the catalogue: *Currency, etc. should be sent only in Registered Letters.* Then time for lunch, and we three girls, plus Florence, from the front, quit the building to nibble whatever we had, in whatever shade we could find on the street. It was relief more than food we wanted, and we could have gone to the park, or down the block to State Street to shop the big store windows, but we hadn't long and we only wanted a lake-sent breeze, really, something resembling fresh air. You'd think all the talk among us would a been about the airship crash and a load of it was so, because hadn't I been there to see for myself and they wanted my account of it, same as the boarders at Bridey's. I showed them the small wound on my neck and we shook our heads over them perished.

"Big loss. I saw one of them airmen myself at Grant Park on Sunday. And I can tell you girls, he was a fine lookin' man," Eveline said and winked, suggesting more than she wanted to let on. Typical of Eveline, that teasing. The newest of us, having started at The Chicago Magic Company less than two months before, we'd become used to her by then and for the most part liked her. Eveline was one implied more than revealed things, so for all we knew she'd slipped away with the airman for a cocktail or a dance before he set off on his fatal crash.

"If it was the pilot you saw, it doesn't matter if he was handsome. He's one of the few who got out alive. Didn't you see in the papers? He landed safely on a roof and that's not fair at all. Not when it was his fault." This from a frowning Ruth. "I don't see how you can feel sorry for a man who caused the death of so many innocents. Just gone to work, same as every day, then poof! Dead. They say it was a German balloon, too."

"I hear they've got him under arrest," said Florence.

Could be hard to hear out there with the motorcars firing and the newsies bawling the latest and all of a sudden a brass band coming from somewhere. Then, too, Ruth spoke in a high, almost whiny voice, childlike. Eveline talked tough and dressed better than the rest of us and not because Mr. R gave her any more in her pay packet. She came to work with nails painted and her lips swollen and rouged. My chum Gladys said Eveline got up to mischief with men, as if she was shocked by it. But maybe Gladys'd like to have been getting up to the same with Charles Francis Brown on the seventeenth floor. She laid her opinion of Eveline on how she dressed and that laugh of hers, which could feel like a slap. Gladys never liked my work mate, but she often came out with us all the same, Gladys did. Some days just the two of us strolled along State, searching for an idea to bring back for Margaret to make for us. Margaret being a crack seamstress could copy anything and Gladys was always one for the latest fashions.

That day, with the stink of the crash still in the air, Eveline held back any smart remarks might a hatched in her mind—employed a respectful tone, in my view. "It was a Goodyear balloon. Same as the tire company. You could see it on the front. Goodyear. You can't blame the Krauts for everything."

"Easy for you to say. But if it wasn't for all them Germans, my Walter would have been here and I wouldn't be spendin' my days with all youse." Florence blinked back the tears fountained up every time she mentioned the name. Her Walter.

The moment must've been specially sharp for her as the brass band passed at the corner, six or eight players in blue with gold braid across the chest leading a cluster of doughboys up Madison, them maybe just come back. The band played the song everyone knew by then, "Till We Meet Again." Could be sad, but less sad on this occasion seeing how the marchers in brown had returned. Not Walter, though.

Even me'd lost someone. Patrick Dwyer was never a soldier, not with that weak arm of his, and despite him trying to strengthen it with exercises didn't do much good, no guarantee it'd ever be good enough for shooting. But the flu came home with the boys and got Packy. No Germans, only the flu. His sweet ways flare in my memory even now, him going on and on about how smart I was, how brave I'd been to leave Ireland on my own—well I'd never told him about the Sisters of Perpetual Grace—how pretty I was, so's he'd almost had me believing it. The sisters said girls must watch the sweet talkers because they knew what they were after trying to accomplish with their sugared words. Too many of them words like too many candies could make you sick, except, in the case of the sweet talkers, you might find yourself the kind of sick that lasts for the rest of your life. They liked to put the fear of God in us, the sisters did, and we guessed their meaning while also knowing it wasn't always true. Things people told me flicker through my thoughts unexpectedly like that and with them come pictures—Sister Mary Theresa, her face squeezed into a raised round biscuit by the white wimple under her black veil, her gums pale red above small teeth when she smiled.

Despite her no doubt good intentions, she was wrong about Pat. He acted proper, not like some of the toughs held up the walls at the club dances in Hamburg and Canaryville looking for an easy girl. We'd tried those dances, Margaret and me. A lot of drinking and fights out back and priests there to oversee the goin's-on and politicians strolling in, some of them not bothering even to take the cigars out of their mouths, but chomping down with one side of their jaw as they leaned into you and shouted over the music, "Havin' fun, honey?" More proper, too, my Pat than them employed young Bridgets—Bridget being what housemaids were called. Rich old fellas tried to have their way with maids like Margaret in the big houses on Prairie Avenue. Despite her weekly pay, plus a room and her meals, and all the things she learned about how fine folk laid the table and groomed themselves, Margaret ran off the first time the man of the house tried to kiss her.

Yes, Packy was a gentle one. I'd seen it right away. Him sitting in the chair just beside me in the church hall, his mother on the other side of him. The youngest of a family of four and the last home, his mammy maybe hanging on to him. But he got her to invite Margaret and me out for ice cream after the show featured some of the parish children dancing. Couldn't a been more genteel. While Mrs. Dwyer was describing her particular sort of hip stitch to Margaret, I found him staring at me, and smiled. Must have encouraged him, because next thing wasn't he asking if he could meet me after my shift at the catalogue company the very next day. Himself he worked for the city. Already moving up in the sanitation department, thanks to his folks being good Democratic voters and him knowing what he was after.

Mere weeks we walked out together before the night he took my arm and steered me across State Street. Stood me to supper at a restaurant with white cloths on the tables and napkins big as a child's shirt, chairs padded with velvet. Me marveling it was Maeve Curragh of old Mill Street, Ennis in the scene, for I hadn't pictured the same, even if they often said at home I'd got the gift same as our mammy. You can see the good people in the night, Mammy'd whispered, when I'd wake, frightened. But I have rarely seen them so much as felt their presence, like a rheumatiz knowing when a storm's about to come.

There he sat across the smooth white napery, Packy, his hair slicked back, color of rust rained on, his eyes shining as he talked about the future he saw for us. Me just going along, nodding, enjoying the gleam of the polished cutlery, the lamps hanging down over us shedding light yellow as cream clotted at the top of a pail, all the while thinking I'd be changing from the leader to the one led and how that would happen, I didn't know. But fat sizzling along the bone of a hefty chop and taties on a platter decorated with parsley, coin-sized carrots sliding in butter. I appreciated a good meal and it felt nice with someone taking care of me. Didn't I remember the evening fondly, too, when things changed that fast, well before Christmas. I never got the ring he promised me, but had only memories, same as I had of home.

~

Finally done for the day, slipped into the stream flowing towards the tall brass doors whirled a body from the vestibule out to the street. Knowing my choice rested between Bridey and her back stairs or our oven of a room, I got off the car at Halsted, as I often did, but instead of heading up to West Monroe I meandered along the street to enjoy a bit of the evening stench, the clouds of it blowing north from the Yards, then also garbage rotting and sweat-dripping horses, the wheezy motor cars and trucks with their billows of gas exhaust, the reek of urine along the walls outside the saloons. More open there on Halsted, brighter so. Even though a dirty sky, I could see more of it here than downtown, where buildings rose so tall they darkened the streets beneath.

I had to walk past the Academy of Music and wasn't I tempted to duck in and see a show, for they played all day and not many days didn't need lightening with a laugh. But I had to choose between a show or supper tonight, because we'd splurged on Sunday, Margaret and me, and it was too hot to sit indoors anyhow. The old ones sat out on stoops, crones with shawls draped around them in the scant shade of doorways. Signs tempting from above, or painted right on the window, *Ice Cream Sundae, 10¢,* and didn't that one wet my mouth with longing. A storefront movie theater, had to be Italian with all the i's in the words. The mission on the corner where a man held a placard said, "Jesus Saves." Lunch counters and proper, if not especially fancy, restaurants, Thompson's cafeteria further down and delicatessens where the proprietor would slice me off a smidge of cheese or meat I could eat in my hand as I walked if I wanted. Oh, yes, and I was famished and the memory of lunch dry as the bread made up that meal. I'd a liked nothing more than a cold soda or one of them lemonades you could buy at the café on the corner where Halsted met Madison.

Thought to myself, wouldn't it be nice to idle here till the sky went pink again and it wasn't so blinding out, blinding even if a layer same as the gauze strips you'd put over a bleeding wound spread over the city of Chicago where my sister Margaret and me'd come to meet our futures. I'd already spent a nickel for my fare, though I might've had it still if Desmond Malloy'd been collecting on my car. Yes, that one, and hadn't he been sneaking into my dreams all day? Good chance he would a let me slip by for free, since he'd made such a fuss yesterday.

But I was left with only four nickels and where to spend them? The sizzle of sausages from one of the Hunky places, that salty cheese you could get from the Greeks if you could suffer the garlic on the vendor's breath. Well, we'd had a grand time, my sister and me, at the show on Sunday. We'd laughed at the vaudeville and we'd cried at the picture, and even if it cost us a good portion of our weekly wages, I never saw one so beautiful. *Broken Blossoms*, and in a movie palace so grand made you forget your near empty pocketbook. Maybe it meant more bread than meat till the next payday. Didn't matter. More than the gut needed satisfying.

Then a tap on my shoulder and me, startled, turning round to see the moss on the friary stones boasting its softness. The hair shooting back from that arrow point and the barest strip of scarlet around the boiled ham forehead, and his hat in his hand, but a boater instead of the conductor's billed cap he wore on the cars.

"Fancy meetin' you on this night of nights. The girl who saw it all, and them still countin' the dead. What's that I see above your collar?"

He gazed down at me, so I wondered if my hat'd gone crooked again, or my shirtwaist'd got soiled as well it might have at the end of such a day. But it's the nick, from yesterday, he saw as he bent down, breezing me with the smell of beer.

"'Tis a souvenir of the disaster yesterday, though I don't need remindin'. But why would this night be special, then?"

Another American holiday or some other occasion I'd missed in my ignorance? No, but the game his men lost, the White Sox, and it's no surprise to me he should a been pinning his dreams on those fellas like most of the rest in the city. I rarely dawdled for long in the sports pages, but I'd seen pictures of the players lined up in their uniforms. They were going to win the World Series of baseball, everyone said it, though the world they talked about included only the U.S. of A., as far as I could tell. No one imagined their precious white would turn to black, all those men be shamed before the year was out.

"That's the tragedy, then, is it? Not the airship crash, or the soldiers returned in one piece can't find jobs to feed themselves?"

It's like he never heard me. He was shaking his head as he was smiling, his lips pursed together. A dimple the size of a pencil eraser dented his left cheek and them eyebrows went up. Still, he did look beat and I was after thinking it had to be more than a game troubling him. But I aimed to keep my gaze hard as the glare of the sea on the rare days sun blessed our crossing, and I drifted—as I do when the past rises—and the seconds ticked along while I tried to think of what to say next, but then he spoke.

"Have you had your supper yet, darlin'? I confess your name has slipped my memory, it bein' such a day, but I'm just off to have my own and would be pleased to have you join me."

I lied, saying of course I'd had my supper, because it'd all of a sudden gone to mid-evening blue—I'd strolled that long—and a girl with a proper family would a been home and come back, if she was out at all.

"Well, then, sit with me while I have mine. You might enjoy a dish of ice cream or a lemonade. What do you say, dear? Cheer me up? There's a café at Madison where they make a nice lemonade. Go down very smooth on a steamin' evenin' like this."

Dear, he said, and darlin', as if he'd known me for months, after just confessing he'd forgotten my name, not remembering I'd never mentioned it. I shrugged, as if I hadn't been thinking of that café myself.

"Cheer you up, is it? Well, then I suppose I could, for a short spell, because I'm after meetin' my sister soon. That'd be Margaret Curragh, while I am Maeve."

I fibbed about Margaret to give myself an escape. Yet, as the hour whiled by, I regretted it, because he persuaded me to have a piece of pie with my drink and winked at the lady—old as Bridey could a been, but looking done-in and wearing a skirt soiled with something must a dropped on it—when she mentioned the à la mode would be extra. It was cherry inside and came lovely with cream dripping over the sugar sparkle of the brown crust. She didn't look at me at all when she set it down, but—smiling, the years as if melted away—asked him if he'd like to take cream in his coffee.

"Thank you, dear. I will." He took out a package of cigarettes, shook one loose and lit it, and his right eye went squinty with the smoke curling up towards the ceiling fan.

"Dickie Kerr's the disappointment. If they wanted to use a southpaw they should a gone with Lefty Williams. He's the man. If they'd asked me I would a said, 'Pull Dickie,' but no one asked and no one listened to the experts in the stands, and so we lost the series when we could a made a clean sweep of it."

The waitress then brought his dinner on a thick white plate, heavenly fumes streaming up from the meat, slices of it drifting in a dark gravy soaked up by a hunk of bread even thicker than the plate. I should a bitten my tongue for thinking it more dainty to pretend to be full when I had enough appetite to finish his plate, my pie, and more still.

"I've had my supper," I'd said, as if I'd never missed a meal. Pride's a virtue suited better to the well fed, but there was nothing for it then but to stretch out the pie forkful by forkful, taking a bit in my mouth and savoring the difference between the soft tart filling and the crisp pastry. Listening, too, for he blathered as he stabbed and cut, pierced, chewed, swallowed. Like a man ought to eat. Despite my own hunger, it was gratifying in itself to watch Desmond Malloy campaigning his way through that meal—juice dribbling onto his bristly chin, him wiping it with the back of his hand between words that described the defeat his beloved White Sox suffered at the hands of the Yankees from New York.

That he was a man of strong feeling I could guess by the way the lights and darks shifted on his face as the story wound out. He grinned at the recollection of one thing, frowned at something else, and the melody of his voice rose and fell and occasionally paused as he gulped and the big knuckle in his throat jogged up and down in a fascinating way. I recalled the picture in yesterday's paper of the dirigible preparing to take off from Grant Park.

The ropes'd held it fast until it rose to its fate. Sitting there across from the streetcar conductor my heart lifted, not entirely off like that airship, but like a conveyance intended to soar, only tethered to the ground for the time being.

It'd gone to near night outside and the waitress had taken our plates and I'd sucked my glass dry, but Desmond Malloy showed no signs of wanting to leave. I wondered if I should get up and say goodbye to make the appointment I'd claimed to have with my sister. But he seemed to have forgotten that or didn't care. He spooned sugar into his coffee and stirred it with a clink, clink and he'd gone from the ball game to the strike that was surely coming, he said, if the Chicago Surface Lines brass didn't budge. A talker, he was, and that suited me because myself I was more a listener, something'd always marked me different at home. He explained why the men ought to get the eighty-five cents per hour they were asking for, and it had nothing to do with the Bolshies, like the company brass'd claimed, said Desmond Malloy, but was only on account of the needs of honest working men like himself.

If they did get it, he would be making as much in a couple of days as I made in a week at The Chicago Magic Company. I'd have to learn one of them tricks created money from wands if I wanted to keep up. Already, as far as I could figure, he earned my salary in three days instead of six, and if the car men went out for long, how would I get to my job, to make what I did make? Margaret could walk to her work at the shirt factory, but she couldn't support the both of us, and with the garment situation being always up to the rim, about to boil over, maybe she would go out like the thousands of others in the city that summer.

As evening deepened, the odd puff of air came in, cooling. If I'd gone back to Bridey's and had a wash before my stroll and hung my shirtwaist in the air to freshen it, or worn tomorrow's, I'd not a been wondering if I smelled bad, or if the grime of the city'd soiled my face. But I would never a met Mr. Desmond Malloy had the weariness of a man at the end of a day, smoking his Camel cigarettes.

Then, so sudden I blinked my eyes, he smiled broad—his teeth good—and dropped altogether the subject of striking car men and losing ball teams. Instead he asked, "Anyone ever tell you you're a dead ringer for Dorothy Phillips?"

The movie star? No one had, and I admitted as much.

"The brown eyes and the curly hair though. Look closer in the mirror, darlin'. You'll see it."

Pouring right across the table, all that charm of his. But Dorothy Phillips was it, herself on the cover of *Photoplay* the very month? Then he switched subjects, asking about the home country, and had I come over with my family and how charming it sounded, my way of speaking, and how had we all made out. The past loomed like an ache, my mammy's face, the blades of her cheekbones, the hollows deepened with each tooth lost. My da, his good nature besting the pain of walking most days, but sometimes the pain besting the good nature and him lashing out with his stick at whoever stood nearest.

The wicket gate, the friary, the whole tangled, startling lot of memories threatening to overtake me in one of them waves I fought through by looking out at the lights on Halsted Street, crowds of people, and peddlers calling still, at this hour, and tunes from a squeeze box. All so busy and joyous, easy to forget any trouble in the bustle. Nothing of the kind in Ennis, only the streets—even the nicest, like Church Street with its curve opening to a view of the cathedral—even Church Street filthy with the dropping of ponies and asses waiting in the harnesses of the traps. Streets so narrow they'd be somber on the sunniest of days.

"It's just me and Margaret came," I told him. "My sister. Our da chose us as the ones likely to succeed in America and we'll be goin' back someday for a visit anyway. We're savin' for it."

But sure we were not. Whenever we put a few bills aside some need forced us to use them. We might as well a been saving for a palace as the price of our passage back to Ennis. He was staring across the table at me, intent like, yet even so the right pupil wandered off to the side of the red-veined white.

"Like us all. Never set eyes on the home country myself, but my ma can get herself weepin' for it, though she was small when she left. Come to think of it, I must have passed you in the crowd Sunday at the flag raisin'. You're a member, aren't you, Maeve, you and your sister Margaret? The Ancient Order of the Hibernians?"

The right side eye joined the left as he stretched them both wide, rolling his r's, playing the clown like he did on the cars. He laughed at his try for an accent same as mine.

"Grand, wasn't it? The flag of the Republic of Ireland flyin' right here in Chicago?"

"'Twas," I nodded, without admitting our absence. Instead of joining the party in Bridgeport, Margaret and me'd been sitting in the theater dabbing at our tears as the Chinese man found the poor little girl dead in the wonderful picture show, *Broken Blossoms*. It was the memory of that caused the mournfulness he read on my face, though he thought it must be me missing the home country.

"Gee, it must be a simpler kind of life. And wouldn't we all go for a life like that, considerin' what's happenin' here in this stew pot. You can't open a letter for wonderin' if there's a Bolshie bomb in it, and even worse than the Bolshies, them niggers just keep streamin' north, when any jobs we have ought to be goin' to the men fought for this country, like you were sayin'. We need some changes around here. It can get a man down. It's a wonder I don't just jump in the lake some days. Do you ever feel like that, Maeve?"

"The big one there? Never that. No."

"You're not a swimmer, then?"

"I am not."

"You've not been to the ball park, and you don't swim at the lake. You're missin' out on all the pleasures of the city, darlin'." Perked up again, stars glinting in them eyes, light shining through a glass bottle greener than anything I ever saw back home, despite the picture his mammy painted for him.

I let my shoulders lift and fall and he went on talking about the fine dunks he'd had in Lake Michigan, contests and all and how his da taught all the Malloy boys—four of them—to swim when they were kids. My da so, too, out at Lahinch, if teaching is what you could call it when he limped into the wild Atlantic and threw us down the waves one after the other, like fishes too meager to make up a decent feed. Even Fiona, the youngest then, and hadn't she caught a terrible fever after, weakened her, Mammy said, and maybe what started her fading, though when we'd left, Margaret and me, she was still in the picture. Always coughing, though. Don't know how it must a been for our da when Fiona finally coughed her last. Don't know because we were looking after coughing ones ourselves, Margaret and me, them children barking even though Florida and all the waters around it had to be bushels warmer than Ireland's Atlantic. So you couldn't blame our da. Fiona wouldn't a liked being left on the shore as out he tossed the rest of us. *It's the way you'll learn*, he said, when we came up sputtering.

But we never got to Lahinch much and my next experience of the sea came on the *Mauretania* with that heaving motion. Thought of it sickened me though it was near to eight years since we'd come over. All of us too nauseated to eat the poor food we were offered, the nuns, too, but the main nun, Sister Mary Brigid, who'd made the trip more than once, assuring us that tomorrow would be better—it wouldn't be rough for the whole crossing. Didn't the sea prove her wrong that trip? Even when we got to St. Augustine, after riding on the train over land sure solid as any I'd walked upon, even then when I saw the sea I smelled sick. How it got in our hair. We had no place to properly wash so the sour travelled with us.

The grand *Titanic,* big as a city sunk down among the icebergs? The *Eastland*, right here in Chicago, almost as many killed as on the *Titanic* even? The stories I'd read of these disasters shouted in the background, nearly deafening me as he babbled on about his fine times at the lake, parties with young friends, picnics. Then my thoughts stilled, for if my ears had not played a trick on me, he was proposing to teach me to swim.

"It's easy and the most refreshin' thing you can do on a summer day. What do you say?"

He tapped another cigarette on the table, struck a match, sucked in the tobacco and his eyebrows went up as his lungs filled, then down again as, squinting, he blew the smoke into the space between us. Me, I must a swallowed, shivered, but I couldn't a said even that same night what I did because as the tobacco smoke drifted up and he leaned across the table, my nose sized up the sun on his shirt, the man-sweat with its whiff of beer and the roast meat smell, the grease of it, because some of it had got onto his necktie. If I'd been one of the girls in the Laura Jean Libbey stories I'd a been swooning right then under the power of all those perfumes, the hair, too, with the oil he'd put in it, dry by then.

I never fainted, no, but I heard the rasp of a blade slicing through the ropes'd held me, though my hands were folded politely on the table and I kept my teeth on my lip. His hand was sliding across towards my wrist. A fine mitt with the long fingers like my da's and golden hairs growing on the section above the first knuckle and nails a bit gray at the edges, but trimmed so, and hadn't he just been out all day? And didn't my da have thick black in the skin as well as under the nails, enough so that our mammy joked about him starting another plot of cabbage right there at his fingertips? Desmond Malloy's hands were nothing like that, but smooth on the backs and a sweet baked bun color from the sun, just a rumor of the veins running beneath. I wanted to touch one of them. I was that trembly I thought he'd surely notice, so I shook myself. Fool, fool, I scolded.

"Whaddya say," he repeated. "You could meet me after work. I've got the early shift Wednesday. Bring your bathin' costume with you and you can change in the bathhouse." He winked. "We'll make an evenin' of it. Some ice cream after? Or maybe a late supper? Tomorrow at five thirty? It's goin' to be another hot one, darlin'. You'll be glad of a swim. It'll be peachy. Whaddya say?"

I had neither a bathing costume nor the money to buy one if I wanted to, but there we sparkled like two people on the cover of *True Story*. Margaret, worried about me since Packy perished of the flu, wouldn't have a care but could move along into married life with her Harry because it seemed to me that Desmond Malloy could be more than a flirt. Him warming me with that emerald fire burned directly through me, Maeve Curragh, made me think I could do anything. Even swim. I patted my mouth with my napkin like the sisters'd taught me and twirled the straw in the glass, which had been truly empty for a long spell.

"It can't be tomorrow."

"Then the next day. It's goin' to be hot all week long."

A powerful man, yes, might have been him holding me in his arms instead of whatever else bound me. The street noise streaming in from Halsted, someone hollering at someone else and boys running past the door shrieking and the patient clop, clop of horses leading their buggies back to the barn. Somewhere a telephone with its shrill ring, ring. All of it making a platform for me to raise myself up. Me thinking, yes, yes, but staying cool, I think, keeping my face straight.

"Thursday, then, and where would you be wantin' to meet, so?"

He laughed a big laugh, filled the café and caused people to search for the cause—like you do when you want to be in on the fun. I pretended to be interested in something going on behind the counter, where a waiter in a white apron cleared dishes and filled drinks, and pearl divers in the kitchen behind scrubbed and smacked plates against one another, for I did not want Desmond Malloy to see my own peepers flashing with excitement. I would have thought it a joke, but didn't he reach across again and try to take my hand before I slipped it away? Oh, yes, I was in for it. I didn't feel the heat of the evening at all or the loneliness'd been my companion as I walked along

Halsted earlier, made smaller by the crowds, the buildings, the noise. No one noticing me at all.

He steered me out to the street and down to the corner stop and we waited until we heard the clacking and the bell. He tipped his hat and said goodnight and made me promise to remember our date.

"It'll be jake, Maeve. I promise."

As I stood in the shadows, stunned by a kind of wonderment same, better, than my first tree of oranges, a colored man sprinted to make the door of the trolley before it started off. The poor fellow tumbled over something, and fell to the cobblestones, just missing the car Desmond Malloy hopped onto, laughing as he waved to me, and the car clicked away.

～

Even then, hours after the last edition, a young newsie held to the corner singing the latest headlines.

FOLKS IN PARACHUTES FLOATED THROUGH SKY!

**READ THE NAMES OF THEM KILLED
AND HURT IN DIRIGIBLE DROP!**

**SANDBURG SEZ, RENTS GO UP
WHEN NEGROES MOVE IN!**

I had my paper from the morning but the news'd got old and I'd promised Bridey, and I never did spend my nickels on supper but made do with pie and ice cream and the breathlessness makes a body lose her appetite. I gave the young tenor his pennies, and grabbed the *Daily News* from him to leave fresh on Bridey's hall table.

Margaret was in and snoring. If I hadn't seen her and heard her, I would a known by the smell. Her man Harry only drove the raw meat, didn't butcher it himself, but the stink clung to him and jumped onto Margaret same as a flea.

My bottom just fit on the sill of the window where Margaret's shirtwaist fluttered in the shy bits of air could never seem to work themselves up into anything truly refreshing. Swim? Sure a dunking in the lake would cool a body, but the Lord only knew what lay beneath the water, them drowned there, including the hundreds tumbled off the deck of that ship, the *Eastland*, and it tipped over right at the dock. Mary and Joseph! Fishes and maybe water snakes like the nuns warned us about. Satan himself ready to coil around my ankles and pull me under for my bushel of sins.

I didn't have to go. But if I did I'd need a bathing costume and fearing water, as we had ever since that ship and later the sight of the creatures crawled out of the water in Florida, we'd found better things to spend our money on. A snort, a toss, but not so reckless a toss she fell onto the space waiting for me. With her mouth slack, Margaret looked younger than her nineteen years, except for the red hands, scarred from the pricks of her trade and the needle once went clear through her thumb.

My eyes wandered down to the lane where some men shambled along home from the taverns, gassing each other about this and that, a mischievous one stopping to tug at one of the clotheslines strung from tenement to tenement. A bit of moon brightened the scene, and the odd yellow light from a building. *As long as the day is, night always falls.* Da said that, and also, *Good luck happens same as bad. Remember, girls.* The words he left us with. *Remember girls, good luck can happen same as bad. You'll find your way better if you keep your heads up. And you, Maeve, born at the hour that you were.*

Of course no lights burned at Bridey's. I had to feel my way down them creaky stairs and hope Bridey and her nosy son were asleep and the other boarders too, despite the caterwauling came from the lane, voices rising in threats. Two flights, then the door with its glass oval and the owner's lace conceit. The sleeping ones might think it cats or rats, never thieves if they heard anything at all, because it wasn't a house with bits and pieces worth stealing. Down the steps to the street, air soft at night, the sort of night we seldom enjoyed at home where all the stones in the land held the coolness.

In my mind I saw them hanging clothes and thought of the opportunity showed directly to me, for I might find myself a bathing costume hanging out there with the sheets and the union suits, the shirtwaists and the baby nappies. Though the night beat black as a sinner's prospects in heaven, my eyes soon adjusted and by the time I got to the corner, it didn't seem nearly so. Maybe it was the moon angling down on the washing pulled me sure as if the clothesline was merely a rack in a store and me coming in with a pocketbook full of dollar bills.

Between the houses I had to steer myself out to the back with the aid of a wall. A bottle rolled and something shrieked, terrifying the life near out of me, for it had to be a rat or a feral cat or some creature I hadn't seen yet, but only heard of—like the alligators in Florida raised their open mouths from the edge of a swamp when you didn't even know they were there. Then the moon went behind a cloud and left me stuck. I could see nothing at all, and in their confidence the crawly things came out and fair chased me down the street, and in my nightdress I tripped and fell.

When you've decided on a thing, there's nothing but to be after doing it. These are my words, not Da's, something taught me by our long way here across the terrible ocean to America, at last to the city where we'd stayed for nearly four years. Yet for a minute there, in Bridey's lav with its smell of Jap Rose soap, which stung the scrape on my knee, I did stop long enough to drift. Never a good idea, that, to let wondering interfere, but there came a thought real as anything outside my head. If he was so keen on my company, why had Desmond Malloy not suggested the pictures, or a stroll through the park? A dance hall, a show, supper? Certainly the heat of the week came into it, but did it have to be swimming? For even if I found the proper clothing and joined him on the lip of the lake so vast it might be the ocean itself—it's that wide you couldn't see across to the other shore—would I have the courage to step deeper into the water when I knew there might well be a part from one of the bodies fell off the *Eastland*? And how many other corpses rising up from the bottom to plague us living and tempt us under?

Margaret's arm had fallen onto my half so I had to lift it, roused her. "Go back to sleep, Peg," said me, stroking a damp strand of hair from her face, squeezing her plump arm while pushing my foot against her arse to make a bit more room.

Wednesday, July 23, 1919

TOO SOON I FELT her climbing over me, rattling the pot, starting the water to boil on our gas plate, then slipping out to use the lav before Bridey and the others formed a line in the hall. I stared out the window at the whiteness constituted dawn there in that big place, and sat up only when the knock of metal against metal told me the tea'd boiled. Margaret returned with a pitcher of water for a good scrub at the basin on the washstand and then it was me telling her my story, about the fella invited me to the pictures.

"To the pictures? And supper, too?"

"I've hit it big, Megs, I think. That'll be me, sittin' somewhere under one of them lazy fans, sippin' a cool drink through a straw. Maybe it'll be an ice cream soda and we'll be talkin' about the show we saw and what did we like best. You know."

"It wouldn't be one of them vaudevillers come into your place, would it? Or that artist fella?"

"George? Never him. It's an office man, works in the same building."

"Don't let your loneliness fool you."

Echoing what the sisters used to say. Mary Brigid, the words rolling out from between the lips of her wimple-pinched face, her voice hoarse and whispery as she described the smallness makes the throbbing space around you big and cold, so you long for a comforting touch. *Pray,* she advised us. *Pray lest you fall into an occasion of sin. God is the only one who can relieve the shadow that darkens the spirits of girls on their own.*

"Never lonely, Meggsie, jewel, not with you. And Harry soon to be my brother, and all them at home."

I mouthed the last as we were going out the door, for Bridey'd reminded us often of the sleep needs of her addled son, John, and though Margaret would be boiling at me for telling her a fib, I'd make it right after, I would. And if I held her one minute longer when we embraced at the corner as we usually did—a habit from the beginning when we had to separate and didn't want to and clung to each other whenever a situation forced it—she took no notice, but turned aside to go her way to the shirt factory while I went mine, down the road to the stop and the crowd of sleepy people, heads down, waiting for the car. The little newsie with the curly hair was hollering everybody awake with his *Trib*. Another rascal across, could be Greek, shouting louder:

CAR MEN READY TO DEAL!

CAPITAL RIOT, TWO DEAD!

WEST DRY AS DUST,
RAIN DANCIN' EVERYWHERE!

CONGRESS OUGHTA REGULATE BLIMP SEZ MAYOR!

Their voices, one bright made you think of sun on a dime, the other husky, as if predicting the size man he'd grow into. The two calls angling against and sometimes crossing one another reminded me of what I heard spilling out the Academy of Music when they had opera singers on the bill. Trying to meddle with our curiosity, they were, the newsies, and it worked, you could tell by the gradual lowering of the stacks of papers alongside them.

ONLY DAUGHTER LOST IN BANK CRASH

the one hollered, while his competition bested him in volume,

HE'S COMING!
PRINCE GONNA VISIT CHICAGO!

With money on my mind as usual, and more so today, what with me needing a bathing costume, I daren't waste a single coin and I could read over the shoulder of the man standing next to me. Yet wasn't it sad, this news. Irene Miles her name, and her small watch found in the rubbish on the floor of the bank the airship crashed into, along with $1,200. Not the $200,000 rumored, and no reports of anyone getting any of it, or what else was found, only the watch engraved on the back with the words, "Irene from Mama," and a locket with an inscription, said the paper, *IGM*. "These are believed to have belonged to Miss Irene G. Miles, a stenographer and the only support of her widowed mother, one of those killed when the dirigible fell."

More stories of the dead filled pages I could not see to read, despite my shifting and craning my neck and just as well so, for I didn't need to be carrying sorrow in my heart. When I did get a seat I looked up to page two and there they were staring me in the face, pictures of the victims, including the smiling Irene Miles among the headlines.

FIRST BLIMP VICTIM FUNERAL HELD TODAY

BOMB IS FOUND IN GARAGE

WARTIME PROHIBITION UPHELD BY U.S. COURT

BREWERS BEGIN LEGAL FIGHT

It was the day the returned soldiers, and anyone else needing a hand, could line up for shoes and clothes and groceries at the settlement house. When I tore my eyes away from the paper to look out the window I saw a queue of them, some of them soldiers still in uniform, or parts of a uniform, there waiting for the house to open at seven thirty. You saw soldiers everywhere then, the worst of them shell shocked, begging. I heard of one fellow made it all the way through the war and shot himself only two days home. But the soldiers left my mind quickly in my preoccupation, me wondering if there might be somewhere a body could line up for beach outfits and those sweet espadrilles I'd seen in the paper ads, or shoes laced all the way up the leg.

The conductor, an old fellow, tired already in the morning—not your Desmond Malloy, but doing his job just the same—this fellow hollered "Dearborn!" I jostled out with the others and fair raced along the street, holding up my skirt with one hand and my hat down with the other, scrambled through the whirly doors of the grand Marquette right into the first elevator without noticing if the head above belonged to Hairy Bear, or Black Hawk, or Keokuk, or the Lord himself.

Although I made it to the ninth floor and the frosted glass door of 902 only minutes after I should have, Florence at the front exposed her little teeth in a way said, *Me? I am never late.* Or maybe it was just she'd seen the piles on my desk kept me slicing and tearing, and printing the sums neat in the ledger, typing out the orders, marking paid with stamp, stamp, stamp. Maybe those teeth were only biting back the words, *Good luck to you, Maeve.* She dressed more swell than the rest of us, for the front, and never passed a day without mentioning her Walter, but Florence was neither so tragic nor so high she avoided the company of us other girls, including my chum Gladys from Cosmo Buttermilk Soap on the floor above. Because that day burned just as hot as the day before, we all gathered again outside in the shade and the smoke at lunchtime and listened to Ruth read out the "True Life Love

Story" you could find in the *Trib*. If you wrote in with your story and they took it, they'd pay you a five-dollar bill.

Ruth's eyes, the bulgy of someone with a bad thyroid, blinked again and again because of the sun sneaking through the weave of her hat, or because of the emotion of it. She read aloud in the thrall of a couple, Mollie and Jack, met aboard a ship travelling the world on the way to Egypt. They got off the boat in Spain and went touring around and visited an old bell tower they saw. There the bell ringer persuaded them to pull the bell rope. Wasn't till later they learned that any couple rang the bell together at the twilight hour were destined to be married someday. Sure enough, as the trip went on they fell in love and announced their engagement, and were married in London.

"Isn't it beautiful," Ruth mooned. Gladys pinched my arm because she thought Ruth not simple exactly, maybe innocent is the word. Poor Ruth longed so for a love story of her own, someone to talk about, to write to, other than the brother over there still, mending in some hospital in France. She lived not far from our work in a residence for women and saved money each week to buy things for her hope chest, she said. We took her at her word, but living where she did, and being who she was with her bulgy eyes and her childlike voice, what hope could there be? An unkind notion, sure, and who was I thinking I was, after just one evening with a handsome man? You had to watch it or they'd trick you, the good people. You had to watch not just what you said but your thoughts, too.

I nodded to show Ruth that, yes, it was a beautiful story, Mollie and Jack, sure, but same as *The Talk of the Town*, starring the very Dorothy Phillips himself said I resembled, the pictures, the stories came from a world seemed altogether different than the one where I lived. Wouldn't I like to visit it, though. Falling in love on a ship? Had to be sailing smoother seas than the one we crossed with the Sisters of Perpetual Grace, Margaret and me, for you'd not have had the strength to raise your head, and when you did you'd be looking at someone sick as you. We heard the cries from something going on in the dark corners of the steerage where we snuggled together, trying to comfort each other with images of the lives we'd have as good nuns if we ever reached the shore we dreamed of, but it sounded more like pain than love. Still, five dollars. Weren't we all thinking the same thought? Easy money, and didn't we have true love stories of our own?

"I'm goin' to write about my Walter. That was true love," Florence said.

"But Walter's gone. Not such a happy ending if you ask me," Eveline reminded her, and then, just like one of the fast types in the pictures, she said, "I guess I've got some love stories I could tell. Question is…" and she winked here, Eveline did, because she was that kind of girl for all you couldn't help getting a laugh from what she said. "Question is, would anyone print them?"

Florence thought Eveline aimed to mock her, but I knew it was just Eveline, a little older, though she never said how much, and maybe cockier because she'd made her own way in the city from the day she moved here young from another state, Indiana or Ohio, or some other state begins with a vowel. Why she left home so young had me puzzling. She never said much about her mam, though there were brothers, and a da—she'd refer to them now and then, never kindly, but in that same cool joking way she had. If I'd asked for more, she might have demanded my own story, to make us even, but only Margaret would ever know the truth, most of it.

The talk of the girls started me plotting. Of course the bells in my story would be the ones we heard every day, clanging as the cars snaked around the rail bends. Not romantic as a castle in Spain, and sure they'd frown on a girl who tried to nick a bathing costume to go off with a fella alone on her first date, so I'd have to change the details some. They called them true-life love stories, but who knows what Mollie and Jack got up to in that castle, or on the decks of that great ship as it sailed whatever seas never made them lose their breakfast. Yet I liked the part about the legend because didn't it smack of the fairy stories, the mischief the good people made to steer the affairs of those mostly couldn't see them but only feel their meddling ways. The piece of cake you saved for yourself under your pillow suddenly gone, to remind you of your selfishness, but a wandering pig miraculously found before she fell into the hands of some family hungrier than your own.

Oh, yes, I'd felt them many times, guiding me same as the Mother of God, even then, that week in Chicago. Hadn't the airship tragedy been the occasion sparked his interest in me? Not that the good people would a caused the blimp to crash, no, I wouldn't think so, not for that reason alone. But was it not a skein sure, everything knotted up in ways you could not divine until later, maybe not even then? And here the opportunity to record what'd already begun to develop in my mind as a story every bit as magical as the one Ruth continued to swoon about.

"Imagine," she said again. "Like it was all planned. I'll write about that soldier I met at Riverview, bought me chop suey, then one of them little paper umbrellas. He even held it over me when it rained. What do you think?"

"Not your bell tower," Eveline laughed, and then we had to go in.

Sears Roebuck and them promised their catalogue customers shipment, even delivery, the same day an order came in. But Sears Roebuck had hundreds of girls on the floor, whereas at our magic outfit only a few of us processed orders came in for illusions and the paper novelties offered by the Rainbow Paper Company. Of course the amusement line did not demand the same hurry you'd imagine for a new suit of clothes for a wedding, to name one thing. Still we had standards and how could we know that the "Disappearing Wand," or the "Improved Bouquet and Card Trick," might not be the effect would turn a parlor magician into a vaudeville star, changing his life? Meaning, most days we worked efficient as those after sending out the more ordinary things people needed.

Same as at the mission school, it came to the old question of the envelopes. I'd become the expert at opening them addressed to The Chicago Magic Company and dividing the contents—the money orders and cash to one side, the catalogue number and a description of the object on the other. Rolling in an order sheet and pressing down hard on the keys, a little thud instead of a tap as the metal key made its mark through three thicknesses—a copy to send to the customer, a copy for the stock boy, and a copy for Mr. R, who made sure the money came in equaled the cost of what we sent out.

No credit in the operation, and precious little cash either, because not many ignored the advice on the second page of the catalogue. But, today, as if I'd done good and fate was steering things my way, I found a five-dollar bill folded into an order for "The Talking Skull." When I saw the number on the bill I left it inside its paper sleeve and shuffled it to the bottom of the pile, deliberately slowed my breath, lowered my shoulders and pressed my arms against my ribs. As much as the price for a love story! The envelope next gave me the opportunity to stall, for the customer had enclosed the catalogue entry itself and I read the trick description as if it was new to me and marvelous. The drawing and all, with the addled white birds lifting right up from that frying pan, "The Wizard's Omelette." The money order got clipped to the copy for Mr. R, the copy for Billy into the tray meant for him. The envelope with the shape of a bill inside smoldered at the bottom of my pile. If I took it right out, Eveline would see—our desks were that close—and if I went ahead and slipped the bill into my pocketbook I didn't know if I'd see judgment or pleasure on her narrow face.

But my fingers'd learned to be smart them days I spent thinning out the donations at the mission so's Margaret and me could make our way north to Chicago. When Billy came to pick up the orders, distracting everyone with his patter—for he never missed an opportunity—I slipped that lucky envelope into my sleeve and waited until he'd pushed through the door to the stock room before I went to the lav in the hall, taking my pocketbook, sure, and rolling my eyes at Florence as I passed, guarding the sleeve in question by placing my arm at my waist and the other hand over that, and wincing a little with the pain I wanted her to think came with my monthlies.

Must it always be this way, I thought to myself, in the hallway, the depths opening black for that one minute before me answering myself in the same thought—*it must, for the time being*. But Desmond Malloy could be the man to lead me out of this life and then wouldn't I make it all good. Him after opening a window I could step through to the future where someone else managed the juggling of the daily needs.

~

Avoiding the other girls at leaving time, I hurried into the first elevator stopped, then sauntered through the marble foyer onto the street with nobody ever suspecting what I carried with me. Not so much I couldn't save and put it back, same as I put a penny into the box for the missions whenever I went to church. Only a five, not a week's pay. Maybe even not enough, paused me a minute. Yet it must be enough, it had to be, for just as if on a regular errand, I joined the State Street throngs and headed towards The Fair, straight to the section where the bathing costumes hung. I could have tried the heaps of clothes in the stalls on Maxwell Street and maybe found what I wanted, but with the plan being to meet my man tomorrow, I had no time to take a chance on Maxwell Street. I knew The Fair well, the dresses and the on-sale goods, the toiletries section where Gladys and me would stop and smell the creams on display while girls our age but dressed fancier, in black with shirt sleeves and collars white as a new tooth, stood behind the counter looking proud as if they owned the creams themselves.

Upstairs then, where mannequin heads modeled the loveliest straw hats for summer, and beyond them the racks of bathing costumes. Cotton jersey, wool, satin. Wouldn't I a loved one of the satin models felt so slick under my hand, shone like a lathered bay horse, the one used to stand in Church Street and let me pet him. No horse for me, Conor Curragh's eldest daughter. No satin bathing costume neither, not for the bill my envelope gave up. Well, the mohair would more than do, and I picked a nice navy one with white piping trimmed the square neckline. Held it up to myself and thought it would sure enough fit.

The saleslady asked, don't you want to try it on and would you like some assistance and have you seen the bathing slippers and stockings, the charming overskirts? Her saying it with a smirk meant *I have to say these words, it's part of the job, but I know who you are.* I never was trying to hide it. How could I, being who I am, small. I have always been small, but I have made my way as I had to. I only opened my pocketbook and snatched out the five rightfully belonged to someone wanted an imitation skull to tell him what to do—as if there weren't enough empty headed ones running the show—plus one dollar of my own and put the bills on the counter. She wrapped the bathing costume in paper and dropped it into a bag. I thanked her and that was that, despite her smile told me what she thought of me and it wasn't much.

I'd got the thing, yes I had, and the store after closing. A light-colored man in a blue uniform, a mulatto with the steel wool hair, but thin lips and a nose straight and haughty as Potter Palmer's, stood at the door and inspected me like he could see inside my mind. I held out the bag, the sack with the name on it, The Fair. This big man would discourage anyone trying to lift goods from the store. But me, I was a shopper like everyone else dribbling out the doors, my glance told him, and why would he think otherwise? Him in the uniform, sure, but no policeman.

You saw colored at the doors, but not shopping, not at The Fair, though you did see them everywhere else, crowding streetcars, some lines. Plenty in Chicago wished these new kind of coloreds would march right back to whatever ship landed them and sail to Africa, or at the least board a train bound for where they'd come from, Mississippi, Alabama, somewhere we'd passed through, Margaret and me, riding north, and saw out the window the shacks, the stick-legged children. 'Twas the colored paper started it all, the *Chicago Defender,* with what they'd called "A Great Northern Drive," trying to get colored folk to leave the South—where they'd been slaves and where they might be strung up for the slightest thing—and get themselves to Chicago for factory jobs and grand times at the hottest night clubs.

Well, they must a believed what they read in the papers because, like Desmond Malloy'd said, there was a stream coming into the city and unsettling those'd come earlier, we Micks and the Polacks like Harry, and all the rest, from every corner of the world. He was one complained about them taking all the jobs at the Yards and steering clear of the union. Made it bad for the rest, said Harry. But Harry never made room in his mind for much more than his job, his kind, and Margaret. Like I said, I got over the fear of folks with skin different than mine when we were in Florida, for it was my job to look after the babies whatever their color, them ivory, or tobacco brown, or caramel, some of them. Really all the tints nature'd mixed.

Oh, but wouldn't I a liked that kind of life, bringing something home every day. Then I looked at the streetcar strike another way, for if the car men got their raise and Desmond Malloy got me, wouldn't the extra money just be more to support this habit I could get into, of strolling the store aisles thinking of what I might like and what I might need and wouldn't Desmond be happy with a new tie same as I'd seen draped on a rack above the counter near the door? *Oh, yes, I'll take that one,* I'd say to the saleslady. *Maybe that one as well, to match his eyes, they're such a lovely green you know,* and her smile would be altogether different than the girl who packed my bathing costume in tissue paper crackling inside the bag I carried close against me as I wrestled through the going home crowds on State Street.

It was suffering hot on the Madison car, people standing sleepy, odors of all kinds insisting. Car crawling along, sometimes you'd think you could have walked faster. Lucky ones sitting near the windows covered by grills the gritty breeze pushed through. Even though later than my usual hour, all the seats filled as it seems they always were and more of us hanging from straps. Not much talk at the end of the day and a sweltering one such as that with everyone's feet stinging like they must be, like mine stung. Some reading the *Daily News* or the *Examiner,* or one of the papers in their own languages, or the *Trib,* gone old since the morning. Me trying to get a glimpse of what'd happened since I last looked.

CAR MEN OFFER WAGE COMPROMISE

WEST PARCHED, SUFFERS

GIRL MISSING IN MYSTERY

while wondering if my crime would make a story one day, one of them small ones on the back pages, headline in short skinny letters, but news all the same.

CLERK DISMISSED FOR THIEVERY

Would it be worth it in the end? And what in heaven would I ever do with a bathing costume if Desmond Malloy stood me up?

She'd be wondering what was keeping me, Margaret, and how would I explain the delay and the bag said The Fair? Yet, seeing the twin towers of St. Pat's, I stepped off the car before my usual stop. In the street the children were glazing their bare arms with the leavings of ice from the free deliveries Mayor Thompson ordered to relieve people couldn't get out of the city, or even out of their rooms. A horse'd folded his legs under himself right on the cobblestones and all the dogs were splayed out in the patches of shade the walls of the church threw on the sidewalk. My conscience guided me around them dogs and in.

Not novena night, but, because dim and cooler than the stoops of the tenements, people, mostly old ones, bent over in scattered pews counting their rosary beads. No priest waited in his box for confessors, not that I planned to confess, not then, for I was having the old argument with Him. The nuns would say Jesus puts temptation in our way to test us, but you could also say he's after offering an opportunity, same as, going all the way back home, he sent the mission sisters into our schoolroom, opened my mind to the possibilities this poor life offered. Same as he gave me the wit to use a typewriter. Same as he planted the idea of this city in my head and saw to it that people sent money in their envelopes to the mission school. If Margaret and me'd never gone with the nuns, if I'd stuck to scullery work, if folks'd sent their donations to the archdiocese as they were supposed to, instead of directly to the mission, if Packy hadn't caught the flu...

The "if" chain linked back to the day my da and my mammy came together in ways they never talked about, though theirs made a true life love story if ever there was one. I would describe every bit, for there's no shortage of paper, and I came upon the habit of writing things down after watching my da lick the end of his pencil and scribble away, raising his craggy face to think a bit, then continuing, the book of his on his knee and him bent as he had been bent since the accident on the railroad and me barely in school. Most Ennis men drank themselves away from their families. With my da it was the dreaming took him, Mammy said. "You might as well be off with the others for your nightly jar, Conor. You're as gone as they are anyway. Praise be it doesn't cost us anythin' but your attention."

Da, hearing her say that, let his pencil drop and hobbled over to where she sat on her straw-bottomed chair by the hearth, where she sits in my memory, her skin browning from the peat smoke, her eyes shining like bright blue stones on a road in the moonlight. He tugged her up, though she resisted, and took her into his arms, and steered her around the square of earthen floor in a pretend dance, though the wheezing and the sleep-whining of us all provided the only music. Then he paraded her to their bed where I heard more protesting before I pushed my face above my sister Margaret's shoulder to see him on his bent arm, kissing her.

Drops of rain blew in under the chimney cap. I shut my eyes and nodded off to the dependable rhythm of the torrent, restless and troubled with feelings I did not recognize. After the accident he could have stayed away, joined the other men jawing away the hours at a cottage down the road behind Mill Street and playing games to gyp each other out of a drink. But he was soft, Da was, and the butt of other men's jokes because of it.

It's them, sure, made me who I am, the firstborn, bold as one of them irons at the front of the car pushed anything blocking the tracks out of its way. I promised to pay it back somehow, what I took. Slip some bills into an envelope and mail them to the person scribbled a return address. It was a promise came from my heart and would right the sin. The promise of money and daily prayers for the sake of the suffering, all this to the Virgin in her sapphire cloak studded with golden stars, for the Virgin seemed more understanding.

The Virgin, who kept her title though she gave birth, had to understand how it could be for a girl alone in the city, and all she needed and wouldn't a man make it a better life and wouldn't it be grand to see him coming in the door every night, from his work or his ball games. We'd certainly have a nicer home than the one Margaret and me shared at Bridey's. Maybe I'd be blessed some day like them saw tears falling down the painted faces of statues. It was something I dreamed of seeing, a real sign from the Virgin knew I did my best to be good.

But nothing that evening. Only the snort of a shrunken one in the last pew, no doubt exhausted from climbing the steps and shouldering open the heavy door, all he could do to save himself from the heat took the lives of the weakest every summer since I'd been there. Terrible. Isn't it human nature, then, to take advantage of what opportunities appear right in front of you? Wouldn't it be as much as a slap in the face of God, or fate, or the good people, to turn your back on them?

~

Margaret sat on the front steps watching the children at their skipping games, watching something anyway as she waited, like the whole city, for a wind to blow up or the temperature to fall. It'd gone to the periwinkle hour of evening, not quite dark but promising, and neighbors perched on the steps of every house I passed, still in my work duds and clutching the bag with my pocketbook up against my chest. It was not so big, the package, that my sister would spy it right off. I wanted to slip on the costume and admire myself in a scrap of mirror, but it would have to wait. I patted the top of her head and promised to return after I used the lav, which I did, but first hid the bag with the costume in the same place I kept my writing book.

"Harry's out tonight, then, is he?"

"He's on with the Teamsters, them decidin' what they're goin' to do if the Yards go out again this week. Your fellow stand you up, Maeve?"

"Tomorrow we're meetin', not tonight, and good thing for it, too, because I need to wash this shirtwaist and pray it dries overnight."

"Or somethin' lighter. I have a flower you could wear at your neck. Is he handsome, Maeve? Do you like his looks?"

I laughed at her curiosity, yet I'd a been the same. "He's ordinary handsome. The nose a little big and sun burnt." That much was true. I didn't go on about the dimples in his cheek or sure she'd know. "Show me the flower when we're up again."

"Have you had your supper?"

Food filled my thoughts every minute of some days, and other days, like that one, I forgot I had a stomach. But I couldn't tell Margaret so. Instead, I packed another fib in that ever-weightier valise I carried in my conscience and told her I hadn't much of an appetite, because of the heat and working late and all.

"Bridey got the ice today and I left a bit of cheese in her box. Do you think we'll ever sleep at all?"

"We will, Meggsie-pegs. When it's cooler. I will help myself to the cheese, and then we'll stroll over to the park and look at the people."

The prospect of a change from Bridey's stoop distracted her from any more questions about my date and anything else might make me squirm. But I swore that, if Desmond kept his promise and we agreed to meet again, I'd insist, I would, on inviting my sister along. And, if she asked why I'd fibbed, I wouldn't confess it was because the sight of Mr. Desmond Malloy caused my heart or something in that vicinity to melt same as a candy in the sun, but explain it's because I knew she feared water as much as me and didn't think much of car men in general and probably less now they threatened to walk off the job.

Maybe she would understand, instead of scolding me about the kind of life I'd be opening myself to—me who'd come so far and worked so hard for my share of Bridey's room, and shows as often as we could get to them, and the papers and what dime novels I could buy or borrow from the girls at work, where we soiled our fingers with ink beneath lamps that jumped and swung on account of blasting going on underground or far away, or some spell Mr. R was after casting to keep us girls alert.

When Riverview'd opened for the season earlier that summer, Harry—trying to help me fill the gap opened when Packy died—proposed we make a day of it with one of his pals from the packing plant. I screamed on the roller coaster along with the thick-fingered fellow whose words I could barely make out.

Him as if talking with stuffing in his mouth, me being more a listener than a talker, yet still unable to make out much of it. Trying to avoid touching, though the coaster and later the tilt-a-whirl threw me right up against him. Mary and Joseph, the fellow stank of packer's blood and man sweat and hadn't he then gone and found himself some cologne to try to smother it. When I threw up the hot dog he treated us to, they all thought it was the ride made me sick.

Thursday, July 24, 1919

STILL ANOTHER STORY satisfied Margaret's curiosity about the package I carried with my pocketbook. Wasn't it my best skirt, then, to change into, for my date? My sleepy sister inquired no further, for even early on we were both that drained by the heat we saved any go we had for the day ahead. But she did remember to give me the bunch of violets she promised, and pinned them at my throat.

There I was at the streetcar stop, the violets tickling my chin and the morning edition soiling my hand because, since I needn't worry about buying my own supper that night, I had two pennies to spare. July 24, ninety-three degrees already, and there's a child missing.

40 HOUR HUNT FAILS TO BARE CLEW TO CHILD

The same missing girl I saw mentioned in a headline I'd skipped over the night before, but this story on the front page grabbed your stomach, where fear prowls same as hunger. Only six years of age and with the sweet face and the bobbed hair of Baby Marie in the pictures. Janet Wilkinson. Gone missing on her way home from school. "Not a trace," wept her mother. Little Janet shambling along, as children do, up to the building where she lived with her mammy and her da in an apartment on the fourth floor. Disappeared, just like that. No trace. Not a schoolbook, a shoe. No screams heard, no signs of a child's nail marks on a doorknob she could a been clinging to. Only a box of chocolates found in the apartment of the janitor, name of Fitzgerald, lived in the same building. A moron, they called him, the papers. Could a been him, Janet's father thought but, as it was, the whereabouts of sweet Janet were a mystery, another mournful element in the day's hash of woe—other strikes brewing, prices going up. The troubles stretched over the city like an elastic band and me wondering what next thing would cause it to snap.

In my daze, I saw a horse rear up and near dump the man driving the wagon behind. People dodged the flying hooves and, in his haste, a man in a seersucker suit slipped on some horse leavings on the tracks. Boys laughed as he fell and rose again quickly, cursing the beast just then suffering his master's whip even as he craned his big horse head around, teeth bared, wanting to bite. Another boy there today, smaller, his father hunched behind him holding a small stack of the extra papers. The little one's voice a tin whistle shrill, threading through the two newsies already'd claimed the corner.

FIRE CAPTAIN DIES ON DUTY!

POLACK TENEMENTS DESTROYED!

**RUSSIAN TROOPS DESERT ALLIES
JOIN BOLSHEVIKI!**

Mr. R was studying Janet's story when I passed through the shop. I could see his shiny hair over the top of the front page. Did he think he could find her? Or bring in Anna Eva, whose powers made a person shiver at all that lay behind the solid world, unsettling as the good people.

Mr. R and Anna Eva could go to that apartment building and call the spirit of little Janet. I believed they could do it, for I'd seen Anna Eva's power at work and not just by means of the cabinet trick first amazed me. Though it'd been only the summer before, when Packy and I were promised and Margaret looking lonely, seemed already years ago I took her to one of them special afternoons Anna Eva put on for women shy of letting their minds be read among men. I made Margaret sit on the aisle and when the assistant—a young man, like there were young women assistants for the men performers—when he strolled up the aisle asking for volunteers, I lifted Margaret's hand, and she tried, but not so hard, to lower it, and didn't they choose her!

The young man—looked a little like Mr. R with the oiled hair and the mustache, but not the wrinkles, of course; no, his face was smooth—he asked Margaret to write a question on a pad of paper, something important on her mind. He then turned to Anna Eva, dressed in white, layers of it making the skirt and the neck nice and modest and her hair done up as it had been in all the pictures I'd seen on the posters. Anna Eva guessed it immediately.

A man. *Will I ever find a husband?* Margaret'd written, and Anna Eva assured her that she would indeed, and she flipped her hands out as if to say, *Presto!* Such certainty beamed from the stage we more or less looked over our shoulders, expecting Margaret's intended to be right there, beside or behind us. Then Anna Eva cautioned Margaret, for the man meant for her might not be who she expected. Not long after came Harry, not the Mick Margaret supposed she would marry, and just as well, for she wouldn't have to worry about the drinking and fighting went on in some households. Not with dependable Harry liked his beer at a picnic, his schnapps—but not much—before he'd snore off, this last something she discovered later.

~

"Mornin', Mr. R," I said, and over the newsprint he shot them blue-black bullets could go right through you. Did he guess what I'd done? Mentioned nothing about any missing money or any missing child, or Anna Eva, or the possibility of him and her finding little Janet, but only nodded as I minced past him to the back.

In my rush to erase the sins of the day preceding, I squared the orders on my desk if they slid so much as an inch off the pile, made a show of rattling the coins that dropped out of an envelope. It was one of them rare days Mr. M made an appearance. He was a more ordinary sort of man, without the dash of Mr. R. Hair thinning already on Mr. M's head, and clothes seemed an afterthought—generally a button missing, a stain on his shirt. A bit of a beard, more a goatee that did not suit him, actually. You wanted to tilt your head, try different angles of looking, to get him all in a piece. Or maybe it was he never showed up often, once a week, if that. Left Eveline to deal with the business of the orders came in for the paper hats and nut cups, the streamers, and the noisemakers and such he peddled in the Rainbow Paper Company catalogue, more a brochure really. He got George busy, too, that day because he needed a new edition of the brochure, with a few additional items, including a line of paper lanterns in the shapes of balls and bells and flowers. Every one of us stopped at George's drawing table to see him work from the model Mr. M had brought in. A distracting day altogether.

I thought of telling my chum Gladys about my date, for we would go out together at lunch, and hadn't I listened for hours to her doubts about Charles Francis Brown, her wondering if he would stop in the Cosmo to say hello, or just pass in the lobby and nod, thinking of something, or someone, obviously not her. Did the maroon shirtwaist she'd worn until spring make her sallow complexion appear yellower? Should she use a bit of rouge on her cheeks to appear younger? For while they were near the same age, she and Charles Francis, maybe he thought her older on account of her complexion. Ah. For all she dwelled on him, Charles Francis Brown never did turn out to be what she wanted. On account of her blindness in that regard, but for other reasons too, the better choice of confidant would have been wiser Eveline, her never without a man, it seemed, and she got them to buy her not only dinners and shows, but necklaces and even a hat.

Eveline. Not as pretty as fair Florence in the front, but sparky with that short upper lip left her mouth a bit open if she forgot to press her full lips closed, and hair so long she could roll it into a chestnut crown. Lanky, she wore her skirts shorter than anyone else in our place—could not get a normal skirt to cover her, she claimed—but she didn't care how much leg showed. And why would she, with stockings too nice for an office girl? No doubt another gift, and one she drew attention to by leaning down and stroking them, as if they'd got wrinkled and needed smoothing. Not cotton or wool but real silk they were.

Not hard to imagine what Eveline might be willing to do for those stockings and the rest of it, and if the "what" some thought was true, love might not even a come into it. Not the kind of love Desmond Malloy'd seeded in me, and so I never did confide in Eveline then, which left me with Gladys. Though I toyed with the notion of spilling the beans when lunch came and we walked over towards State with the idea of looking at the Boston Store window, at a particular hat she thought Margaret could copy, we happened to get caught up in a welcome home parade of colored soldiers. Them marching in uniform, many lined along the road cheering, including children waving the flags of the men's unit and the Stars and Stripes. Band playing some of the ragtime tunes you heard then. The opportunity to spill my secret to Gladys never came, nor did we see the hat, for we could not cross through the soldiers marching, some dancing, them had the limbs for it.

Despite the commotion Mr. M caused, and even though my mind wandered toward evening as I patted the hair springing out from my damp scalp—it was that stifling in our place, despite the fan turned lazily above—no one could fault the dutifulness of Maeve Curragh that afternoon. Slice an envelope open, roll an order form into my machine, type, type, hit the carriage return. A soothing sort of rhythm to the work. Just before leaving I went to the lav to damp my face and do my hair over and fix the violets at my throat, and they were a lovely color. But it crossed my mind Desmond Malloy could have forgotten in these almost two days passed since we sat across from one another in the café. A strike looming and his ball team winning and losing and maybe another lady hopped on his car caught his fancy. For all that—my dark Ennis eyes fair brimming with possibilities thrilling and sad—my thoughts strayed to Janet Wilkinson. Little Janet, and I whispered a prayer for her safe return.

Eveline stood near Clyde's desk in the lobby, gassing with the doorman as he surveyed the comings and goings of all the people passed through the grand foyer. Gladys lingered nearer the door. Of course the hat, the one we couldn't see during the lunch hour. But more than the hat, I knew my chum wanted to talk about Charles Francis and did I think he loved her and would he be faithful, and if he was truly interested—as he must've been to stand her to lunch that winter day—why did he insist on working most nights, so the only time they spent together he was bent over his drawing board, while she chattered from the high stool he generally waved her to. Always suffered over that man, Gladys did.

Of course I couldn't go with her that evening to study the store windows, and though Gladys would only smile and her eyebrows would go up at the inside corners, and she would go all big on me and hug me and say, *I knew it*—as though she could peer into my private space and understand—I didn't want anyone knowing about Desmond. Not yet, no. I wanted to keep him for myself. That's what it was caused me to make up a story about having to meet my sister to look for fabric for her wedding dress.

"Then I should come right along with you. It would be perfect, Maeve. Good practice, for our turns will come soon enough. Where does she plan to start? The Fair's always good to give you ideas, or The Boston Store. Or is she thinkin' a specialty shop? More expensive, but if she's goin' to be makin' it herself, costs nothing to look."

"That I can't tell, Gladys. She made me promise not to, for doesn't she want to keep it a secret until the day itself."

"Oh, well then."

"Another day? Maybe even tomorrow? For the hat?"

Just then Eveline laughed that laugh of hers, unmistakable, kind of breathy and trumpety at once, and Clyde, too, snickered, though with his head lowered, I saw, for we'd both turned. Gladys blushed like they were laughing at her. Then I was sorry to have put her off because she'd been my friend for nearly as long as I'd lived in Chicago, and if she wasn't worldly in the same way as Eveline, she'd always been kind to me, Gladys. She was one for fashion, sure, and I told her so, and complimented her on her shirtwaist, the one with a square collar like in a sailor's suit and with navy stripes around the edges. Too, I promised to ask Margaret if she might come along next time, for Gladys could give advice if anyone could, better advice than me. She nodded as she headed for the whirly doors, and looked back and waved before she stepped into them. But her face had that pinch beneath the eyes showed her hurt. Maybe I'd convinced her, and I hoped I had, for I never aimed to trample on her feelings. Well, isn't it true fibs are only stories after all, a matter of replacing one set of words with another?

~

Finally I was free, like Margaret and me got to be free of the mission school with the money I pinched for our dream of Chicago, the good life we'd heard of there and no snakes and no alligators. A place to make your fortune. There was nothing for it but to go ahead now I'd dug myself this far in. Wait at the corner of Clark and Van Buren, he'd said, and there's where I stood listening to the clack-clack music of the trains on the El threw a shadow

I sheltered in, for the day had not begun to cool, though a breeze snuck down, sifting soot through the air. The crowds hurrying, everybody always hurrying, and bigger crowds it seemed, with the soldiers back—some in uniform like it was the cloth itself'd made them who they were—and they'd look at me, not all, but a few, because wasn't I standing there with my pocketbook and a bag besides and those crazy violets at my throat. I kept my lips straight and refused to catch any of the glances tossed my way.

Over all the racket, newsboys hollering what a body could read in the late editions.

NEW SUSPECT TAKEN IN LOST GIRL HUNT!

FLAT FAMINE RAISES RENTS!

ZOOKEEPER FIRED!

CAR PARLEY STUCK ON 8 HOUR DEMAND!

While I wanted to know about Janet, it's true, my taste for stories about all transpiring in our city, and indeed the world, that day waned in anticipation of the evening. The great din of the motorcars and horns blaring and the elevated above and me waiting for my man. More motorcars here at this corner, aiming towards Michigan Avenue, a grand parade of them. With precious few rules to keep everyone where they were supposed to be, automobiles battled for road space, just as the office workers jostled for sidewalk. Some of the men after loosening their collars, taking off and carrying their jackets over their shoulders, hooked on a thumb. A man with his boater pushed back on his head, tie like a noose hanging round his neck, carrying a satchel, strode towards the avenue like there was free beer and he's the fella wanted to drink it. Across the street a few other men gathered around one holding up a pair of pants, white pants, and Lord only knew why they'd be conducting their business there in the middle of the street, but it mesmerized me all the same to see the pants go from hand to hand, one matching them up to himself, then passing them to the next.

Girls strolled by in pairs, and I saw one of them reach around and pick her dress loose from where it must have been sticking to her arse this hot day, me thinking she might have left her bloomers at home and how daring. Thrilling to be out of my normal routine of life, more thrilling because secret, but after today, after today, if we made another date, then I'd bear Margaret's tendency to scold, and tell her she had nothing to fear from this car man at least. For all they're known to be flirts, we were not above a little flirting ourselves, to save the fare. A nickel was a nickel and if a girl could save one for the price of a smile, we smiled and let them think what they wanted.

It came down to me counting the bolts worked into the steel beams held up the El tracks. Counting them and noting the little cinders in the grit layered them. Must've been nearing six, but I had no watch. Me a girl without a watch, when just yesterday was found a watch without a girl. *To Irene with love from Mama.* That suffering woman, so good to her daughter, somehow gave her a watch. I could a stopped one of the passing men with chains bounced and glittered across the front of their waistcoats, but sure it could not have been as long as it felt I'd been idling there. I wouldn't wait forever, but I'd wait until forever was on the doorsill.

My stomach grumbled despite my little sandwich and the treat of a cake Florence'd brought in to celebrate her birthday. Baked by her mother and carried from home for us all. Oh, yes, it'd been a big day—the cake, singing Happy Birthday to Florence, Mr. M and the paper lanterns. Desmond Malloy'd mentioned supper, he said we'd make an evening of it. Maybe he'd bring a picnic and I could dawdle with whatever it was he'd packed until it went too dark to venture into the water, for I wouldn't be the fool and claim again to have eaten already, like one of them girls in the pictures, Dorothy Phillips included. So slim, life barely touched them as they spectered through it.

I tried to concentrate on the foot traffic, looking for a tall man with the peak aiming down his forehead. Terrible aching my feet were, though, standing there. What felt good for the novelty after sitting at my desk most of the day had worn with the minutes. More of them passed than ought to have and then I started thinking, praise be to Mother Mary for not having to test myself against the smooth ways of Mr. Desmond Malloy. Wasn't this a gift from the God I'd been talking to only yesterday? Yes, it'd been long enough. The copper on the corner, the one directing traffic, had been looking my way smiling, me nodding, then drawing my eyes back out to the street to make it clear I was looking for someone. God only knew what he suspected of me. It had to be near to an hour I'd waited.

Just then a small group gathered across, a man and two women, all three in somber missionary wear, as if the word of God was serious indeed. How they must have been dripping under them clothes, but in the spaces between the trains, their voices spiraled sweet in some hymn I didn't know, though it comforted me all the same. Whatever disappointment rose in me could not compare to the grief poor Janet's mother had to be feeling.

The shadows shifted and if the letdown caused my feet to sting all the more, relief let me bear the suffering, for I could tell Margaret he'd stood me up—she didn't have to know who—and, feeling sorry for me, she'd ply me with something, as our mammy used to do. Let me cook you an egg, she'd say, for we had eggs for comfort more than anything else. A nice soft-boiled egg with the skin clinging to the rounded knob at the end I'd pop in my mouth while she salted the rest, scooped it into a cup. Two mouthfuls and gone. Something so delicious coming out of that button-eyed hen clucked at the back stoop and wouldn't lay in a proper nest, but wherever she felt like it, so some went wasted even though we thought we knew all her hidey places.

Thinking of home, more than eight years after I squeaked open the wicket gate and crossed into the single room housed us all. Even though I could buy myself eggs and eat them every day, they never tasted savory as that surprise Mammy would find for one of us. To think she might find only one, too, while there in the shops along Halsted were dozens displayed, creamy white, fawn brown, and speckled.

I crossed the street, right past the policeman winked at me as I went, must a been he'd decided me an honest woman. I tried to look up and admire the buildings and thought I might even stroll into the Palmer House a few blocks away, as once I'd done, venturing past the liveried boys, onto the marble walkway, up the stairs into the grand lobby with the ceiling painted like a cathedral, angels and cherubs and gold leaf. The same year we arrived in Chicago, me just turned sixteen, and one of them in livery thinking me there to pick up the laundry or polish the silver. The gilt, the marvelous designs in the plaster, the chandeliers with lights Bridey never would have believed, bright, yet spreading gently onto the seating area as if breathed down from the ceiling by one of them broad-winged angels. The liveried one took my arm and tried steering me over to the housekeeping department, thinking I wanted a job.

But my bold words saved me, me who doesn't talk much, something made me different from the start at home where, if talk were money, we'd all a given Potter Palmer and his kind a run for theirs. I lifted my chin and said, "No, I am not here for work, but to meet my father." Did he believe me, the bell captain? If not, he pretended to and escorted me to a straight chair, velvet, in my favorite blue, color of twilight. I rested from the outside bustle, imagining my da limping up them marble stairs in his cap and his black jacket going orange with age, collarless shirt, stubble on his cheek, the way he'd come through the door at home some days, smiling, smiling, like he'd a secret when he was only imagining something and how he would be reaching for his book to describe every thought.

When the bellman left, I slipped back down them marble stairs. But I'd been there and when we wrote Mammy, the first occasion we had a few dollars to send, I would tell her so, how a body could just walk in to admire the carpets, the marble, the wonderful patterns above.

~

I was after composing another letter so when he appeared, strutting along towards me, bundle under his arm.

"Maeve, darlin'," he said, guiding me over to the curb. "Did ye think I'd forgotten you? And you lookin' even prettier with flowers at your neck."

The scolding words stopped in my throat, because he was a fine figure, Desmond Malloy. He had to be ten inches taller than me, requiring him to bend down to speak and I got the scent of him with its history of the day, the coffee and tobacco and the sandwich he'd chewed for lunch. Made me forget my stomach hunger, the stories I'd been making up. His hand came down on my shoulder and he turned me towards the streetcar stop, talking all the while about the ball team winning, the lateness of the hour, and did I have supper. This time I said no.

"Are you perishin' from hunger, then?"

"Not at all."

The truth is, suddenly, I was not. Wouldn't it be wonderful if hunger, like magic, according to Mr. R, rested mainly in the mind? When the streetcar arrived Desmond took my arm and helped me up.

"We'll take this up Clark Street to Lincoln Park. There's nice bathing spots up that way."

He winked at the conductor, a pal, and we got our ride free, and he talked all the while we rode. But with the motor cars grinding, streetcar bells clanging, the El rattling over, and "I'm Forever Blowing Bubbles" drifting into our window from an upstairs dance hall must a run all day, I couldn't make real sense of what he was jawing about, only catch the odd word.

At North Avenue we hopped off and crossed over to the grass of the park from where we could see that big lake—pretty for all its frightfulness, for the sun had fallen to the level of the haze unfolded like a great blue-brown sash across the city and, nestled there, a lovely cherry color. The lake itself calm as milk. I was thinking it would be all right and anyhow his hand at my back guided me along the paths for a while, and then he was pushing me across uneven ground till we got to a copse of bushes where he stopped and smiled down at me.

"Here we are then, Maeve. Isn't it grand?"

He threw down the bag he was carrying and lit one of his Camels.

"Here?" I said, surprised, because I'd expected a public beach with lifeguards and everything and the change rooms where you could put your clothes in a bin, and refreshments from a cart, cold drinks and the like, when all we had here were some bushes dividing the grand city and its soaring buildings from the great lake and all the secrets I feared from it. He got my drift right away.

"I know what you're thinkin', but the big beaches further along are too crowded with swells and most of the ones in the south are dirty with niggers. You get your fights breakin' out regular, a lot of gamblin' goin' on, right on the beach. We'll have this little spot all to ourselves, don't you know? Better a quiet place when you're learnin' and I promise to be a gentleman, so you go right ahead and change, Maeve. It'll be jake."

I heard my sister's voice warning me, *You can't believe a t'ing. You be careful*, she'd a said, echoing the words I'd spoke to her when I'd stepped out with Packy and left her alone and worried that curiosity and loneliness might drive her to places she shouldn't go. But this Desmond already different than what worried her, because he'd come along when he said he would, or near enough, and here we were just like he promised, and while he thought we had the spot all to ourselves I saw a pile of garments behind one of the trees, meaning others enjoyed the place, must be good. I never saw anyone else, but I did hear laughter once. Maybe all of us trying to avoid charges for the change rooms. Maybe a charge even to step into the lake, if they did charge. Me, I wouldn't a known, not being one who frequented the bathing beaches of Chicago that week or any other week in any other city. Only those few times at Lahinch, and so long before, when it'd been all about our da and us thrashing and sputtering through the water back to him as fast as we could.

Afraid of showing hesitation, I separated the bushes and stepped through to a clear space big enough to accommodate me wrestling with my clothes, disrobing there, right outside, as if it was common for me, though whenever we undressed, Margaret and me, we never took everything off at once, and not in front of each other—not at home, not at the mission, not even in our rooms. We managed ways of leaving the top layer on while we stepped out of our bloomers and slid our nightdresses up under. There, in the bushes, with the buzzing of some insect near and the twittering of a little bird could a been snickering at me, the skirt came off first, then the shirtwaist with the violets, the corset underneath. Thrilling, the air a muggy kiss on skin never got so bare.

Hurrying, working too fast to fall, it came back to me, the scene of Margaret and me scrambling into clothes we nicked from the stacks donated to the mission. Chose ones made us look like women and not the girls we actually were, changing in the washroom of the station before the train pulled out of St. Augustine and laughing so, girls playing dress up. Margaret near tripping on the skirt too long until she'd found the means to raise the hem, for even then she knew how to use a needle. But that'd been years ago, a lifetime, and even though it's hot as blazes still and midges were whining around my ears as I stepped into the suit I bought with money not all mine, I felt like a woman of the world. I'd have stories to match any of them I'd heard from the girls at work, if I wanted to tell them, which I might not want to, seeing as how I was not much of a talker to start.

Then up with the costume, my first time in it, and lucky it hid everything'd interest a man, but my arms showing white, so white, and only then, idjit though I was, did I remember that once I got wet I'd need a towel to dry myself. What a stupid one he would think me when there must a been a towel hanging from that line I could a yanked off the night I prowled the alley. Something for the trouble'd left my knee blemished.

"You'll see I made a nice nest for us here, Maeve," he called, from the other side of the bushes, and it was do or die, same as when the nuns called out for them had vocations and I raised my hand and Margaret seeing me, raised hers.

"There you are, all set, but you'll have to take your shoes off, darlin', or they'll drag ye under and we wouldn't want that. Though I'm a champ swimmer I don't know how good I'd be at life guardin'."

Of course I looked the fool and more with my button-up boots, and once I reached the robe he'd spread on the sand fronting the bushes, I took them off and arranged myself in a pose such as I'd seen on the cover of *Dream World*. Leaning back, legs nicely crossed in front of me, surveying the sky as if I could tell the weather from it or expect something to drop, a bundle of money maybe or, more likely, a surprise from one of the gulls screaming like someone'd just died.

"Just give me a minute to change myself," he said, taking my place in the copse.

Oh, yes, I enjoyed the air that evening, it being like the petal of a wild rose—that soft, that moist. Not that roses mixed among the weeds we'd climbed through. I could hear some bird, maybe the same, mocking him, too, and wind stirring the dried leaves on the taller shrubs, the lake slopping up the shore. He sang, humming really, "Baba, daba, daba, said the monkey to the chimp." If I didn't have a good idea of what she'd a said if she saw me, I'd a liked Margaret to be there to take a gander at the pose, like Theda Bara herself, though without the kohl smudges around the eyes and without her glam clothes. My foot, with the imprint of my boots still on the stockings, the foot tapping in space, me humming along, but quietly with his silly tune, because wasn't it swell sitting there, watching the tint of the sky change, the boats way out.

Unable to fully relax, what with wearing fewer clothes in public than I'd ever wore, I held myself tight and let my thoughts drift to food for a minute, wondered what he'd packed in his sack. That subject faded as soon as he appeared in his costume, legs and arms proving he'd been in the sun regularly, and muscled so, though he was not a man did hard labor. Long legs with that same sandy hair on them as on his wrists, and hair mussed from the shirt coming off, I expect. Didn't those restless feelings force my eyes from him and direct them to the long view, the watery one. Mother of God, he was a fellow to take notice of, cocky with that smile said he knew it. Entered my mind the thought, *What does he want with me, when he might have chosen Dorothy Phillips herself?*

Shouts from way off, and when I squinted over I saw bobbing shapes in the waves, maybe belonging to whoever clothes lay yonder. Pretty as the card we sent home at Christmas showing the lake and the buildings behind, all of it more swell sure than Limerick. Come Easter, when Mammy sent her letter, she wrote she was glad the nuns'd settled in Chicago, for she'd never seen how we'd manage a place as foreign as Florida, with all the wild Indians and the darkies and trees she'd seen only in the magazines brought around by the missionary orders. Although I felt uneasy that Mammy should think us still with the nuns, I was not thinking of Mammy just then, but surveying Mr. Desmond Malloy, the length of him bent to fetch something out of his sack, and how it'd already come to seem natural to be lolling there together. A beautiful man standing with the lake at his back. The grin and his good straight teeth, the broad shoulders with their islets of freckles. He held a flask of something I rightly bet was whiskey.

"A little courage, Maeve. The water can be cold, but you can trust me. I'll not letchya drown, or even get your hair wet, if you don't want."

I shook my head and he cocked his and raised them thick eyebrows I liked, and in the low angle of sunlight I could see red hairs and gold ones mixed with the brown of a deep bay horse, the kind I would have chosen if my da had been one of the landholders in Clare. I needed something to swallow down whatever was in my throat, but I'd hardly a taken a drop from a nearly strange man in a lonesome place, both of us half dressed. Seeing he couldn't persuade me, he shrugged and took a long swallow himself. I smelled it when he sat down, not room for another body between us.

"Look at the lake, Maeve. Isn't it grand? Does it remind you of the sea over there? For all I've never been, I feel I know it from my old people talkin' of it when we lads were growin' up. Especially after a night at the Hall, on one of them music evenings they have there with the tin whistle players and the fiddlers and the school girls dancin' the jigs with their hands at their waists. Mother said it was easy for our da to miss it, when there was no chance he'd go back and risk starvin', cuttin' turf and liftin' potatoes, hopin' some farmer would take pity on him and pay him in coin instead of cabbage. Was it like that for you?"

It startled me, him wanting me to go back there, if only in my mind. The poverty worse than down along Halsted Street. "It was poor," I said, and it didn't matter the sparsity of the description, because he continued on, as if I'd said nothing.

"Oh, she used to be a terrible sharp-tongued one, my mother, but she's settled quieter since her boys are grown. She's one who's bathed in the lake, Maeve. My old mother and my old dad. Both of them. It's the best thing for you in summer. Are you ready?"

I wanted to ask how his da had got into the water if he had no legs—or was it just one he'd lost?—because I remembered the story the man told on the car one evening before Desmond

Malloy knew I existed. Maybe they'd carried the old fella in, Desmond and his brothers. Or maybe the old one'd gone in when he still had all his parts. Could it a been something in the water caused him to lose them? Any of these questions might have stalled us there on the shore, which would a been fine with me, for wasn't my empty stomach after knotting up like the letters on the crosses in St. Patrick's church, and— though still plenty hot out—goose bumps stippled my flesh where it was bare because of the light breeze skimming across the water and ruffling it prettily, if also disguising the surface.

He stood without effort and held out his hand. I reached for it automatically, and as I came upright he pulled me towards himself so I nearly bumped my nose into that broad chest with the hair curling over the top of his costume. Nearly. It not being a regular public bathing beach, stones in the sand made it cobbly, with some edges sharp enough I cried out when I stepped on one, and he offered to carry me over. Wanted to get his paws on me, he did, but no. No. I pulled my hand out of his because there we were then, at the edge, and for a minute I forgot everything else but the water with its scummy foam nudging my toes, and my stomach gurgling—though the lapping noise thankfully covered it, rude lying sound that it was. It's that makes me think hunger is not in the mind. But magic?

Did Margaret meet Harry because Anna Eva contrived it, or because it was meant to be and Anna Eva could see into the future? Could Anna Eva be as powerful as God and the Blessed V I'd been praying to, hoping for just such a man as Desmond Malloy, but never expecting him to turn up handsome so, frisky as a colt, winking as he encouraged me, on the edge of a dare, like the boys at home would dare me to jump from the highest stone step of the friary? I did jump, for I was the oldest of the Curragh girls and I had to face fear for the sake of the rest of them. To show them it could be done.

"There y'are. Just take another step. You'll like the way the bottom squeezes through your toes, just like jam comin' up."

I heard his big laugh, same as I heard the words, but for all they touched me, he might a been out on one of those ships whose masts I could see, if I was seeing straight. My mind was after spooling out stories of snakes, eels, like, and how they could wrap around a body's ankles once you were out to where you could barely stand, and if they got a good hold they'd tow you beneath. And once you were under you'd see the bones of all them'd gone before, like the folks on the *Eastland*. Them poor people—nearly a thousand there'd been—bought their white clothes for the holiday excursion the electrical company'd promised their employees, then hadn't the lot of them, whole families, toppled off the listing ship into the water. Right from the dock in the river, too, hadn't even made it to the lake, but their white clothes, like their spirits, might a drifted there.

Had to be things on the bottom'd break your heart—a child's lost shoe, a watch same as they found in the ruins of the bank, that watch belonged to Irene Miles, whose name stayed with me, for I could only imagine what her mammy felt when she got the news of the crash. Just gone to work, typing her way through the days, like any of the other girls, Irene, then smashed and burned. How would our mammy feel when Margaret told her? *She said she was going to the pictures,* Margaret would wail. *With a new fella. I never would have let her go swimming, and not with a car man!* And Mammy maybe still believing us to be nuns.

All these thoughts strummed my brain to the beat of my jumping heart, my tossing innards, me not even aware I was clutching my upper arms and shivering, while he'd given up on me for the moment, striding down the shore till the lake reached his knees.

"Come on then," he said, splashing and laughing, diving in and coming up all slick like a water creature. "It's peachy, Maeve."

Fear was fighting a fierce desire to follow him anywhere till he scooped up a big handful and splashed me with it, and instead of cooling me it burned me like a hundred tiny sparks on my skin.

"There's nothin' to worry about, I'll protect you. But you've got to get out here where you can float, Maeve, darlin'. You're gonna love it, come on, give it a try."

Darlin' was it, and him standing there in his costume wet so and outlining all his man parts, a sin to be looking there and I looked away but I'd never seen poor Packy in such a pose, and his arms—Desmond's arms—stretched out for me to fall into, same as we used to hold out our arms for the little ones learning to toddle, Margaret and me, with Nuala the last, at home, and then when we lived at the mission in that broiling Florida. He was drawing me to him with something powerful, Desmond Malloy, and I took another step till the wet stuff reached up to my calves anyway and he cheered same as if I was the Joe Jackson everyone talked about.

"There you go, come on. A few more steps and you'll be up to your knees. There's a girl."

The bottom did squish up, warm, but also slimy in a dangerous sort of way to my thinking. Yet his smile brighter than the electric along State Street lured me and sure the next step would have brought the water nearly to my bloomers, but didn't a little boat appear, barely bigger than a plaything yet carrying two boys associated with the yacht club, must have been. Careless in the way the rich can be, for weren't they singing and hollering just a short distance beyond, where Desmond Malloy stood with his arms stretched out towards me? The sail wrinkling, and them trying to straighten it, made me realize there was more wind than I'd thought gathering that evening, and who knew if one of them storms might whip up powerful gusts, tornadoes, hurling purple clouds pouring down with rain?

Desmond hollered at them. "Watch it, lads!"

Two of them wobbled in that wee boat, in bathing costumes

and one with a sort of captain's hat on and this one turned suddenly. His companion screamed at him not to upset the balance, but before he could turn back, didn't it tip and them boys go over, right in front of my eyes?

"Mother of God," I shouted to Desmond. "Save them if you can."

He laughed as the boys came up sputtering on the other side of the boat, their wet heads, the cap gone. There was no danger to them, it being that shallow Desmond could stand with his head above water as he helped them in their struggle to right the craft. Their voices clanged against one another in argument and laughter until the mast pointed up again to the deepening blue. I hard gripped each arm with the hand opposite as I stood there and waited and waited while he nattered with them. Our connection broken, I might as well have been sitting on the shore. I stood there and listened dreamily and noticed little fish in the water lapping around my lower legs, schooling like so many grains of silver rice, and marveled to be sharing the water with the cold-blooded creatures I feared.

Didn't it turn out to be my lifeboat, that little craft, for all the activity out there took the minutes he might have been getting me in deeper. While he was chatting with them, inspecting their boat, sharing the flask they'd saved from the toss, seeing them off as their dripping sail filled and they headed back to where they'd come from, I saw there would be no swimming for Maeve Curragh that evening. He said it himself as he strode through the water. "There'll be no swimmin' for Maeve Curragh, this evenin', not with the dark comin' so quick. Funny how the day goes, isn't it?"

It's what my da'd said, about the day being long and night always coming, and it softened me to think of the connection, though I doubt my da would've liked imagining Desmond's wet hand on my elbow steering me across the beach to the bushes. Same hand sliding up further, to my neck and getting tangled in my hair, for of course I'd left my hat with my clothes.

"But we'll do it again, won't we? And then you'll get your bloomers wet. Look at them, like they've just come off the clothesline on a sunny day."

The midges had gathered in numbers would challenge an army and they were singing around my ears as I tried to cover myself before they could feast on me. Once I'd buttoned my shirtwaist, I stepped out and let him take his turn because he was the one wet and all, though I saw he was warming himself with another sip from his flask and having a smoke, smiling as he surveyed me with my arms up, trying to pin my hair so that it'd fit beneath the hat.

"I'd like to see you again with your hair curlin' out like that, darlin'. It's lovely hair, and you're a peach and if we didn't do all I thought we'd do, you got your feet wet, didn't you?" He laughed at himself for using an expression described what actually happened. Didn't know my feet were still wet inside my shoes because I'd been that daft I never thought of bringing another pair of stockings, and paid the next day, blisters being the cost of stupidity.

"Hmm?" he said, stepping right close to me and tipping my chin up with his thumb, then angling in, hand on my throat. Was he going to strangle me or kiss me? Neither, only straighten the violets in danger of falling off, fasten them with the pin, breathing on me, all the while speaking. "You don't have much to say, then, do you, Maeve? I like that in a girl. Most of them chatterin' away so's they don't know what's goin' on around them. Still waters run deep, they say." Another laugh, for referring to the water, must a been. Water kept coming into it.

~

Back across the park in dusk, him sure footed, pulling me by the wrist to the avenue with its traffic and noise, me believing he had a plan and I could trust him to carry me along with it. It'd gone past the usual hour for supper, sure, and a picture of fried chicken and mashed taties nudged into my head, along with visions of ice cream sodas and pies and every good thing I ever ate or imagined eating. Consumed me, those pictures, and the warmth of the man's hand at my back, till all at once it stiffened and I felt the fingers claw in and heard laughter coming up behind us. I turned to see two boys, their white teeth big in their brown faces, two young colored fellas full of high spirits, must a been kitchen help at one of the hotels, or some of the garbage collectors got their jobs last year during the city strike.

Packy'd complained about it, how they brought the darkies in and kept some of 'em after the strike, meaning our kind never got back in. So Packy said. Desmond tensed and asked in a voice loud enough to best the din of the street, "You all right, Maeve? Are you havin' any difficulty?" Me? Then I understood he meant the question for their benefit, as if saying, *Keep away, clear out of my sight, out of town.* Feelings were running hard then, harder than I remembered, unless I'd never noticed, what with all else there was to take in when we arrived.

But, now, thinking back, I see them numbers flowing north'd cemented the hard feelings. Even my own sister had come to dislike them, surprising and all considering that she, like me, held the little ones in our arms and dried their tears sparkled clear in trails down their dusky cheeks. Beautiful so, and didn't we love them as much as those sisters we left behind, another since Nuala, Mammy wrote. Kathleen, a little sister I'd never meet. At the mission Margaret'd spent much of the day in the kitchen where she worked alongside a woman mixed of colored and Indian blood. A skinny, long-browed woman, more pious than the nuns themselves.

Then Margaret got with Harry, who told her the women might be fine—women couldn't help what their men did—but the coloreds he took exception to were them came up north in trains and by the truckload to take the jobs of union men walked out of their places to get a decent wage for the people worked there. Same folks who thought they could eat anywhere they wanted, sit on the main floor in a theater, instead of the balcony where they'd always sat.

"Blacks are spreading through the city like a sewer overflowing," said Harry. "Man works hard all his life to buy his own house, then some nigger agent comes in and buys up a building and the values of the whole neighborhood drop." The papers told the same story, 'specially when there'd been an explosion or a fire meant to drive the colored out. "It isn't fair," Margaret complained, and though I hate to think mean of her suffered so much alongside me, I can't deny she was a follower, my sister, except, before Harry, it used to be me she followed.

The boys stopped laughing when they saw the look on Desmond's puss, and they shuffled back to the store window behind us, pretended to be looking at the display in there of sheet music and piano rolls and such.

Satisfied to have put them in their place, Desmond Malloy looked up and down the street and took out his car man's watch to check it, and when we did duck into a café, he ordered us coffee and pie gone stale by that hour, and lit one of his Camel cigarettes, blew the smoke out in rings. Through the smoke I noticed that right eye of his drifting. I can't say disappointment didn't enter it, but he saw it right away, Desmond did, and explained that when he'd planned on supper, he'd forgot about a meeting tonight of the car men's association, for it's serious, this strike business, and he had to play his part, if he expected a bright future with the Chicago Surface Lines, which he no doubt did. It must have been getting onto nine by then, a queer time for a meeting, and I said as much, my empty stomach boosting the petulance.

"Queer time for a meetin'."

"It is that, but these are queer times, and with the shift work… Well, you understand, don't you, dear?" Dear. His collar open and a whiff of the lake from the skin of his throat, and them fingers with the shining hairs on them tapping the wood of the table, cloudy with water stains, and me wondering if he was keeping me hungry for some reason but what it could be, and if so, what could I do?

He threw his nickels down and herded me out to the street and up to the streetcar stop. "These are tryin' days, but we'll best them, Maeve. We'll meet again this week and if you wait for me, I'll save you your fare tomorrow. For tonight, take this." He pressed a few coins into my hand, pockets must a been thick with them, and realizing I would neither have to spend the coins I had left, nor go to bed gnawing inside but stop for a bite before I climbed Bridey's stairs, I waved out the window. He jogged along with the car for a minute before it gathered a little speed. I wouldn't go to bed hungry, but I wouldn't be sitting across a table like I'd sat with Packy, tapping at my lips with a linen napkin and sipping a drink dainty.

In the paper beside me, left behind, but with a story torn out at the bottom, a headline right across the front made me smile—and that was rare enough when it came to the papers.

ANIMAL PALS MOURN FOR CY

He was the zookeeper these last thirty years, fired for drunkenness or saying his mind, maybe both. The papers had the lions roaring dismally, monkeys stopping their chatter, as the news spread through the zoo. Reports, too, of lower prices near the Hull House neighborhood. Ten cents a pound for tomatoes near enough where we could pick them up, and wouldn't we be needing to save if Bridey turned out to be the taking advantage type, and put our rent up. Little Janet still not found, though a suspect'd been taken in. God help her, the poor child.

FRIDAY, JULY 25, 1919

MARGARET LIKED THE comedians and the singers at the shows. There could never be enough Uncle Josh to satisfy her, whereas me—even before Mr. R, but more so after—it was the magicians held me. Of course, I came to know how some of them managed the tricks, and I learned how to juggle, not that juggling is magic, though the children thought it so and were always after asking me to demonstrate, bringing me oranges or rubber balls of some kind, begging me, even when I'd already got too old to hold one ball steady, let alone juggle it with another or two.

When my sister and me first arrived in Chicago all those years ago, we two girls in our borrowed dresses, we'd never seen so many theaters, let alone a show in any of them. Margaret lived-in and had but the one day off. Me, being on my own, except for the girls worked all round me in the big catalogue place would never a gone by myself. But Gladys, worked at the desk alongside me then, invited me to that first show. I pretended it would be no great event, while mimicking Gladys's every move, and her noticing, but only laughing to think someone could reach the age of eighteen without having been to the vaudeville. Already past twenty, Gladys knew it all, yet she'd never been too high and mighty about it. Well, I'd fibbed about my age, hadn't I, and it didn't matter because I could do the catalogue job as well as any of them. Just sixteen still, but Gladys or nobody had to know.

From the balcony seats we could see the faces of the lovely singers and laugh at the comics, and in the play they were after putting on—about the girl pining for her fellow lost at war—dab at our tears, and later sing along to the words on the picture screen with a piano player seemed to know every song. Best of the lot, Anna Eva, small, as I have always been small, and her dazzling performance in the cabinet. I thought to myself, *I'll have to bring Margaret, seeing as how I know where to go and what to do, and no one'll stare at us and think something mean.*

On her next day off we did so, but to another theater, even fancier, for Margaret could pay her own way and we spent it on the good seats. There, towards the end of a show Margaret remembered for it being her first look at Uncle Josh, was a girl in a beautiful dress, pink as a wild rose and glistening with sequins, the scalloped neckline draped with crystal beads. The Great Sebastian so-called, a mind reader, sent her out to the audience, and that lovely girl spotted me on the aisle. When Sebastian asked for someone to offer up a personal article, my eyes were resting on him, the handsome man with the turban on his head and the mustache, but it was the pretty girl with a flower in her hair tapped me on the shoulder and asked for something.

Margaret nudged me and what did I have save a handkerchief, a clean one, though, and the girl snatched it away. Margaret grabbed onto my arm and the man in the turban said, "The object you're holding? Why I believe...yes, it's a handkerchief." Not so brilliant, perhaps, but it could have been a necklace or a key or a coin, and it was not so much the right answer gave me the shivers, because they might a worked out a code—the Great Sebastian and his lovely assistant—but I wondered if in fact a line ran from him to me, something connecting us, with me supposedly possessing the famous gift came from having been born in the wee hours, as my mammy had been.

Oh, yes, the vaudeville could carry you away, and we hadn't had much occasion for that. The evenings at St. Patrick's, and before we left home, travelling shows'd come to Ennis. But I don't remember them as much as the stories would be told at Uncle Thomas's house, of the meddling wee folk, the banshees would plague my mind when I had an errand at night. I'd never take to the road alone after one of them nights at Uncle T's, but cling to my limping da, and Mammy with the baby in a bundle on her back. The very first performance she saw began Margaret's crush on Uncle Josh, her still laughing at the things he'd said, as she and I kissed goodbye at the Prairie Avenue stop. It made the days ahead easier for her. She wanted to go every week.

We tried the neighborhood theaters as well the downtown palaces, one grander than the next. We learned the popular songs, we even saw the famous Alexander, would bring people onto the stage and study his crystal ball and tell a person her prospects. But, after the handkerchief, I shied away, and even though Mr. R told us it was a trick, like all the others and explained how the common mentalists could convince an audience by pointing out things about an individual applied, in fact, to people in general, even Mr. R did not know all the secrets. He'd said so himself.

"You believe in magic, don't you?" he'd asked, that slatey glare of his boring into me as it had that first day. Truth was, I did—it was all that blather about the gift, my knack for seeing things others could not, started it—and so, whenever they called for volunteers from the audience, I never budged an inch and wouldn't let anyone volunteer me again. I didn't want the world and all to know what dwelled in my mind. Especially Margaret, especially on the Friday morning that fated week in July when she poked me awake and asked me about the evening and what did we eat and did he like the violets.

"Was it grand then, Maeve? What picture did you see? Tell me his name again."

In the eggshell light of the morning, the first words on my tongue, Desmond Malloy, started a flood of warmth same as the morning tea Margaret pushed at me so a wave of it sloshed near over the edge.

"We'll have plenty occasion to talk later, tonight, but yes, it was grand. Desmond he's called. Desmond Malloy."

"But it can't be tonight, unless you wait up for me, because it's the baptism party for Harry's nephew. I told you yesterday, but I see you are distracted. You could come along, if you like, Maeve. Harry never minds."

All bustle she was, Margaret, pinning her hair, buttoning her sleeves, shaking the skirt free of what'd gathered on it since she took it off last night—hair, dust, soot. Me savoring the breeze she created for its reminder of the air off the lake against my bare arms, him standing there watching me clutch each arm opposite, as if chilled. Laughing at the odd possibility of someone feeling cold on an evening so warm. Laughing at something. Desmond. Didn't the name dissolve in my mouth and sweeten it while Meggsie went on about her plans and hurried me along.

~

Desmond'd said to wait for him, but if I'd let another car pass by I would a been late for work. Hadn't I been that daft and dreamy I forgot to ask the shift he'd be working? Wait for him, but when? The newsies sounded more like goats bleating than singers.

CAR CRISIS TODAY! STRIKE NEAR!

FITZGERALD'S WIFE ARRESTED!

JANET STILL MISSING!

Two cents for the Friday paper, a nickel for my fare, and a shame, so, me knowing somebody with a pocketful, and a soft spot for the likes of me. July 25, seventy-five degrees, cooler then, and there's more about the little missing girl, Janet. Something draws a body to sad stories, a natural sympathy that puddles around curiosity. I prayed to the Blessed V that Janet had come to no harm while at the same time feeling certain she had. Fitzgerald still the fellow most suspect.

But them hollering about the strike of the car men yanked my thoughts away from little Janet because I saw I'd been wrong to doubt Desmond. A worry for him sure, the strike, and despite all he'd said about the Reds and the Bolshies, him no doubt voting with the others, for people had to make a stand. He'd said it himself. I pictured him doing that actually, standing up and raising his hand when the vote was called—memory of me still on his mind—his hair combed back neat so the peak pointed down, and his collar buttoned up. Gave me something to dream about as the car jolted to a stop, and started up again, rattling we passengers until we got to the Loop and all the hurrying.

Wait for me, he'd said, Desmond Malloy had, and weren't those the words pealed through the day, me once including them as I typed out the orders, so I had to roll that form up and out and roll another in and down, for imagine an order called "The Ideal Handkerchief *wait for me* Wand." I thought of the boy had printed out the request, if it was a boy. Pictured him trying to fool his friends by passing a square of silk from one cone to another. He didn't know, maybe, he'd have to buy his own silk. Smiling at that, me who never found too much to smile at.

"What's on your mind, Maeve?" Eveline asked me. "It's still only Friday and we have a day to go till we're free to dream. Unless we make like Houdini himself and manage to dazzle Mr. R by escaping into thin air. Are you planning something? You've got the look of someone with a plot."

"And what would I be after plottin' then?" said me, but for all my experience with secrets it was the joy gave me away, the memory, the anticipation, and Eveline'd seen it before.

"A fellow. That's it, isn't it?"

"Get on with you."

"She can't help it, Maeve. It's all she ever thinks about." This from Ruth, who seldom had the opportunity to get back at Eveline.

"It is, isn't it?" She had the bit and she did not intend to let it go.

I rolled another order form into my machine. Eveline leaned across and pinched me. I didn't dare look or she would a known for sure. *Wait for me, wait for me.*

"It don't take a magician to guess what's on your mind, my friend of few words. And if you don't want to talk today, the time will come when you do and you know where to find me." She shook her shoulders in a little dance and sighed, and then addressed herself to the orders on her desk, for nut cups and paper streamers. Not so remarkable as them I processed. Ruth rolled her goggly eyes at me and shook her head and soon after found an excuse to go to the front and gossip with Florence. With just us two in the back Eveline spoke again. "I mean it. If you've got need of anything where a man is concerned, I'm your girl. Do you catch my drift?"

Mr. R had callers that day, Florence told us when lunch hour struck and we stepped out of the building as we liked to do. He'd closed himself in his office, Mr. R, with a couple. The woman, *Could it be Anna Eva?* I wondered for a minute, then accepted it couldn't be her, because Florence said the woman was almost as big as her husband, or whoever he was in the bowler and the pin-striped suit, and so would be taller than Anna Eva. Anyhow, I'd never seen her in black, only white, flowing, so she never seemed evil, despite what the papers said later about her using trickery to make it seem she was a true seer. I never believed her to be anything but good, a body you could trust with your heart's wishes.

"Someone famous?" Ruth wanted to know.

"I can't say." Florence squeezed her lips together, turned her head away. Pretty Florence'd given up wearing her mourning clothes. Must a been because a year had passed since her Walter'd died, or because black didn't go in summer. Not in the kind of heat we had that week. Mr. R'd felt sorry for her or liked her looks to hire her on, near the same day as me, but she didn't need the job as much as the rest of us. She lived across the bridge, on the north side. Close to Lincoln Park, with her mammy and da and a little brother'd been safe from the war on account of him being too young. "Thank God for that," Florence would say when she spoke of him.

She had the light hair my sister had, but she wore it more severe, gave her a dramatic look. The hairstyle, the violet eyes often cast down, as if she was contemplating something deep, and the lovely clothes she wore, always with a bit of lace, or a drape to the skirt. Whatever it was she wore, or did, boosted your view of her as someone wounded, and I believe Eveline thought she'd designed it all to get our sympathy. But of course Florence'd had her true tragedy in Walter. Nothing designed about that.

She refused to say who the famous or not famous visitors were that day because Mr. R'd sworn her to secrecy, like the rest of us. But that didn't stop curiosity from gnawing at us.

"The thing about starting to say something, but leaving the good parts unsaid, it's teasing," said Eveline, before we went back in. "Is that what you used to do with your Walter?" she asked Florence, while directing a glance at me. It startled me, the notion Eveline wanted to be my friend.

Ruth giggled, but Florence's already pink skin burned redder with whatever sad or shaming memories Eveline'd tweaked. Me, though, I didn't take sides, didn't say much at all, only touched Florence's arm to turn her and we thronged back through the whirly doors into the building, past our watchful Clyde, without saying more.

~

Finally, day's end, and all we office workers on the street at once. A car pulled up, clanging. No Desmond Malloy, though if he didn't stick his head out the opened windows, how would I a known, with the pushing crowds blocked the view. Had to be steaming in there with all those bodies, but a lovely gale swept through the canyon between the tall buildings, and it being shady, I could wait. There was even a water fountain and a trough for watering horses, but filled so with garbage. In the going-home bustle of the streets, I took refuge in the pages of the newspaper I had yet to study, though it was the early edition I'd hung onto and there'd been more news since then as the strong-throated ones hollered.

FITZGERALD'S WIFE SAYS HE KNOWS!

COURTS DECIDE BEER IS BEER!

BROWNS AND SOX IN HOT FIGHT FOR SECOND!

NEGRO CRIME TALES A LOT OF BUNK SEZ SANDBURG!

Soon I was bargaining with myself as another car pulled up, people jostled on, it clacked off. If I didn't see his mug craning out the window of the very next car I'd better step on anyway for my waistband's loosening around my body. I'd enough paper left to feed my curiosity and entertain myself with the funnies—Mutt and Jeff, Dorothy Darnit—while I enjoyed a piece of pie and a second cup of coffee in the Halsted Thompson's. I'd sit there with all the other single girls came to find a new life in the city and ended up under the glaring lights hung from the ceiling of the room where individual chairs—with their one arm wide enough for your plate and your cup—ensured they'd stay single.

Not so many horses and good so, for the streets were cleaner, but here stood one, a poor creature, dirty gray, though it could have been white as a fairy horse if somebody'd given it a good scrub. Exhausted, stopped in the car tracks. Wouldn't move, despite the driver pleading with it, then whipping it with a switch, then getting down and applying his boot directly to the horse's rump. The nag shifted herself as far as the curb, then stopped, as if she'd reached her barn. One of them ladies looked like the speakers on the women's voting, always sported the big hats and the spectacles, marched over and spoke to the owner, waved her finger at him, no doubt scolding.

There were ladies took it on themselves to fix all the wrongs they saw. Women with an education and fathers rich enough they didn't have to work, but could go round meddling in other people's business. Or so said a letter to the editor in the *Daily News*. State Street soon wouldn't allow the horses and buggies, not with the future going to motorcars. But we were in the in-between stage, had bits of what'd gone before and all that was to come. The horse planned to stay right where she'd planted herself, thankfully off the tracks, because another car came clanging up. Desmond Malloy had not forgot me. I saw his smile beaming brighter than the brass buttons on his jacket and I knew I'd be going home with an extra nickel to spend at Thompson's.

"There y'are darlin'."

He squeezed my arm, all the while grinning over at me with one eye wandering to the box, making sure no one snuck on board without depositing their fares unless he gave them a sign. Grinning at me, Maeve Curragh, and didn't it make me forget the crowding, the stink, poor Irene Miles and Janet Wilkinson, the trouble at the car barn, coloreds and whites fighting each other right outside President Wilson's door, and every other tragic thing, as we moved up Madison towards Halsted, him calling out the street names in his own comical way—"Clinton, Jefferson, Desplaines. Dis dem dere plains for dose of you lookin' for it!"

I nodded as if speaking to the woman sitting down in front of me, the one's face'd wrinkled with a question. *That's right. This is Clinton coming up and he's the man will tell you the next, if this is not your stop. And, if you didn't notice, by the way, it's me his smile is meant for.* Then he's standing next to me, talking in a voice whispery enough no one else could hear, them eyebrows of his framing a gaze trickled over me like a cool stream.

"There's more trouble down at the barns, Maeve, dear. I had to take another shift so's my pal could go speak to the bosses, as he's one of the big union men. We'll have to make Sunday your next lesson. Whaddya say? You won't disappoint me, will you?"

Disappoint *him*? He took my wide-open eyes to mean surprise, not knowing my true thoughts concerning the situation, that anyone should think me the body with power to disappoint. Gentler then, and closer, like a blessing on my head, the smell of tobacco assuring me he'd had a break. I turned up a face displayed what? The tingle between my shoulder blades? My hopes? While in the scheming part of my mind I was thinking I'd be able to put together a better outfit. Find a proper towel, maybe line up for shoes, after all, because you never knew what'd be left from bundle day. Or go to the open market on Maxwell Street, with money to spend since tomorrow's the day Mr. R would be coming around with our pay envelopes. It wasn't like Desmond'd stood me up. In fact he was trying to sit me down. Bulled over to a young colored man sprawling on a bench at the back, his arm slung across the rim of the bench, discouraging office workers from sitting down next to him, because his loose clothes took up as much or more room than he did on account of their ripe smell.

"No one taught you your manners?" Desmond said, kicking right at the fellow's scuffed boot to get his attention. "Don't you know to offer your seat when there's a lady nearby standin'?"

Sleepy eyes widened in a face itself no wider than a Bible's spine. I wouldn't mind sitting, sure, though some ladies took it as an insult when a colored offered a seat, as if their skin were not naturally dark, but dirty and had soiled the place somehow. Letters in the papers said they didn't know how to behave in the city, those colored farm folk hopped the train north. They didn't know you were not supposed to wear your overalls without a shirt underneath, didn't know you were supposed to give yourself a good scrub everyday. This is how it was done in America. For all I could say about the Sisters of Perpetual Grace, they had taught us customs our mammy wouldn't a known to teach us. We'd never been as clean as we got to be at that mission, and since, but no one'd ever worried about it so much at home, where some sort of wash on the Saturday before church'd always been sufficient, with the whole bath saved for Christmas and Easter. The way the boy got up and hunched over to the strap nearest the back exit made my stomach shrink.

"There you go, darlin'," said Desmond, proud of himself. I couldn't refuse, could I, and the seat still warm from that fella's skinny arse, him studying the window with narrowed eyes, wouldn't a heard if I troubled to say thank you.

~

There were as many papers in the evening as the morning, including your final editions, with the box scores entranced the city. On that Friday evening, every paper there on every pile at the Halsted stop had pictures of little Janet on the front page, though on the bigger papers her sweet face had moved beneath the fold. She would disappear from the news altogether if they didn't find her soon. It's just one child after all and, sad as it was, working people wouldn't be able to get to their employment if the car men went out, and with the prices of everything gone up, how could you pay for anything if you couldn't get to work? Trouble everywhere.

JEWELRY STORE ROBBED OF $8,000!

GUARD ATTACKED IN DAYLIGHT!

MAYOR SEZ SEND WAR PROFITEERS TO POKEY

The newsies like beads on a string all along Halsted, but I turned in at Thompson's, where I chose a seat with a view to the door and watched the girls coming in. Plenty like me, the young ones. But older ones too, a man and wife had to be Bridey's age, him steering her forward and her looking at him like he knew everything in the world. Maybe they'd been married as long as the couple whose picture I saw in the paper, fifty years, and they're merely stopping that evening to save her fixing a meal. Or maybe there was some other story behind them.

They left my thoughts as quickly as they entered and found their place, because a fellow in a car man's uniform stepped in next. My heart dropped because the first sight of him made me think he was Desmond. He was that tall, but his pug face and hair that lay almost over one ear denied it, thankfully, because a chippy girl hung on his arm, curl pasted to her forehead and big spots of rouge on her cheeks, like the kewpie dolls you could win at Riverview.

Smell of hamburger steak. Mashed potatoes gone crusty, but enough gravy would perk them up. Thanks to my man, and the carfare he'd saved me, I ate my fill and was lingering with the second cup of coffee, like I'd promised myself. Not reading the funnies as I'd planned, but basking in the memory of that sweet whisper came down through the weave of my hat. Disappoint *me*? I was gazing towards the food counter at the farm scene above, made out of little colored tiles, same as the discovery of Chicago in the Marquette Building'd been formed out of tiles—that being the fashion then, making whole pictures out of little pieces of various colors—when a pair of ladies entered and looked around for a place to sit.

Ladies like the kind talked to the man with the horse. Their eyes lit on the two chairs across from me, empty as if waiting for them. I pretended to be fumbling with something in my bag, but it did no good because they'd noticed me notice them and soon they were there, and one of them, with a voice like a river, said, "Good evening, dear." I was reminded of the nuns would talk to me that way sometime. "Dear," not the way Desmond said it, and—knowing the nuns and what they turned out to be, some of them—I took a big gulp of my coffee and it burned my mouth and didn't I yelp despite myself.

"Oh, my, you must have hurt yourself, miss. Sir, sir!" She hurried up to the counter calling to the fellow there for a glass of water, which came in an instant—she had that way about her everybody listened. "Just let it sit there in your mouth for a minute."

They introduced themselves, Harriet and Clare, and if it'd been Margaret instead of me, she'd have chattered on about Clare being the name of the county we came from in Ireland, and telling most of our story, not all, for Margaret and I never confessed why we ran from the nuns, or how, only that we'd decided we hadn't a vocation. These ladies, especially Clare with her river voice, were not so bad as that letter-to-the-editor writer made them out to be. They fanned themselves with one of the newspapers had sometimes called them man-haters and commented on the weather, and then didn't they offer to buy me some ice cream to soothe my burned tongue.

If they were not the company I wanted, they were company all the same, and ice cream was ice cream, and my mouth did burn. I knew there's nothing in this life came absolutely free, and yet the price of dessert seemed to be nothing but information— where I came from, where I lived, where I worked. Sneaking in a way to find out my age, which was plenty old enough to be on my own, and how long have you called Chicago your home and do you have a beau?

Not more than a sentence did it take to satisfy them I'd established myself in rooms with my sister, and the flu'd got my beau, for I didn't know that I should mention Desmond Malloy. Even the name in my head, wanting to spill out, made me burn the same as if the coffee'd scalded me all the way down.

"You're one of the fortunate ones then, despite the sad loss of your intended. What are you called, dear? Here we are talking like old friends and we don't even know your name!"

She laughed at this, as if hours instead of minutes'd passed here among the clatter of dishes and the shouts of the cooks and the countermen. I answered her at the same time running my finger over another name in fancy script on the outside of my coffee cup, spelled Thompson.

They were out that night, Clare and Harriet, visiting the tenements to tell people in the neighborhood about the goings-on at Hull House. "You must know it, Maeve," they said. And who wouldn't a known that building sprawled along Halsted? A promise you wouldn't die of it, whatever the trouble was. Shabby, but solid, sitting there, and the odd sights you saw from the windows of the streetcar. A woman covered in flour and her carrying an empty sack and standing on the doorstep. The people lined up for whatever was being handed out on food day.

"I guess you know that we've a fine apartment building for working girls, they run it themselves. Girls like you, Maeve, and your sister. Just over on Polk Street. So if you're ever in a spot, you know, you can come over and take a look. You ask for me, should you need to."

When Margaret lived-in, I pondered such places. Cheaper than the women-only residences downtown, like the one where Ruth lived. When I passed the West Side YWCA, and that was often enough, it being in the neighborhood, I looked over and even stepped inside once, but didn't it smell like charity, remind me of the mission and all we'd been made to feel there—thankful, inferior, ashamed? Charity didn't come free, neither.

This Clare then unpinned her hat and took it off and I saw her hair matched the pale wheaten color of Margaret's and I liked her looks better without the hat. She had a wide mouth and her smile unhid a gold tooth, not far back. Added some years to her. She could a been Mammy's age, or older even. My heart opened a bit. She was that kind I thought of telling her something would bind us, the way confidences do, but what? Never Desmond. Not the story of us hiding out in the bushes near naked. No, women like that would reel off all the dangers before grabbing my arms and sweeping me off to their Hull House or Polk Street or somewhere they could keep me safe. Weren't there people already coming into our office building and distributing them pamphlets showed men in black fedoras waiting to nab girls from the train station?

Yet, for all the warnings, the saddest thing'd been, nobody'd ever noticed me. Nobody'd tried to accost me or lure me. I didn't seem to make an impression on the city at all until the evening Packy found me at the church hall. Then Desmond Malloy picked me out from among all the others on his car. I couldn't talk about Desmond so soon, but something. My sister? How she'd settled on a man and what would I do when she went off with him? The thought sprung up as if freed, and pressed against my skin, something I never knew'd been crouching there inside.

"I might consider it. Because Margaret will be leaving with her Harry soon. They're going to be married at Christmas and they'll want their own place, sure."

Clare reached across the space between our one-armed chairs and patted my knee, as if I needed comforting. "Why don't you pay a visit to the Polk Street building? You'd be surprised to find girls just like you. You'd never be lonely there. They go out in the evenings together. It wouldn't be your sister, but the next best thing."

Lonely was not something I planned to be ever again, but what she didn't know wouldn't hurt her.

"Just remember where we are if you need anything, dear."

Their suppers were getting cold and they set about eating and we all fell silent for a spell until I saw there was nothing for it but to leave.

~

Margaret got in with her talk of the baptism party and Harry's fear the Union Stock Yards would go out again and the teamsters support them, how she would have to work for the both of them and it would be okay because the garment manufacturers foresaw an increase in work with the demand for winter coats. A cold winter predicted, and the prediction came true, sure, but all we expected then was somebody'd be working and maybe they wouldn't have to put off their wedding after all.

As if she'd read my mind same as the Great Alexander or them, she asked, "What about you, Maeve? Do you think this new man, this Desmond, might be the one?"

"Don't be after frettin' about me," I huffed, for hadn't I already lived on my own, me in the great city of Chicago while she slept high on Prairie Avenue? Me just sixteen kept my arms close to my body and my head down and lied straight out, said I was eighteen, a trained stenographer, not a full lie because the nuns'd showed me how to type and had begun to teach me shorthand. So I got the job for the big catalogue company, riding the cars back to a room smaller than Bridey's, taking my meals in silence, afraid a what'd spill out of my mouth if I opened it. Maybe I'd a stayed in that situation if it hadn't been for Packy and then me catching enough of the flu myself to have to miss weeks of work and lose my place. Margaret gone by then from Prairie Avenue and hiring out for piecework barely covered the room rent, much less food for us.

My sister fell to sleep smooth faced, her big problem solved, despite the little problems remaining. But me, I couldn't sleep, not at all, not with the heat and the thoughts in my mind running like the creatures rustled at night looking for opportunities in the alleyways of Chicago.

Back to the sill of the window, dreaming, when the good people gathered as dark shapes among the piles of cast-off bricks and metal and whatever else'd cluttered the dirty ground between the buildings. Maybe only someone strolling home from the tavern, or a couple snuggling, or even dogs, I thought at first, but no sound drifted up, meaning it must a been the good people wrestling, one against the other, as in the long ago hill battles in

Munster. Fierce, as if they're out to slaughter one another or some common enemy I couldn't see with the few lamps sputtered out as stars behind swift-moving clouds. I could see no faces, only whirling outlines made it more fearful so's my heart jumped up to my shoulder and beat there madly. Them being out of our usual time and from some world not altogether ours kept the cause of the struggle a mystery. It couldn't a been me, yet why had they showed themselves?

Dizzy, faint even, I tried to raise Margaret, tell her I was sick. But wasn't she that used to my prodding and jostling, the two of us thrashing away like the forms outside, she only turned and mumbled and the tapioca pudding feel of her shoulder recalled the cafeteria over on Halsted and the vision of a little cherry sitting in the middle of the gluey stuff and the kindness of that lady, Clare.

I nodded off to my sister's moaning, and soon entered dreams of a big full moon, the lake gleamy as the fine chalice the priest raises at the Mass and not watery at all, the lake, but solid, so when Desmond led me towards it we walked on top. I trusted it, as I trusted him, and lifted my face to his mouth, which I wanted to kiss the way I never wanted to kiss Packy, nor in the rough way that man on the ship tried to kiss me, nor in the way my da and mammy kissed me, with all the love in the world while a kind of resignation stuck to my face so they never knew my thoughts at all.

Wasn't it lucky I got to be the expert? Started young to hide what went on inside my head?

Such a dream. Me waking from it with a troubling feeling, had to be sin. I never slept much at all, nor did many people in the city. It was that hot, the weather and all what else boiling. And my tongue still sore from the coffee'd scalded it, despite the ice cream. Margaret, mumbling as she tossed, about rashers and being careful to wash your hands so worms didn't get into them.

I fixed the sheet over her and went back to the sill, lifted my arms to dry the slickness under them and fancied myself flying over the buildings like that doomed *Wingfoot Express*, seeing everything down there and making sense of it, maybe learning whatever happened to the Wilkinson girl, God help her, and knowing where himself'd gone, for he'd been shy of telling me too much. Lived over in Bridgeport still, he said, helping out his mammy and his da, who had finished with working. No wonder he'd finished if he'd lost his legs, but Desmond had not explained how yet and I'd forgotten to ask him, what with our meetings being so rushed. But the opportunity would come. Sounded like a big family—hadn't the man on the car said four boys? Were there sisters, too? I wondered when he'd want to introduce me and if they'd take to me.

That hour vermin owned the town, displacing even them battling shapes sent me to the side of my sister. I heard rat tails sliding, imagined their pointy noses poking into the meager leavings made it to the trash, and then I spied a shadow. Someone roaming the lanes like I'd done, and before the cloud rolled back over the moon I saw a shadow enter the tenement across. Wasn't I hoping he belonged there, because I'd hate to a been called as a witness to testify against some murdering fellow who snuck into a house at night. Then a candle flamed in a black square across the way. There wouldn't be anyone snatched like young Janet, not in this neighborhood had only the writhings of people couldn't rest, the faeries battling it out for causes only they knew, and the whiskered critters came out in the night.

Saturday, July 26, 1919

**JANET'S PHOTO FAILS TO BRING CONFESSION
PLEADING EYES OF LOST GIRL
DO NOT MOVE FITZGERALD**

CAR PARLEY BRINGS HOPE

**FRENCH PROTEST AMERICAN
SOLDIER ACTS TO COLORED**

I SCANNED THE DAMP ink as I waited, but I never bought a copy from the curly-haired fella with the dago lilt to his words, nor from the ruffian on the other side of the street trying to disguise his station with a necktie he must've lifted from somewheres. Not that day, it being payday, and me, after my feast at Thompson's, with just enough to get downtown.

Came through the mail, the pieces of a fortune-telling ball, and the customer after pestering us for a refund. The ball didn't work, not as advertised, not as Mr. Howard Thurston made it work, and the customer in question'd embarrassed himself, having been the butt of laughter from the group he set himself up to entrance. Instead of moving up and down its rod, as expected, to answer the common questions—How many children will I have? Will I be rich? When will my beau propose to me?—the ball'd dropped to the bottom of the base and never budged. The performer shamed, his audience wanting their money back.

He should a known the ball couldn't answer without the magician contriving a spell. Magic was no matter of mechanics alone, as Mr. R had well taught us. Not to give anything away, Mr. R would start, in one of the moods'd come over him, appearing without warning in the back, dressed in his usual neat business suit, but as if wearing a cape or something conferred on him a theatrical, sort of swashbuckling air. He would pick up a trick—an illusion we were to call them—"The Ideal Handkerchief Wand," or a deck of cards. He'd practice for the lot of us at the back, and while flipping the cards from hand to hand and fanning them out, then sweeping them back into his hand, he would ruminate, as he did less with us than with his cronies who visited.

"The real magic, girls, comes from the magician. Watch closely. You see it is not so much what I do with the apparatus, but that you *want* to believe. Yes, you do, don't try to deny it. The audience has to be willing to believe, and it is the magician who opens the door for them to that opportunity. No illusion that. Are you ready, girls?"

He would cause a broach, for example, to move from Ruth's shirtwaist to his pocket. Even we who knew it a trick were fooled. But hadn't I guessed this all along, operated as such? It is the magician creates the magic, and before you can convince anyone else of your unearthly powers, you have to convince yourself. Sad to say, no such advice appeared in the catalogue distributed by The Chicago Magic Company, and so the unfortunate customer who'd bought the fortune-telling ball'd failed, perhaps was bound to fail.

With Mr. R gone on his usual Saturday lunch, not to return till the hour came to hand out the pay packets, I tried to put the ball together, see if it would work for me, answer my questions and all. For the tube of that hourglass marked time as sand trickled through, that space between the past and future'd magnified so the present seemed everything—the what-to-come far off as the roof of the building looked like a palace, the Art Institute, with its big lions, and the past so far behind I could barely remember the music of my family's voices and the squeak of the wicket gate. There in the middle was me, stretched out between that distant future and the just as distant past, waiting, waiting.

"Do you think that'll really work, Maeve?" Eveline, laughing, a flake of lipstick on her front tooth, though I didn't tell her, not with her thinking me the fool.

"I'm tryin' to see if the customer was right."

"And then what? We're not supposed to send any refunds."

She waited for a reply never came, but another laugh neither. Hard Eveline softened a little. "I think you really believe in that stuff. Who would a thought? It's a shill game, Maeve. There's always some trick to it."

"I know it. It's just the trick makes me curious is all."

She winked, she did, as if we shared more than I imagined. A bit of a seer herself, Eveline, and though I'd never been much against her from the start—not as much as Ruth and Gladys—I'd begun to open to her more, because we don't know all there is to know about a person, do we? *Let he who is without sin cast the first stone.* Who was that said about, then, was it Mary Magdalene?

Normally we sent damaged goods back with Billy, who kept them behind the swinging door in the storeroom. Mr. R would sometimes be able to fix a problem so's we could mail out the article again. Yet he seldom got up to that task and a pile of broken things gathered dust on a shelf near the floor. Nobody'd miss the ball is why I thought of smuggling it home, but hadn't I already done worse and, with all the strikes, I couldn't risk losing the job. I put the pieces in a drawer in my desk and there they remained. Then it was just waiting for Mr. R to come in with our pay. He always made a bit of a show of it, too, holding the envelopes up while a little thrill'd go through us all, even Eveline. I knew it, because I'd seen her shoulders rising same as mine, the oft-stained teeth biting on her red lips.

The girls lived at home might be planning a shopping trip, if they could make it to the stores before early closing. Gladys surely would want to go somewheres and I'd seen her at our front, lunchtime, talking to fair Florence. Didn't say a word to me, only smiled when I passed. Maybe she'd given up on me as a confidant on account of me snubbing her on the Thursday. Maybe the two of them would go off together, and wouldn't I like so, too, but we without relatives to put us up had to satisfy their rent first. With Thompson's asking more for meals, and Bridey, on account of some missing butter, threatening to cut off our kitchen "privliges," as she called them. I saw my pay shrinking—price of bacon doubled since we could afford to buy it, tea gone up by a full dime per pound.

Yes, Florence might make a better companion for Gladys, them better matched on account of her living with her aunt and Florence still at home, so naturally having more to spend than the rest of us. Even if Gladys had to pay something for her room, it wasn't much, and her aunt wouldn't throw her out if she was short. That left Eveline, Ruth, and me as the independents. Eveline seemed to not care what went on with anyone. She'd be out the door as soon as the long hand on the clock moved up to the top. She'd already spent ten minutes buffing her nails and smoothing her stockings, using a little silver compact with a mirror to powder her nose. I'd a liked one of those and maybe I'd get one when I was promised to Desmond. He'd favor all the newest styles and I imagined he'd want his wife to look her best. Eveline noticed me watching.

"Want to try some?"

"Oh, don't," Ruth warned. "It's cheap."

Eveline laughed, but not in a mean way. "You try it, too, Ruthie. It washes off, you know."

"Doesn't seem to be much traffic in the party business if you have the opportunity to do all that."

"Come on, try it. You first."

She held out the silver case to Ruth, who—though she looked at it suspicious like, as if there was a spider and not powder inside—took it and held it in her hands, opened it and touched the powder with her finger.

"It does smell good."

We'd divided, we three in the back and Florence up front with my pal Gladys who'd never even worked at The Chicago Magic Company.

"You're not going to try it?"

Ruth blinked and sucked in a breath and handed the compact to me. "Not today. I'm perfectly happy with myself as I am, thank you."

It felt lovely, the shiny silver smudged a bit from going around from hand to hand, but cool against my skin. It snapped open and in the little round mirror I saw the middle of my face, without the hair, without the neck of my shirtwaist. Dorothy Phillips was it? Well, I'd do it then. I patted the puff into the pressed powder and daubed it on myself, my cheeks, my nose, under my eyes. Ruth couldn't help watching for all she might a disapproved.

"It does smell good, you're right about that. How does it look?"

I didn't like it that Ruth stuck out so. Awkward. Might a been me. Was me, before Desmond. But I had someone, and Eveline too, had to be, while Ruth had only the company she found in the building where she lived with the other women who worked downtown. For all the ladies in the big hats, Clare and her friend, had praised them buildings where girls could live together, couldn't a been their first choice.

"Not so bad," she admitted.

"Brings out your eyes," said Eveline, then laughed, because if this is what it did, then for sure it was better Ruth'd declined. Maybe she'd missed Eveline's meaning. I know she didn't like our mate's brazen way, but she was fascinated with her same as me.

"But I wouldn't want to get in the makeup habit. I've got better things to save for."

"Better? Like what, Ruthie?"

She chewed on the inside of her cheek, maybe considering whether or not she wanted to say, then decided to go ahead. "The Normal College. I'll be starting after Christmas. My brother is sure to be settled home by then."

"An educated woman you're going to be."

Ruth frowned as if injured. "A teacher. Nothing wrong with that."

"I never said there was, Ruthie. I think it's swell."

If I couldn't go out with Florence, and nowadays Gladys alongside her, I could dream of the fine displays at The Fair, the mannequins in simple afternoon dresses patterned with flowers and looking so cool, the creams and perfumes, the gold necklaces shining in the glass cases. And my mind drifted to Desmond Malloy, the raise the car men would get to stay on the job, and what a life would be possible with money like that. We didn't know for certain there would not be a surprise in the pay envelope. Mr. R'd given them all an extra dollar at Christmas, according to Ruth, and sure we could use a bit more, Christmas or not.

It's that hope anyway caused me to use the letter opener, and nudge the blade along the seal, slow, like combing tangles out of Margaret's fine hair, in place of ripping the paper, and not reaching in and grabbing, but opening just enough to see the pay packet's no fatter after all. A glance around told me the others'd got the same, not that any of us'd expected a windfall. But it was the hope for one we hadn't lost yet, the some of us had it to begin with.

⁓

It was leaving time and that sweltering again I might not a hung my shirt to dry at all. I could feel it sticking to my back and twisted my spine around to release the cloth from there and the cleft between my buds. That's what Mammy called them, buds, and Da said buds turn into beautiful flowers and Mammy said to keep his poetry out of the ears of his own daughters so. Da only laughed at her. A gentle fellow he was, him taking what he earned and bringing it home, more than some did, as Mam's letters reminded us. "A good man still abides by the Christian spirit despite everything, you girls will be happy to learn." Of course, Mammy never knew right off when we quit the convent and the mission and, save for Sunday Mass, most things holy.

Was it the thought of Mammy stopped me, or the dread I felt about facing the woman in the bathing costume department, the one'd looked at me like she did? I should a forgot it. Her thinking if she'd been the one choosing people ought to be in this world, she would a left me out. Me, who was barely in. Didn't want to meet that one again, no. So there I was standing on the street corner, dreaming about The Fair—the bonnet would complete my outfit, or at least a proper pair of bathing stockings—wondering where my famous boldness hid, in the moments I cowered undecided. Then up came a boy with the *Daily News* Home edition changed my fantasies of shopping altogether. 'Twas an Extra reporting on the little girl.

POLICE ORDER LAKE DRAGGED TO FIND GIRL

TELEPHONE CALLS INQUIRE WHETHER REPORTS ARE TRUE THAT BODY OF LOST CHILD HAS BEEN FOUND IN BASEMENT OF VIRGINIA HOTEL

A cinder blown into one of my eyes started them both watering. Either the cinder or the laced air threaded through with murder and anger and cruelty. Janet Wilkinson maybe already tossed into that lake held all I feared, and me—daft with love—forgetting the terrors, enjoying instead the little fish like grains of silver rising round me the evening I lingered with Desmond. Them same fish could be pooling around Janet's sweet pale face. Hah! Saturday night supposed to be cheerful, a full day off looming and me with a date for tomorrow. There was no advantage in standing around reading sad tales of murdered children and watching the man on the corner beat a horse almost dead to begin with, for on the other side of the road boys chased after pigeons flew up before them as if happiness existed still. Sparks from the wires made a pretty light and a breeze stirred the poisonous haze over Chicago, a promise, if it kept up, we'd sleep tonight.

STRIKE NEARER!

UNIONS BOLT PARLEY, CALL MASS MEETING!

FALL KILLS JUDGE DOLAN!

BROWNS BREAK TIE, GET LEAD IN 7TH!

Because it was Harry at a meeting Saturday night—the situation that serious, for the teamsters, for everyone—Margaret waited for me on the stoop and a look at my face told her something had me down in the dumps.

"He's disappointed you. And when you were just gettin' goin'. How much do you know about him anyway? Is he just one of the louts like them over at the Hamburg used to try to sweet talk us out the back of the club? Don't be lettin' your loneliness drive you to a fellow like that. Remember what the sisters told us."

"It's tomorrow we're after meeting. A stroll in the park. He's not disappointed me, no, Meggsie. You have it wrong." Oh, yes, wrong. Her, quoting the sisters like that. I had to hold my tongue. But she was changing, Margaret was. She'd had her waltz with adventure when we ran away from the mission, but then, imagining a comfortable life ahead, she'd swung back to where she believed she belonged. Influence of Harry was part of it. But then, too, she was going to turn twenty before I even turned twenty-one. A new decade for her to start, with a wedding planned, a house to find, children to birth, the shop they would eventually open. No magician was Margaret and, if her vision was strained by sewing, she could see a plan clear as she could see herself in a store mirror, and she often looked. I want to study the dress, she'd say, but I'd notice her turn this way and that, flirting with her reflection, squinting at it and patting her hair, drawing her shoulders back. Of course there was no mirror to speak of at Bridey's. We didn't get the chance much.

I walked her down to the same café where himself had stood me to the pie and the lemonade, and the menu board at the front distracted her. I could see by the way her tongue stabbed at the corner of her mouth.

"It's payday and I'm goin' to have the roast beef special. You have it, too. I've seen it come out and its grand, lots of gravy, and you get dessert with it, too."

"Does sound good."

"I'll stand you to it." For I'd promised Mammy I'd look out for her, even though it's her peering over at me suddenly, exploring my face for a clue as to what might a befallen me. Why my new fella left me free on a Saturday night when most every other couple would be dancing somewheres. "He had a home emergency. His mother. He's good to her, and you know what Da told us about putting our trust in such a man, for he'll honor us same as her." Oh, they rolled out, they did, the stories.

But it was a long speech for me and Margaret showed she noticed by her worried blinking. We didn't know then the degree of her short sightedness, but she'd eventually lose her job because of the handicap and have to buy herself specs.

"Is it his mother you're sad about then, Maeve? Because you can't fool them that's knowed you since we were little ones, and what we've been through together and all. You cannot pretend somethin's not sittin' on you."

I raised the paper. "They think she's in the lake. They think he threw her there."

"Ah, the lake! No wonder, you poor t'ing. Not to mention her. Oh, that devil. But you shouldn't be readin' all that."

Margaret reached across and patted my arm and urged me to put the paper away, for wasn't there enough sadness in our lives without inviting it in through the papers? Advice easy enough to follow as the waiter approached our table with the plates, both of them steaming and us forgetting how hot we'd been just an hour ago, and our mouths already watering and my stomach howling in anticipation.

We saw a show after, like always on Saturday night, and this night at the Academy of Music someone almost as good as Nora Bayes performed the song we went home humming, Nora's most popular, "Shine on, shine on harvest moo-oon up in the sky," the hit of the show. But didn't we laugh at the monkey in the picture, too, it dressed in clothes like a child. The magic act, a simple one of card tricks I knew all about. Wasn't magic to me, only a trick anybody with a head on her shoulders could practice until she got good enough to do it in front of a crowd. Seemed there had to be a good dose of the unknown, a mystery that teased, before you could believe it magic. There had to be a flourish and the magician crying out, or sometimes whispering, "Presto!" You'd come to the end before you ever knew how everything happened. But I clapped all the same at the card trick, for politeness sake.

My mood had changed so, when we passed the posters pasted to the side of the building, including one with Dorothy Phillips in *Talk of the Town*, I told Margaret someone had said I resembled her. Margaret laughed. "Dorothy Phillips herself, is it?" Stung it did, and Margaret saw and tried to console. "But I can see why, Maeve, with your dark hair and your brown eyes. You never think you're pretty, but you are."

Some of the tenants lingered on the stoop and we stopped for a while to gab with them and Bridey about the show, herself in an easy mood and all because we'd paid our rent. Even smiling she was, Bridey, and encouraging Margaret to remind her of how that song went. Teasing, must've been she was, because you heard it everywhere. Even Bridey had to a heard it. But she felt that good, Margaret went along. "Shine on, shine on harvest moon up in the sky. I ain't had no lovin' since January, February, June, or July," she sang, her eyes aimed up and to the side, like Nora Bayes in the shows. She didn't go right through, but stopped at that first line, and curtsied instead of taking a bow. Bridey and the others applauded her.

We were good for another week. Despite all the unemployed, she could count on us had the regular pay. Saturdays Bridey was happy as we ever saw her. Yet, she steered us from the show to the story of Janet quick enough, and asked if we'd seen another edition, if any more news'd come out about the awful fellow suspected. She never raised any similarities between her John and Fitzgerald, the janitor thought to be involved in the poor girl's disappearance. Maybe there were none, but she had to wonder, she did, what her grown-up boy might be capable of doing.

Whole minutes passed when I didn't think of my man and the swimming lesson set up for the next day, if no one was murdered before then, or the cars stopped, or a bomb go off somewhere, a Bolshie bomb or one of them meant to scare Negroes out of white neighborhoods. Or maybe another war would start in some country we had yet to hear of.

SUNDAY, JULY 27, 1919

LOWDEN FIGHTS CAR STRIKE!

NEW EVIDENCE TIGHTENS NET ON FITZGERALD!

$2,500 FOR JANET!
TO RELIEVE THE SUSPENSE OF
JANET'S PARENTS AND FRIENDS,
THE CHICAGO TRIBUNE WILL PAY $2,500 FOR
EXCLUSIVE INFORMATION
LEADING TO THE DISCOVERY OF JANET WILKINSON

$2,500! But Margaret steered me right away from the piles of papers, fewer stacks of them Sunday. She did not want me distracted at Mass and I did not protest, really, though I could not help but hear the newsie hollering the temperature would be the hottest all week. It got me pondering the moment I would step into the lake, him with his arms outstretched, encouraging me. Could I do it thinking little Janet might be floating in there somewhere?

"There's only bound to be more trouble. Keep the papers out of your head, Maeve. There's the girl and all to pray for and peace with the workers."

She dipped her fingers in the holy water font, whispering the last, and wasn't the church nearly full, though we stepped in a good ten minutes early. We always chose the same pew, because it was situated away from the incense made Margaret sneeze, yet also nearest the window featured St. Brigid, who'd been a girl like us, and we were not much more than girls still. For me, I hoped St. Brigid and the Virgin would be my path to forgiveness for all the lying and thieving I'd done. Yet I wondered if those two even judged me so, knowing what they must know about the lives we were fated to live, being who we were and where we'd come from. Brigid herself famous for her kindness to the poor.

We chose the nine o'clock Mass for the children's choir, voices like cherubim made me think of our younger sisters—Nuala, had to be nine already, and little Kathleen, the baby then. Not to mention that poor child would never fully leave my thoughts but come and go for years—Janet Wilkinson. Little Janet. Margaret was smarter where feeling came into it. If she thought about our family, the thought had wings, for I noticed her examining the hats, the picture hats the ladies wore, wide all round like the edge of a plate circling the crown, and those with one side pinned up by a flower or a feather, the cloches, some of them with veils.

You could always see the latest fashions at Mass on Sunday—the hats, the summer frocks, the shoes—because the world and all met at St. Patrick's, it being the oldest for we Irish in the city. Beautiful with the stained glass Mr. Shaughnessy made, another window or two each year, too, until the whole church filled with colored light rivaled the marvelous panels in the ceiling. You felt holy just sitting in the rays came through the shapes like a bishop's miter, the knots, the deep emeralds and ruby reds, the fierce glare of St. Patrick, the more modest cast down eyes of Brigid, Mary of the Gael.

The church like a stove despite the stone walls. The chorus of young swallows singing the mass, *Kyrie Eleison*—God have mercy. And wasn't it heartfelt, the echo in my chest, for I knew God did forgive and he would be too busy with all the more important goings on to do more than nod my way. A dip of that sacred head would absolve any sins born of the mischief in my soul. Mischief I excused, because hadn't it sprung from need?

When the sermon came, the pastor spent it not on the labor troubles, or the plight of the poor and the soldiers just returned. Not the coloreds moving up north, nor the innocent folks died that week in the blimp crash, nor the missing girl. Instead he preached the words of Archbishop Mundelein, himself concerned with those who strayed towards temptation.

"For this disaster is usually the end and culmination of other evils, of sinful habits, of neglect of prayer and the sacraments, of cowardice in the face of hostility to one's belief, of weakness in yielding to the wishes of kindred or friends, of social ambition and the hope of advantage in business or public career."

There I drifted, and not the only one either. Actual whistles and snorts rose from a snoozer somewhere close. But me, I wondered if the archbishop wrote them words with special intention for the famous Catholics in our town, the businessmen starving their employees. Wouldn't that be a sin in some category, sure?

"It is essential, in the first place, that clean living before marriage be equally obligatory on men and women. The toleration of vicious courses in one party, while the other is strictly held to the practice of virtue, may rest on convention or custom, but it is ethically false, and it is plainly at variance with the law of God, which enjoins personal purity upon each and all. Those who contemplate marriage should further make sure that their motives are upright. Where the dominant aim is selfish, where choice is controlled by ambition or greed, and where superficial qualities are preferred to character, genuine love is out of the question. Such marriages are bargains rather than unions, and their only result is discord."

He'd have me and lose me, same as others who nodded off in the torpor. Motives? I never did know one to be absolutely pure. Sure we girls wanted to marry, and comfort came into it, yet how could it be otherwise?

We strolled slowly back to Bridey's—Harry due to collect Margaret, but not for an hour or so—and found John on the front stoop, his face shiny with grease from whatever Bridey'd given him to eat, and all of a sudden I had to run to the lav.

"You're not sick, Maeve?" Margaret peering at me. I can see her now, smoothing her flowered Sunday dress, fixing a curl at the side of her cheek, a bit of the young miss in her for all she wanted to be old. Harry that day taking her for a picnic with his kind, and wouldn't she come back holding her own stomach that night on account of the trouble she had, even then, digesting all that meat.

"Just butterflies must be. We'll plan a picnic for the four of us, next Sunday. I am excited for you, Maeve," she said, hugging me. So sure she was then, Margaret. Then gone, leaving me time enough to give myself a good wash and let my skin dry—as much as it would dry that muggy day—before I slipped the chemise up and rolled my stockings on. Started me sweating it did in that room of ours hotter than the day outside. Up with the knickers, the petticoat—plain except for the border of lace Margaret'd stitched around the hem, for she kept her eyes out for trimmings, Margaret did. Buttoning up my shirtwaist and the skirt. I had two skirts for summer and I chose the one with the extra piece flaring out from the waist, another of my sister's accomplishments.

The bathing costume came out from the place it nestled, small thing it was. I flapped it out our square of window where the lines strung between the buildings dangled clothes would maybe never dry at all, it being that still. They might a been flags, the white of the nappies, some garment striped, the red of a man's shirt. Grains of sand escaping from the mohair sparkled in the fingers of sunlight and flew nearly weightless before disappearing into the alley'd often been the source of my fright.

Not that Sunday. I never saw the junk tossed out, nor the feral creatures. Never smelled whatever'd landed there and soaked into the struggling weeds. No, but held the costume up for a minute to admire it before rolling it back up and putting into my bag with a second pair of stockings and the towel I'd reminded myself to pack. I consulted the square of mirror in the lav before I left, but it only told me I was no more Dorothy Phillips than I was the Queen of Sheba, and then I was off, too, tiptoeing down the hall past the sounds of snorts and farts from Bridey's room.

~

In the Laura Jean Libbey stories unfolded in summer, you did not find your dirty-necked, collar-loosed folks, sweat sluicing their mugs as they hung from a strap on a car shouldn't a been packed, it being Sunday. But sure something drew us to the lake, and the open land along its edge, where—in voices just as loud as the newsies owned the street corners—peddlers hollered out the freshness of their popcorn, the coolness of their drinks.

"Ice cold lemonade!"

"Getchyer refreshin' soda pop!"

A monkey danced at the end of the leash fixed to his bright collar, and a fellow played the tin whistle—him in a cloth cap and maybe not so long arrived in Chicago he didn't know 'twas the custom to lay the hat on the ground.

Desmond appeared in his summer suit and the boater, rushing right up to where I'd been waiting, but not for long, and blathering words I couldn't hear in the hubbub. Took my elbow to steer me across to the streetcar stop, us heading to the same place as before, though I'd thought we might go to a proper bathing beach. Once we reached Lincoln Park we saw children playing catch and whirling hoops on the lawn gone yellow. In the dimmer quarters beneath the tree branches, families sat on blankets laid out for their picnics, while on the paths you saw women strolling arm in arm, and old couples resting on the benches placed there, watching all go by, including Desmond and myself, racing as if we had a train to catch.

He stopped, all of a sudden, and pushed his hat back on his head. We were both panting heavy with the sprinting and the heat and I could feel my toes inside my shoes, imagined the cherry red and worse I would see when I peeled off my stockings.

"Am I torturin' you, Maeve?"

He was smiling down onto me and my body was all airy like, so, if it was torture, it was a wonderful sort and him knowing I didn't speak much, didn't expect much of an answer. I piped up, though, because we'd passed a wagon on the avenue and I was perishing of thirst.

"Though I've always been a stout walker, I wouldn't mind a drink."

He strode back to where the traffic streamed to buy me a drink from the peddler closest. I waited in the shelter of one of the big trees arched over the path behind. Suspended so, as if holding my breath, which I didn't, couldn't do, naturally, but all of a sudden him who'd made the earth bigger—just as if he'd swept his hand across the city and said, "Presto!" and me'd expanded to the edges of it—all of a sudden that atmosphere vanished same as if a curtain'd come down. I shrank back to myself and the sweat dripping down my front, and my back, and my hurting feet, and closed my eyes for a second, hoping to recreate the spell.

When I opened them I saw a lanky woman with a loops of reddish-brown hair at her neck and heard that laugh I knew from The Chicago Magic Company, the trill had ironic depths to it, the sarcasm, and wasn't it Eveline strolling by. Not by herself, neither, but with a man even taller, sporting a vanilla suit and a straw fedora, and didn't the lightness of them articles of clothing just emphasize the color of his skin, same as the stone flashing from his gold ring as he waved his hand to describe some point he must a been making, then chuckled right along with Eveline, the two of them so absorbed in one another they, too, seemed in another, charmed, world.

Eveline stepped close to a tree, to lean on it while she fetched something from inside her shoe, and I heard the whistle he let loose when she exposed her leg, as she liked to do, it being long and shapely and sheathed in them lovely stockings. More attractive really than her face, which you'd a called clever more than beautiful. Then she laughed again, and said something in that particular voice made him roar, and they continued, her gait a sort of sashay dared people to confront her.

Eveline with a colored man? Him the same fancy one gave her the stockings, the jewelry, the silver compact we'd looked in? It flummoxed me, it did, me who only the day before'd decided Eveline to be made of more than the impression she gave. What to think? I followed the bob of her hat—a fluffy confection of feathers and ribbon made a nest for a tiny silk canary—until the path they strolled curved and I could no longer see them or hear their voices. She had her nerve, Eveline did. A colored man. You didn't see that much, but I'd heard of it and seen examples of the children made from such matches, in Florida and plenty here, the lighter skin folk you found more often in jobs involved the public. Light like that one of hers, tea with a drip of milk in it.

But soon my own man was striding towards me, gripping the necks of two bottles of Dr. Pepper with one hand and, just as suddenly as it disappeared, the enchantment returned and I forgot all about Eveline.

The world and all had taken to the lake that day. As we got closer I could hear the shouts of children, maybe boys swimming naked as some of them'd do, and someone far off playing music on a trumpet or some such. Desmond moved his hand down from my elbow and took my slick hand into his.

"All right, darlin'?" He squeezed and then I did not feel hot but cold, like February slush in my shoes, my eyes swimming before I did, and then, how many minutes later I don't know, we were there. Ten minutes, half an hour, two days? And me thinking of that old priest talked about marriage, and thinking, too, of Eveline and even though she didn't go to church, even if I knew she went with coloreds, I did not think her a bad sort, though the priest would have thought her so.

It wasn't done much. People said it was unnatural to mix the races, same ones thought everything should be separate—separate places in the cars, in the theaters, separate restaurants, separate neighborhoods, separate schools. He looked good enough, a gentleman in that suit of his and the hat. Later, when I got to know him, I found he *was* a gentleman. Still, Eveline had her nerve. Not as simple as good and bad, life and its complications, is what I came to understand.

Back then I couldn't say what I thought, not with Desmond parting the bushes like they were the loveliest glass-beaded curtains and inviting me into that dappled copse already cleared, the weeds flat as if he'd prepared it for me. But no, there'd been others before us, you could see it in the left behinds, papers from sandwiches or some such thing stuck to the bushes. And there beyond, as before, the lake doubling all the light sent down by the blazing midday sun.

"Here we are then, darlin', just as I promised. And isn't it better without the crowds. Like we're the only ones on earth, wouldn't you say? Just like Adam and Eve?"

He peered down at me, grinning, and I rolled my lips together, wondering if he wanted to go for a kiss, and would it be right? No question it would not be right, not by what the priest said, but weren't the voices of the priests lost in the din of romance novels and movies like the wonderful *Broken Blossoms*, while me, I was thinking again of how life unfolds if you let it, and could something naturally rolling out of events be wrong? Just a flicker in my mind in that standing moment before he turned.

"I'm goin' to test the water while you put your bathin' costume on," said Desmond. "I bet it's peachy warm today and better this time of day without the midges."

Loved the swimming, he did, and my mind moved ahead to the children we'd have—as many as the Lord'd give us, but I hoped for four, two of each—and how he'd want them all to swim and what a fight there would be if I gathered them round me for safety. How he'd laugh at me, but maybe not with the affection he was after showing me that afternoon, the joking. The thought worried me as I undid what I'd done up a couple hours before—unbuttoned the shirtwaist and spread it on the bush nearest, stepped out of the skirt and put it on the same, lifted the petticoat up over my head and shook it before it, too, came to rest on that sustaining bush, its few leaves a sick green for want of water. The air met my skin for the seconds before I tugged the bathing costume up over the bloomers were part of it. I managed to get the top under the loosened chemise and then I slipped that off. Onto the bush.

There I stood decent, my drawers hid in my cloth bag with the extra stockings I'd thought to bring, though I still lacked the slippers girls wore in the photographs I saw in the Sunday supplements. It was still shoes for me, ordinary shoes I took off when I spread my towel and lay my hat on top my cloth bag. Then I could breathe and I did, eyes closed, till I heard the rustling meant he was coming back, and didn't I bite my lip to stall the cry wanted to rise from all the wanting inside me, the dimple when he smiled, him tilting his head to the space beyond our nest.

"I'll be just a minute, Maeve."

Directly in front there's only the lake lapping at the sand and the little stones, no froth on the curling waves today—it was that calm, lovely—and not far off, on either side, there were pairs and a group of children splashing. More lovely still when he dropped down beside me on a towel of his own and, as if it were not warm enough, flames licked at the small space between our two bodies. He took out his flask.

"Courage?" he asked, extending it to me.

I turned him down.

"You're not one of them temperance types, I hope."

That dimple again and his brow wrinkling as he squinted against the sun. I assured him no, I was not, but I'd wait a bit, for what if the drink made me senseless and I lost my footing and went under? Wasn't courage, so much as a trap, I saw in that bottle but I never said. No, instead I got him talking about himself and the war and how he'd been ready to go but they didn't want him because of that eye of his wandered sometime.

"Have you noticed?"

Wouldn't a took Anna Eva or Houdini himself to read the mind of Mr. Desmond Malloy, but a body resists, tells herself stories. We were there for the swimming, like half the city spread out along the grit bordered the lake, and it was kind of him to offer to instruct me. If he thought I looked like Dorothy Phillips, well, I didn't mind opening myself to the comparison. And if it might be his Bridgeport political connections the reason for him missing the war, as much as the eye tended to stray, couldn't it be the good people after compensating me for Packy? Putting in my path a man whole save for that eye, and a car man about to accept an increase in pay? He was a sort of magician, Desmond, with the power he had to make me believe.

"But they'll be plenty of time for that talk, later, darlin'. Let's make the most of the day. Come to me."

He stood and extended his hands, but I got myself up, trying, trying to avoid that touch, all the while him blathering about how this was the hour, and there couldn't be a better place, and wasn't it why he'd brought me here instead of one a them spots where the people crowded and splashed, and some you'd never want to be sharing the water with anyhow. "There aren't but a few bits of stone on the bottom. There…that's right…come, Maeve, come with me."

A spout of cool water shooting up my spine, circling my neck, my shoulders, joining all them little blue streams beneath the skin, goose bumped again. Him leaving me at the edge to go deeper, standing out where the lake covered his knees, bending down and scooping up the water and laughing. Me saying, "Don't," and him only laughing more, and urging me.

"It's grand, it's grand, Maeve. I can't give you any kind of lesson if you don't go past your ankles."

Me recalling the Thursday last, the little fishes not so bad, the truth being it not as deep and frightening as I'd thought. *Remember, remember,* said me to myself as he shook his head and dove under and came up again and there he stood, his wet costume bulging in places I was not supposed to look, just as I'd not been meant to look when first my eyes darted there and away, then back again. His hair flopping over his face, white skin luminous as the moon in my dream and the actual water not cold as what ran in my veins at all, but not as hot as the air, and me moving forward till I was in to my knees and squealing.

"Does it get any worse?"

Him laughing. "'Course it does, darlin', if by worse you mean the deep of it. There's enough water to float a ship big as the *Titanic.*"

Was it the mention of the disaster came the year after Margaret and me boarded the *Mauretania* and suffered our first crossing stopped me before I'd got halfway out to where Desmond stood? Or was it Janet, the thought of her maybe out there, under the water somewhere, because weren't there invisible currents could have carried the dear child from the north of the city down here?

He scowled, impatient, like. "Suit yourself," he said. "I'm only offerin' an opportunity." Aimed himself right into and under the lake so I couldn't see him for what seemed a terrible length of time. Angry with me then? Ready to toss me over for some other girl, prettier, not only prettier but more fun, liked to swim?

Didn't that get me moving out towards him till I felt something on my leg. I screamed, thinking it one of them eels, when it was only himself, Desmond Malloy, his hand where it should not have been on my stockinged leg, pinching me, pretending to be a big fish, then rising up dripping and gasping and putting his wet arms right around me, and me with the fright sinking into them. Oh. Then I could feel the bulge I was not supposed to feel and pulled myself away, tried to, and thought of Margaret and St. Patrick's and Mammy and Da and the young ones we'd left and the Sisters of Perpetual Grace and the Blessed Virgin herself, who'd never known a man.

But I was in a trance like some magician'd worked, for my head turned up to Desmond's down coming one and we were kissing and oh, I should a got away, but I didn't and he was pressing closer in, his body arching over me, and me thinking this is not the gentleman he promised to be, but that thought, too, a sparrow you see in the verge so quickly you're not sure you see it at all. A flock of them thoughts rose up. Me with no leisure to imagine where they would nest, and if I'd ever needed to speak up it was then, but his tongue was after sneaking through his lips right into my mouth, and then I did pull away because I was out of breath. Another tongue touching mine. His tongue! My stockings were wet all the way to my bloomers and my parts lit up like the Palmer House at Christmas holidays. For once in my life I was stopped where I stood.

His voice'd gone husky. Him frowning like he wasn't happy, and saying, "Maeve, darlin'. You don't have to swim if it frightens you, dear. You've had a splash, and you're cooler, aren't you? And I've heard the stories of them immigrant ships. It's a wonder you're here at all."

"It's not that so much but little Janet. The police want to drag this very same lake where they think he threw her body."

"It's that worryin', is it?"

Nice, understanding, and maybe the music in my head would stop, a player piano speeded up like, warping the melody. I could dress and we would stroll back to the park and find a lacy tree limb to sit beneath and he'd buy us slices of watermelon and we'd listen to the fellow on the squeezebox or one of the others with their hats on the ground to collect coins. Except he was leading me back to the copse and arranging our towels side by side while me, I was thinking about the clammy feel of my wet stockings. He coaxed me down and took out his flask again and then I did take a gulp to stop the shaking came from the wet stockings, or was it my own heart beating so fierce it got me trembly.

Also, because what else was I not after doing that day? Kissing a man in the middle of Lake Michigan, drinking whiskey. Shouts occasionally rose and drifted over on the still air and he's saying, "There, there, dear heart, don't worry yourself about the child. She's probably just fallen asleep somewhere in the sun." And didn't I want to accept that as the answer to the mystery, improbable as it was, but then he was lowering me and caressing my buds through my bathing costume and didn't I understand then what my da meant about them blooming and I rolled away.

"No, no," I said, getting to my knees, my feet, pushing through the bushes where my clothes awaited me. I heard him laughing, even singing, and daft as I was I realized my towel lay behind, with him. There I was standing in my wet stockings—having forgotten I'd brought dry ones—and struggling to get the chemise right over my damp skin. Did. Hurried with the petticoat, so it was only my over clothes missing when he rustled through them same shrubs and held the towel up.

"Forget somethin', darlin'?" His voice deeper and softer so with the whiskey. Him reaching out and me falling towards him and us shuffling, would have been comical but no, not to us, nothing comical about that fierce yearning drove us back to our poor bed where he found it easier then to find my buds, and didn't he kiss them and didn't they blossom then into the most tender white flowers. And then his hand was moving down to where it shouldn't and I moved it away, not opening my eyes but the once to see his face near mine, eyes half closed and the tiny red gold hairs sprouting in his beard and chafing me as he whispered, "Shh, shh, Maeve, darlin'. I'll be gentle, I will, dearest, my own."

This is what I mean. This is what I mean about it all being so natural, one thing leading to the next and no planning involved. But me, I wasn't thinking so much then, only feeling slickness down there—not the same sweat'd lathered my hands minutes before when we hurried over the trampled grass to our wedding bower there. Then him fumbling with his bathing costume and climbing on top and that club—which is how I recall it, the feel of it, even though it's dirty to even think such thoughts—oh, yes, but that, like a billy bare against my skin.

Poking, poking at my most private place, hurtful it was and I bit my lip but never hollered and him saying over and over, "Shh, shh, my own. Maeve, don't worry," like a lullaby and then he's in, in me, us joined the way men and women do, and I never felt anything like it, lovely full, in the one moment I relaxed before he started moving. The two of us coupled, the emptiness filled.

In the pictures, the orchestra music swells in a wave when lovers embrace and the screen shows a sky with billowy clouds, or some grand body of water sparkling. I saw the sky above me, not a cloud, only the haze same as hung over the city most days that summer. But for the most of it, I kept my eyes closed, as if not seeing meant it didn't happen. Was that it? Also, with my eyes closed the touches, the kisses, the parts of my body I never knew pressed deep into memory. I could feel them long after, even now.

Furious moving, chug-chug, a train forcing me into the ground beneath the weeds, caught sand maybe wounding something tender, him saying he's sorry and it wouldn't hurt for long and next time, next time… Odd how we are driven to it despite the pain, even him, because he cried out same as if he'd injured himself, and then he sighed and it was over. He kissed me and flopped over onto his back. "You're a peach, darlin'." It's what he said and me after believing it, and caressing the stubbled cheek of him whose eyes went droopy, him being drowsy with the sun and the swimming. Nodded off.

But me? How could I sleep with all ran through my mind, and I am sorry to say it was not poor Janet anchoring my thoughts at that moment. But not sorry then, no, though I knew we'd done wrong, at least wrong as the priest saw it. It never felt wrong. Uncomfortable yes, but it would not always be so. No. We'd be in a bed soon. I smiled, thinking, dreaming and not of food, but of the future we'd have, me and Desmond. If this was the bargain, I'd kept my part and Desmond had shown up when he said he would, dependable as dependable could be when you thought of all was going on.

Margaret need not worry at all, at all, for here I had someone with a future as bright as the city itself. Even if trouble nibbled here and there, Mayor Thompson and all the big men at City Hall would make it right, not that I was pondering the mayor, not that Sunday afternoon in Chicago, with the sweet whistle of his snore coming through my ear. Growing late by then, the sun angled in across the tops of the bushes and our little hideaway truly dim, but it still hot, even hotter with his half-clothed body so near, and me considering, despite my fear, maybe I would sit in the shallow part of the lake for a spell, be just the thing.

But I must a dozed a little too before something woke us both. Laughter? Boys was it, startled us? I looked over at the man meant to be the husband Packy never got to be, face bunched, gathered, wrinkled. He sat up and shook his head.

"What a day," said he, and I smiled—not with my teeth showing, just gentle like, understanding.

"Sorry, darlin'. Are ye all right? We should a been in a grander place, with soft pillows. Will you forgive me?"

I reached up to smooth that hair of his back from the peak and he grabbed it, my hand, and pulled me to standing next to him, and I have to say I didn't mind at all sinking into that manly chest where I could hear his thundering heart.

"We've got to go. I should a been down at the barns. You better finish dressing."

"Isn't the big meetin' for tomorrow night?"

He peered at me. "How would you know that? Oh, yes, you're the one for the papers. Thing the papers don't tell everyone is there's a meetin' every night."

"But it's your day off, sure?" I called from the tangle where my skirt hung, and the shirtwaist. I could feel the wetness around the vent in my drawers and already schemed how I'd rinse them out while Margaret slept.

"May be a string of them off if the bosses don't give in to us. And don't believe all you read in the papers. There's no Bolshie tryin' to influence us. I'd never go for that. We're just ordinary men after a fair wage."

It pained me a bit to follow him out onto the grass, him walking that fast, and a chafing down there, and though I'd finally remembered to put on my dry stockings, I must have rolled a pebble into them. I said nothing.

The park looked tired after such a day, yet people were lingering, some of them maybe tired, too. Others packing their baskets, resigned, and didn't it seem God had tossed us all down on the earth like so many dice and some of us came up a six. The dream Desmond and me'd been in began to fray at the edges and spill right open as we neared the streaming streets. He let go my hand and hurried ahead as if late for an appointment, which he was so. At the car barn. There'd be no supper, not even coffee, should we want it on such a day, but he stopped for another Dr. Pepper, a soda I never drank after that week. It was not a taste I liked, but how could I refuse Desmond, parched as I was?

When we reached the Loop once again a pall of soot layered everything beneath the elevated tracks. It was there he took both my hands. Would he kiss me right there on the corner of Adams Street, with the world and all going by? I feasted on the sight of him, my Desmond Malloy—a man taller than me by half as much again, shirt open at the collar, jacket loose, too, and trousers wrinkled as they might be from any activity on a day like that one, even from sitting at the ballpark. His brown hair combed back, he'd seen to that, and his boater at a cheerful angle covering his head.

Despite the hat, his face'd gone red from the sun and the heat and the whiskey he'd been sipping, and the regret he felt for me, that my debut should be on such a hard bed. Debut, he'd said, as if he'd been after introducing me to society at a fancy dress ball. Gave me power, that, so it was me who said, "If you've got to get down to your barn, go ahead then. I'll just continue on to Bridey's. Margaret will be looking for me. And you've your future to think about." Our future.

Him holding my hands still, then pursing his lips in such a way deepened that dimple. Staring into my face, the eye drifting off. But he never kissed me, no, not there at the streetcar stop where his workmates might have seen him. I could understand him not wanting to be teased and it having happened fast, him and me. Presto! But why not fast? Packy gone so sudden, and people dying here and there, unpredictably. Irene Miles, and little Janet maybe sleeping, but not in the sun, with it fallen, and maybe a sleep she'd never wake from, and all them didn't come back from the war. I never even stopped at St. Patrick's to beg forgiveness because, like I always said, if God didn't want us to feel like we did, why had he given us those feelings?

Monday, July 28, 1919

W E NEVER HEARD anything that night. Nothing like the screams going on less than five miles away, not the clubbing, the hollering, the mean words spit from thin-lipped mouths, broad-lipped mouths. Never knew of the men dragged off the streetcars. No, not them killed neither, until the Monday morning, me as fresh as I could make myself, my hair washed and still damp, the Jap Rose soap smell rising off my skin and my clothes aired and them stained drawers hidden where I hid all my material secrets—my writing book, the bathing costume. There was me marching towards the stop full of happiness as if going to a party, not another day at my job. Margaret urging me to slow down, shouting, "So he's there at the office is he, and that's why you're hurryin' so." She didn't know it would be even before then I saw my man if the right car came along, and so I skipped a little until I heard the voice of the little newsie hollering, "Getchyer paper and read all about it!"

FULL CONFESSION!
JANET'S SLAYER TALKS!

People gathered round him, and plenty too across, where the smaller fellow yelled.

LITTLE GIRL'S BODY UNDER COAL
IN VIRGINIA HOTEL BASEMENT!

and the papers after flying off the stacks, the blaring headlines multiplied in the hands of men and women whose faces you couldn't see for them gobbling up the news.

TWO KILLED, FIFTY HURT IN RACE RIOTS!

BATHING BEACH FIGHT SPREADS TO BLACK BELT

CAR PEACE NEARER

FARES TO GO UP TO 7¢

So her, the sweet child, sleeping yes, but under coal dust not the sun, despite himself tried to comfort me with that image of her, tried to make me believe everything'd be all right. But her sleep eternal and him, Fitzgerald, guilty as everyone'd thought from the beginning. Oh, if it had not been so, if some kind of miracle'd come to reward all we who prayed for one. Better if she'd fallen under one of those fits could take people, amnesia or something, only to have the spell pass and her wake smiling to the relief of her family and of us all.

But how to properly feel the sadness owed the event when another tragedy competed? It took your breath away, it did. Riot in Chicago? Dead? Injured? Shivering, looking around like the trouble stood next to me, meeting the eyes of others lifted away from a hum of opinion more than actual sensible words, to see who stood near. Yet the cars were still running and we could hear the clack-clack of the one meant for us.

The world had not stopped, and some colored folks—ones I hardly noticed on regular days—lined up along the rails like always. A woman held her head up, her chin pointing out. Her in a stylish suit of white clothes, her hat just as white, with a single feather pointing out. Never directed her eyes anywhere but straight ahead. A gentleman in his summer seersucker, a bow tie, him carrying a case could be a lawyer or a businessman. Some younger, not dressed so well, pearl divers they might be at one of the big downtown hotels. I'd got used to them there, never appeared unusual at the stop, but only fanned themselves and yawned and shooed away flies rose up from the horse droppings, like all the rest of us did.

The same today, except I was not the only one glancing over at them. All of a sudden we were noticing differences we'd been living right along. All the races and people from every nation on earth mixed up. You could feel wobbly, not sure of the ground you were standing on, and it was best—sure easiest—when we kept with our kind. But how could a body manage that in a city like this? My own Margaret about to graft herself onto a Polack?

As the streetcar clacked up, my mind was split between anticipation of who I'd see craning his head out the door of the car, sadness about little Janet, and some fear concerning the riot started at the beach just a few miles away from where we— Desmond and I—were after knowing each other in the way the nuns used the word. A Negro boy stoned as he swam across the invisible dividing line in the lake marked where whites should swim on one side and colored on the other. His pals challenging the men threw the stones and then the riot began, said the papers.

A colored rioter is said to have died from wounds inflicted by Policeman John O'Brien, who fired into a mob at Twenty-ninth Street and Cottage Grove. The body, it is said, was spirited away by colored men. Minor rioting continued through the night all over the South Side. Negroes who were found in streetcars were dragged to the street and beaten. They were first ordered to the street by white men and, if they refused, the trolley was jerked off the wires.

Yet, not a sign of any thugs there at the Halsted stop on the Madison line, only we weary ones beginning our week, suddenly anxious at what all the news could mean. Riots spreading, but how far? Would we be safe? Would Margaret be, walking her way to the shirt factory? And if safe from the rioters, then from the Bolsheviks sent bombs in the mail, and airships that fell from the sky, and morons like Fitzgerald free to work in a building where normal folks lived? And if safe from those, then starved because of labor trouble at the Union Stock Yards, or forced to walk to the Loop because of the strike on the cars?

But, no, the car men were not striking today, maybe not at all, only the fares going up by nearly half, and how would Margaret and I manage, with me paying equal to the price of lunch in a café just to get to work and back? Still, there was Desmond, yes, and the promise he represented. Not only the tendency he'd developed to keep that hand touched me in such secret places, that same hand of his over the fare box, but more, the moment when he would ask me to become his wife.

Desmond was not on the car stopped first, and the colored kept to themselves, and Clyde said good morning same as always when I bustled past his desk in the Marquette Building on my way to the cages to ride up with the other workers. A thinner group that day, and when I walked into Mr. R's magic shop, didn't it seem like I entered a different age? Sure a different world, yes, where people believed they could get out of any mess same as the master himself, as long as they possessed "The Sensational Handcuff Act," available by mail order only, for thirty-five dollars.

Mr. R startled me by greeting me himself, from behind the counter Florence generally presided over.

"Morning, Miss Curragh, any trouble up your way?"

"Not to my eyes, though the papers say it's everywhere."

"You've got the *Trib* I see. Well, there's trouble here. Our Florence, who is always prompt, is missing today. George and Eveline, as well. Frightened, I suspect. You're the brave one, Miss Curragh, to ride the cars today. Your face shows it though, particularly rosy this morning."

"Already roastin' then, isn't it?"

He'd seldom spoke to me as long, Mr. R, not since the moment he hired me and showed me to my desk at the back. Directions came through Florence, while Mr. R held himself apart, half hid by the cigar smoke clouds puffed around him.

"City's considering barring coloreds from the cars altogether till things settle."

Did he expect me to stay and chat? Me, the quiet one? When nothing more came out of his mouth I continued on as always to my place where, true enough, only me and Ruth would occupy our desks that day. No Florence, no George, and no Eveline. Her, oh, I could only imagine, and with dread, where she might have found herself. Her with her light-skinned dark fellow, the mulatto, and wasn't she the brazen one? But in times like this I hoped they'd gone home to where they each belonged. Where that was I didn't know, but I found out soon enough.

Midway through the morning Mr. R asked me to cover the front while he stepped out to take care of some business. Didn't say how long he'd be nor what the nature of the business was and I never asked, for it was a novelty to be standing somewheres I'd only passed through before then. I planted myself behind the counter as Mr. R and Florence would do and imagined a conversation with one of the magicians might come in looking for supplies. Puffed me up it did to picture how I'd slide open a case lined with velvet, where crystals said to have magic powers nestled around a set of magician's cups looked like they were made of real silver. It wasn't long before the door opened a crack and I straightened up for a potential customer. But wasn't it Eveline herself.

Finger to her lips, whispering "shh," she beckoned me into the hall where her fancy man stood waiting in that same outfit I'd seen the day before. Ice cream suit and straw fedora, which he took off and tipped when Eveline introduced us. "Mr. Robert Jordan, I'd like ya to meet my pal Maeve. Mr. Jordan is a real estate man." He smiled that big lit up smile must have made him good at his job. "An agent, you know, and he found me a swell place on State, not too far south, but criminy with all that's goin' on, I can't stay there."

"You know Jesse Binga, do you, miss? Name's been in the papers just about every week. I wish I could say it's been good news, but they're tryin' to bomb out Jesse. Unfortunately, it so happens to be one of Mr. Binga's buildings where I found suitable accommodation for Miss Eveline."

They never said they were staying together, and I didn't want to know.

"Suitable, he says." Here I thought she'd break out with that ironic laugh of hers, but Mr. Jordan wasn't finished.

"It's on account of all the people moving up from the south and needing somewhere to stay, spreading into neighborhoods where white folks live. White folks don't like it. I'm talking about the bombings."

"Mr. Jordan," (and here she winked at him) "thinks I oughta get out of town for a while. Visit my cousin in Madison, Wisconsin. Well, Madison is not so far."

"In the United States of America, a man is supposed to be free as a U.S. dollar bill no matter his color." Mr. Jordan was not smiling anymore, but shaking his head, addressing someone was not Eveline nor me. "A man ought to be able to find a place for his family anywhere in the city he can pay for it, but huh-uh. They say colored folks have no civic pride. They say let the coloreds into a neighborhood and soon enough you're gonna have your gambling dens and bawdy houses. Well, miss, thing is—"

Eveline cut in. "Mr. Jordan, my pal Maeve don't need a lecture. All you say might be true enough, but I'm not going to risk my neck for that or any fight's not mine. If I have to stay up in Madison a week, I'll stay a week. Maeve, you make Mr. R understand, willya? I don't want to lose my place here, not with what it takes to get a job in this burg."

"They want to blame that on us too. Not good enough that colored folks died right alongside white folks over there in the fields of France. No, these thugs like to forget that. They say the only reason our boys signed up was so's they could find themselves a white French lady."

I'm looking from one to the other as they're talking to me, both tall, both looking down as if I'm the student and they're after giving me a lesson. It was dim in the hall, but Mr. Jordan's gold ring flashed as he waved his hand from here to there. He was a hand waver, all right, but not the light hearted fella'd shocked me for his ease with Eveline the day before.

"There's talk of the National Guard coming in to quiet things. It'd be better than the Chicago cops who started the trouble."

"They didn't arrest the guy who threw the rock and killed that colored boy, Maeve. That got things going. That's what he means."

"It started long before that, Miss Eveline, Miss Maeve. I was born here and my daddy was born here and I ought to know. They treat us like we're just off the train, like the plantation colored." It looked like his hand wanted to touch her like his eyes did, but he pulled it back and fingered the tie know at his throat instead. Tie had a floral pattern as I recall, and the scent of bay rum rose off his milky-tea skin, and it must a been the same lotion caused the mustache above his full lips to glisten. When we heard the elevator mechanism whirring, he edged himself back against the wall and sort of slid along it, towards the stairway exit.

"Maeve, we are flat in luck to find you here. I thought'd be Florence. Guess she didn't want to risk her pretty little blonde head."

She kept talking as Mr. Jordan continued to back away, doors down from the Chicago Magic Company office and she moved as if he had a string pulling her, and because she did, I did. All the while I'm wondering, what if it's Mr. R gets off the elevator and finds me outside when I said I'd look after the front and what would he have to say about Eveline and her fellow, if he was her fellow, and I don't know why I was still asking the question.

~

Everyone was scared. Hot and scared and if not angry, sad—and hot. Everyone hot. The wave of scorching temperatures lasted and lasted, made you think you were in Florida where Margaret and me'd been, or some place never knew snow and cold rain pelted Chicago in November. Yet faithful Billy got in with the envelopes, even earlier than normal, and dropped them off at our desks, and picked up the orders we had for him and, if he was in no hurry to get back to the storeroom to fill them, we didn't mind him hanging around a bit, asking us what we'd seen and making up stories about being mistaken for a colored himself.

"How?" Ruth asked. "And who would do the mistaking? You may not be as pale skinned as Maeve, but there's nothing about you says Negro."

"If it was night, though, and my head was down."

She only laughed for him exaggerating, our Billy. Him skinny and tousle-haired, mixed of some kind of ancestry did tint him darker than me, but not as much as he imagined. It's just that he always wanted to be part of things, Billy.

"Hey, Ruth," he said, before ducking back into the storeroom. "Do ya know what kind of fruit here is always in season?"

She thought for a minute, despite also grimacing at the way he wouldn't let up.

"An apple?"

"A date!"

He laughed as he shuffled back, as if offstage. That Billy. Ruth was blushing, but could she a thought he was after flirting with her?

It was that distracting, inside and out. But I did my share of work ripping open the envelopes and making out the forms and passing the money along. Mr. R went out again to look for the latest edition of the papers, told us he was going to lock the door this time. Wouldn't be gone long. When he came back in he told us his cronies in the café off the lobby'd said the colored council

135

members had to ride the line between pleasing their white voters and being loyal to their kind. Didn't seem to trouble him, though. Despite people of every hue battling each other all over the city, Mr. R himself seemed somehow outside it all.

But me, who'd expected to spend the day wrenching my thoughts away from that scene by the lake, his body over mine, my eyes closed but feeling him, letting his hands and his fingers, and that other part of him, come into me the way I'd never known, wasn't I distracted by news of the terrible ruction'd started while I dozed beside my man, not really sleeping, because my mind made a stage where the romance played out again and again. *Darlin'*, he'd said, and that pinch beneath the water scared me half to death, and his voice like pink smoke in my ear when he apologized for it being the way it'd been on the hard ground and my debut. Hah!

Oh, but why did I have to mix Janet into those thoughts? Not her so much as the man who'd had his way with her, and her so small. It could not have felt a bit thrilling to the child, only terrifying, unless she was already gone and if so, how could he? How could it be that same act expressed love drove men who could not love at all? I wanted to confide this thought to Desmond, would confide it, when we next met. I imagined the twist of his head. How ashamed he must feel sometimes for being a man, same as Fitzgerald.

The morning passed, tension building, so when lunchtime came, Ruth and me, we thought we ought to stay indoors and took our lunches to the mezzanine and, though there were no chairs or benches, we could walk around below the heads of them Indians guarded our place. Lucky, too, considering. Ruth confessed she hoped Eveline was okay, because I knew, didn't I, that Eveline liked to go to what they called then a Black and Tan resort, where colored and white folks mixed and listened to wild music, and all the black men wanted a white woman. She'd read about it, but not in one of her "True Life Love Stories."

"Think of what they might have done to her!" Ruth's eyes could a popped right out. I never said a word about what I knew, but if Eveline'd been there she would a laughed that laugh of hers and cocked her head to the side and said if we wanted the real dope, it was no wonder the paper didn't want to hear what she had to say, for they wouldn't a wanted to print the juicy details. But Eveline was not there, and I didn't tell what I knew because Mr. Jordan and Eveline herself had sworn me to secrecy. Our nervous mood caused both Ruth and me to wonder if she'd ever be back again.

Cooler there where we sat on the marble stairs across from the wonderful picture made of all the little tiles, me concentrating on the raised hand of Père Marquette blessing the near-naked Indians stepping out of their boat, their canoe. A paltry breeze snuck up from the whirly doors to where we perched, since no one was going up or coming down.

"They say the whole city's going to get mixed up in it. Are you frightened, Maeve?"

"I am so, but this mornin', on my way here, with the rioters not even in bed yet, I didn't know until I saw the paper and I wasn't scared at all. I was thinkin' of my beau..."

I needed to tell someone, make it actual. Desmond. Not tell all but let on this'd begun it for me, the life I hoped to have, as didn't we all? Ruth loved stories of romance and she would not tease me as Eveline might a, making me confess more than I intended.

"A new fella, then, Maeve. Oh," said she, "I am happy for you, and it was not so long, too long, after your Patrick. I am happy for you, Maeve," she repeated and me like accepting her congratulations, same as would come my way once I made the announcement at Bridey's.

"It's Desmond," said I. "We had a grand time of it yesterday by the lake and all. Would never guess trouble boilin' up so close."

"Is he handsome?"

"Oh, he is," said me. "Wonderful soft thick eyebrows over eyes the green of moss, and brown hair with the wave in it, and tall." It surprised me, the poetry spilled out so natural. Oh I missed him.

"To you any man would look tall."

"It's true, but he's taller than Packy, as tall, sure, as Mr. R, and he likes his baseball, and…"

"So, it's serious, is it?"

"I think he's the one. I think I'll have news for y'es all before long."

"Then we might both be leaving the Magic. I'll be at the Normal College and you'll be setting up a home with your man."

I smiled with the happiness of the telling confirmed it, and didn't I feel satisfied, like something'd been accomplished. All the letters answered, all the clothes clean and mended, all the floors scrubbed and the water thrown on the lane, all the taties forked off the plate and gravy wiped up with the heel of the loaf. Prayers said. Bed covers torn back. A good first step into our future because what we'd done proved my Desmond wanted me. We would walk forward together like we'd marched hand and hand across the browning grass of the park bright with picnic blankets and children dressed in their summer clothes.

Was it that tempted them, the good people? They are not partial to smugness, nor even satisfaction seems like, for didn't I pay for it when the morning *Trib* came out on Tuesday and there in the list of names of them wounded in the melee, D. Malloy. D. Malloy? D. Malloy! Could a been Donnie, could a been Declan, could a been Douglas, Daniel, David, Dennis, but the sick in my stomach when I saw that name, it had to be him, Desmond, and then didn't the world and all crash.

~

That night, though, the Monday, I didn't have the news, nor know much of anything except the fear went round the house at Bridey's, and all of it aimed toward the south of us, where most of the tens of thousands of Negroes'd come up from the south'd settled and spread out from there to neighborhoods more white and trying to stay white, as Mr. Jordan'd reminded me. Near enough, the riots could spread to West Monroe. And then wouldn't we be hiding in our beds? Addled John, sensing the fear, started to bawl and Bridey scowled at us and told him, "There, there, John, there is nothin' to worry about," and wouldn't he like another spoon of potatoes?—because food always quieted him.

Harry drove his truck by to see we were all right, and told of gangs lying in wait for the niggers—he called them niggers then and until the day he died, even when the papers later said that kind of name calling was part of all made the trouble—for those people to show up for their jobs at the Yards, places'd opened for them on account of all the men went to war. But those men, many of them, had come back from war and deserved to have their jobs back. The colored workers were only servants of big money, whether they knew it or not, Harry said. Margaret walked him down the fire escape, so called, from Bridey's place.

Me? I never knew fear could turn to hatefulness in such a flash, me with my dreaming of Desmond Malloy and all we'd done, he'd done to me, and the feel of his lips so soft, and the taste of lake water on them, didn't seem poisoned at all, for everything said about the lake. Never could think in a straight line, but the temper of the conversation pulled me back to it.

When she came up from the street again—my sister who'd held the chocolate-skinned babies in her arms same as me and laughed at the comical expressions in their saucer eyes those years we spent at the mission in Florida—Margaret joined in with the rest. Bridey, her other boarders, Lucille and Frances, and Bridey's old woman relative from somewhere, not Ireland. Mrs. Smith, who said less than me, and shared Bridey's table and ate every scrap, Bridey complained, though John's the one needed it. Them from Bridey's and the two fellas from the floor below. Everyone talking mean, even Mrs. Smith, and egging each other on in a spirit made them into a body big enough to stand up to any threat.

You could feel it. There, perched on the stair landings at the back, where we tended to gather, Margaret noticed my quietness, and challenged me. "Don't you think so, Maeve?"

"It's too hot to think and there's too much goin' on out there. It makes a body dizzy."

"But what if your fella and you marry, and want a place of your own, same as me and Harry. What will you find, with all them movin' in, takin' over?"

"It's a big city, sure."

"Be careful out there, though. They're pullin' 'em off the cars, and well they should, but they can't pull all of 'em off, and you got to think this will give 'em the excuse they need to go after white girls. They're always after the white girls, you must a heard. Just months ago, maybe not even that, some upstandin' married woman was dragged into an alley on the South Side. Didn't you see the story? Lucky her screams saved her."

One of the young men from the second floor said this, nodding, as if he knew it all, and maybe entertaining himself with pictures of a colored man ravishing a white woman. You saw crude cartoons like that on handbills plastered up on fences in some corners. A memory of Eveline sailed through my mind and caused me to shiver in its wake. But she'd never looked scared.

"We don't know there'll be cars tomorrow."

True, what Lucille reminded us of, and I did not have my inside knowledge then, not having seen my man on the coming-home car, not knowing he lay in a hospital where he should not have been taken, feelings running as they were.

We washed our clothes and hung them to dry, Margaret and me, her continuing her prattle about what would happen, and how would it turn out, and how would we all feel after. With her chatter and her expectations, she would fit in well with the other wives in the neighborhood where she and Harry planned to stay. He had his eye on the upper floor of a two flat, but they would have to wait till all the strikes were settled. She blamed that on the coloreds, too, Margaret did, even then parroting the man'd be her husband. But, in truth, wasn't there always someone needed whatever they could get? Somebody from a place worse off than Chicago, in that summer when each new edition of the papers blared more complications to a tangled mess destined maybe never to be unknotted?

COLORED PASSENGERS DRAGGED FROM CARS

THREE HUNDRED ARMED NEGROES GATHER

JANET'S BIER AWES CROWDS

JACK DEMPSEY IN CITY

The last light fell through the window onto my *Daily News*. Mayor Thompson'd been out West, but he was back, praise be.

MAYOR HOME IN HAPPY MOOD
HOPES RACE RIOTS WILL CEASE
AND CAR WAGE DISPUTE BE SOLVED

Tuesday, July 29, 1919

STRIKE IS ON; CARS STOP!

There it was, the men'd gone out, as if we needed the newsies to tell us what the silence on the tracks screamed louder. But, just as prominent, as if them two stories were in a race to make it first to the top of the *Herald-Examiner* and the *Trib...*

20 SLAIN IN RACE RIOT

And, in smaller print below

LIST OF SLAIN IN DAY'S RIOTING

Partial list of wounded, too, starting with the policeman injured, him from the Cottage Grove station, 155 whites, 151 black hurt. Later, it would turn out they weren't so evenly distributed, the injuries, between dark and light—more colored than whites wounded. Not that color concerned me much then as my eyes raced down the list of names, my heart speeding as if knowing I was going to see.

D. Malloy, Bridgeport, head injuries, broken leg, taken to Provident Hospital.

Yes, it could a been Donnie, or Declan, or Diarmid, or some other name began with D, but D. Malloy, and Bridgeport, too? It had to be my man, and didn't I feel the beginnings of the same fear ran through the crowd last night on Bridey's back stairs and turned toward hatred? In another part of my mind, though, I was just thirteen and homesick and holding them babies lost their mothers somehow like I'd lost mine—squeezing them out of guilt, maybe, because while they'd been put at the mission because their mammies abandoned them or died, or been shamed into giving them up, hadn't I gone willfully away, dragging my sister with me, at that?

Yes, but that day in Chicago was a day different from when I played with the little ones in the thin Florida dirt outside the mission and pried the bugs out of their fingers, and wiped their faces and kissed them and opened my nightdress to bring that one screaming to my breast, which wasn't much of a breast then, but it comforted him, it did. Wasn't that worth every bit of the scolding, the terrible beating Sister Mary Theresa gave me with a switch, rose welts on my chest, when she came upon us and pulled him away hollering?

Because of them, because of all the people we'd come across in America, in every shade skin could be, I'd lost the fear I had of coloreds when first I saw one on the *Mauretania*. Even the proud ones, like that guard at The Fair, looking me over, like I was a thief. No cause for him to think himself better than me, that one. But… what to think, knowing what I'd learned from the papers? For D. Malloy *had* to be Desmond. He lived in Bridgeport, must be him, and there he lay in Provident Hospital, somewhere I couldn't get to, not with the cars out. Couldn't sit by his bedside to comfort him. And what terrible thing'd put him there?

It being Tuesday, I was supposed to be at work, but didn't I have to set out on foot with all the rest of Chicago? We walked in a mob over the river bridges into the Loop, the weather being the only thing to be thankful for, cooler so. The talk rising around me, the anger, impatience, people complaining, and some of 'em—me—walking her thoughts out. Thoughts mostly of Desmond. Head injury? How bad they didn't say.

But also the coloreds, the car men, and then a thought of poor Janet rushing in and what would happen to Fitzgerald? Would they put him to death at Joliet? Everyone was calling for it, most of us strangers to each other, all of us worried, and me plotting. How long could the cars stay out?

Would my man even be safe at Provident, it being the colored hospital? And him already the victim of some hard Negro or he wouldn't a been there in the first place. Unless it'd been him who went too far, maybe threw somebody off his car, bullying, as he had made the young man give up his seat for me. But that was for me. Had he gone too far with someone had more nerve than that fella slunk off when Desmond told him to? How far would it be to walk to Provident? No matter, I could do it. We'd walked, half run, actually, Margaret and me, to the train station in St. Augustine and did so before day broke. I would get myself to Provident Hospital, too, but where was it exactly?

My feet were after burning from the pinch of my boots, and the toe rubbed raw by sand'd collected in my stocking on the Sunday. I'd considered the selection there might be at Hull House on bundle day, yet the shame of visiting the settlement house when both Margaret and me had jobs stopped me. I was not as bad off as I might be.

Pound, pound, over the cobblestones, stepping around the horse droppings, the trash gathered alongside the streets, the YWCA on the West Side, where ladies like that Clare and Elizabeth I'd met at Thompson's might be working in an office. Past Thomas Elevator, small factories, corner stores, Italian, Greek, Jew, and, with little enough in it, my stomach after turning from the smells came from their open doors. The green spaces, some of them with a bench and a water fountain called themselves parks, other lots empty, save for grass too long and too yellow and the remains of things tossed there, but even at those places people stopped for a rest. Never a shortage of people. There clopped by a produce wagon, then the blurt of a motorcycle, its sidecar filled.

I stuck to West Monroe, though a look over my left shoulder told me most were tramping Madison, same as if the streetcar still ran there. Habit, I suppose, and I had to laugh too—despite the troubles and me sick with worry for Desmond—at the enterprises immediately sprung up along the route. People selling cold drinks, and more papers, another edition, but the news no better. A little to the south I could see St. Pat's, the steeple anyway, but temptation never caused me to veer off and say a prayer for Desmond or anyone else. My church going would come to an end altogether before long, though I did then, and still do, think fondly of them heavenly windows, the brilliant light pouring in and the smell of the wax on the wood pews. A marvelous place to pray, sure, but to a God didn't care, seemed.

Soon the grand post office and Union Station and then the bridge and it recalling Ennis, same as himself did with his eyebrows being reminders of the old friary. I thought of how I used to stand on the Bindon bridge, scaring myself by imagining the running Fergus the backs of brown animals herded there by some giant figure our mammy would call upon to frighten us into behaving. With my feet moving automatic by then and stamping me deeper into my thoughts, I never stopped to stare down at the river in Chicago that day. Head injury, could be bad. How soon could I get to Provident Hospital? And what could I do for him there but pat his hand and assure him I loved him? Was this to be my fate? Finding a man, imagining a future, only to have the fella knocked down by illness or injury, and none of it the fault of the man himself, but only circumstance, that queer combination of events comes from whose hand? If God's, sure a meddling god, worse than the good people, or maybe 'twas them punishing me for the lying and thieving I'd done. But how else could we have got to where we needed to go better ourselves and our lives and ease the burden from our poor parents?

~

The answer didn't come like magic, but not much work got done at the almost empty office of The Chicago Magic Company, neither. No Billy, still no Florence. Eveline, of course, gone to her cousin's. Mr. R himself missing for half the day left me free to search the directory for the location of Provident Hospital. It would be a long walk and not a safe one, sure, not for someone skin light as mine in a neighborhood belonged to all those people at the heart of the trouble. Oh, what to do? But safe not even around us in the Loop when a colored man could be attacked and shot on his way home from work, something I learned when I took the elevator down and stepped outside and saw the story in another paper, all the papers plastered up to the board at the corner and me not the only one crowding in to read.

NEGRO FIGHTS FUTILELY
AGAINST CROWD IN LOOP
SHOT WHEN HE STOPS
TO BATTLE WHITES SECOND TIME

Happened two blocks from where I stood with the others, and me having to angle in from the side, since there were few shoulders low enough for me to see above. Two blocks away only, the poor fella'd run from the mob chasing him. And he'd not been the only one hounded, though he was the only one killed.

One hundred whites, led by five sailors, marched through the Loop early this morning in search of Negro employees. The mob was dispersed by a squad of policemen from the central station, but there was no violence. A Negro employed at Weeghman's restaurant on Madison, near Dearborn, was driven into the kitchen. He escaped by jumping through a window and running down the alley. Later the mob chased a Negro busboy into a restaurant in the McVickers building. He took refuge in an ice box.

Oh, and the oddness of it having started on the Sunday Desmond and I lazed at the beach, me lost in the smile, them nice teeth, the beauty of the lake shining behind him. *Come on, Maeve…* In my dream I stepped right on top of the water and never broke through and we walked right across it to somewhere such misery'd never visited.

Provident, though, the Negro hospital? Why had they put him there?

Back on the ninth floor, still no Mr. R, only Ruth at the back and her using the occasion to write a letter to her brother not home yet from the hospital where he'd been put to recover from whatever got him during the war. Ruth never identified it, his malady. We couldn't let the front stand empty so, door open, not knowing if Mr. R'd come back soon, or at all. I turned the key locked it, in case any murdering types had in mind the sacking of the Marquette Building, not that Clyde would let them pass, no. Clyde stood solid at his post no matter all the goin's-on outside the building.

Feeling more comfortable since I'd stood at the same place yesterday, I slid behind the counter at the front, ran my palm over the glass case, thought of Anna Eva. Mr. R had the keys for the cases behind the counter, the tall ones held the most expensive illusions, and the secrets contained in them, and some others, like the cotton bandage test, not so dear. But I already knew how Anna Eva would get herself tied into a cabinet alongside noise-making things, and, with her still tied, as far as any of the audience knew, objects would come flying out, banjos would strum, tambourines would rattle. Mr. R'd explained how the cotton bandages were fixed so as to let her reach through the iron loop supposed to hold her, reach through and play, or even throw them objects outside. A good trick, comical it was with her head sticking out the top. *My goodness, doesn't that banjo have a mind of its own.* People would laugh even if they knew it to be a trick. No, it was the other things Anna Eva could do interested me, the mind reading and the way she communed with the dead. There were them called that a trick, too, though the great Houdini himself thought her a true medium, and if Houdini didn't know, who did?

A mystery, so, but would any person be referring to some*where* the good people danced in the night, where lovely women called on the spirits of those already gone, and men and ladies both flocked to shows and shops such as ours, and consulted the mind readers you could find everywhere—would all that happen if such a place never existed? A place we felt, but could not see, that we knew of, but could not verify, could not look up in the directory or on a map?

It drew me then, and in the years followed, when the news came out about Professor Einstein's discoveries, and the jokes went round, the cartoons showed him with the wild hair. "Sorry I'm late honey, but don't worry. Time is just an illusion." Them too nodded to the mystery. There was some*thing* more beyond the labor troubles and the cruelty, people torturing each other and taking advantage, like'd happened with poor Janet Wilkinson. Some*thing* accepted. Not only accepted but assumed by Mr. R and Houdini himself, the Great Sebastian, all the magicians and tellers of the future and those called upon spirits. The mystery. *It is all in the power to make people believe,* Mr. R liked to say, sure. But believe *what,* or *in what,* that was my question then and one continued to weave through my destiny, a single nagging thread always dangling just out of reach.

Even now, maybe more so now, it tickles me in a bothersome way, for when you are close to leaving life, looking back on all unfolded in what was given you, you see that while you thought there to be a single reality, in truth the day-to-day living was more like the top of a cake expertly covered with thick icing so you could not see the layers made its height. Yet if…just if…I'd been able to summon the powers I supposedly possessed—those said to a been given me because of the hour I slipped out of my mammy's womb—if I'd considered the possibilities, even thought of them layers I'm aware of today, on the doorstep to wherever it is I am going, would it have made a difference in that week of weeks? Believe, believe. The nuns said it, the priests, Mr. R. You had your believe, sure, and then you had your make-believe.

I looked at the book titles on the shelves behind the front counter of The Chicago Magic Company, thinking I might find an answer there, but no. Fact is, I was not sure of my question. I would write to Anna Eva, for I'd heard she answered letters and then she could tell me—if not *how* she knew what she knew, then simply if the man in the hospital would live and when we would marry. But could I get the letter to her? I found no listing in the directory, and though Mr. R might know where to find her, he wasn't there to tell me and, if I asked, wouldn't he be curious to know what business I had with the woman? It was something I did not want him or anyone to know.

With a cloth I found beneath the counter I polished the glass over them locked cases. I'd seen Florence doing the same, rubbing at the glass, dusting the dark wood behind. The electric light hung down burning yellow and burnishing it so, the wood, and then I touched something gave and the case angled open to the office where lay Mr. R. Not gone at all but there in the flesh, snoring on the satin settee he kept for his visiting cronies. Nothing for it but to slip back into the shop before the case angled shut again and he woke and saw me there. But on top of a letter from the Illinois Trust and Savings Bank sat a slim, leather-covered book like people used for addresses and such. I swept it away before I ever thought how I'd get it back, while also wondering what made him hide there when he must a heard us in the office. Did the bottle of whiskey on the floor beside him say all? Had he slept through everything?

Mr. R, drunk?

All the uncertainty bruised me, and, though I did nothing

to bid it, a picture popped into my brain and pressed on me like a headache. Himself, my man Desmond, lying in that hospital bed breathing his last, alone, the coloreds there wanting to keep their distance, despite his gaping mouth said he was parched. The image weighing me down and me clamoring out from under with resolve, just the same as when Margaret and me quietly shut the mission door and ran along that sandy road, and dogs barking at us and some lights meant the grand station was not so far off we couldn't get there and happiness spurred us. Same as hope spurred us from Ennis. But what was this? Had to be love, though I'd never read or seen a love story like this was turning out to be.

Nothing in the book but scribbled notes. No addresses, and though I thought later I might a found a secret in those pages would help me divine what I needed to know about the some*things*, the some*wheres*, I let the book fall instead, as if he'd dropped it himself before he snuck away with his bottle. If he ever imagined different, if he even suspected I'd spied him there—with his arm after dangling to the square of oriental carpet between the desk and the scarlet settee, his jacket open and that perfect hair mussed—he didn't say. Not long after I forgot myself what I'd seen. The surprising sight of Mr. R got pushed to the far borders of a mind beset.

I left the front and returned to my desk and watched Ruth braid her hair, and listened to her talk about her brother and how they would move out of the city once she finished her studies, for wasn't it getting too dangerous, didn't I agree? I nodded while looking at the few orders on my desk and wondered if the world and all would ever get back to normal. But what was normal? Nothing stopped long enough for me to answer myself. For just then, late to be appearing for the workday, our artist fellow George walked in. His narrow face with its droopy mustache as much as said, *Where else can I go?* He homed to his drawing table as usual and sat there, staring down, without taking off his hat, the soft, floppy-brimmed ones the artist-types favored then.

"I want to be out there drawing the people," said he, "but the fact is I haven't the guts. Not like the photographers from the papers, but not even them got there in time. Did you hear what happened down the block, just this morning? Men in soldier and sailor uniforms, too, chasing a Negro down and beating him to death. Right here! Men with experience in killing, like as not can't get the instinct out of themselves after all the practice they got. Yet wearing the uniform of a United States soldier!"

We knew the story, sure, but what we didn't know is how George'd come close to seeing the dead body, did see the police, did feel the fright electric as any bulb sputtering in the lamps along State Street and retreated to Charles Francis Brown's office on the seventeenth floor, where he'd been since, him and Charles Francis both being artists and understanding each other, liking to talk. I knew this from my chum Gladys, how Charles Francis would blather for hours to his pals, but clammed up on her. Gladys, whom I'd forgot in all the ruckus. I asked George if he'd seen her.

"Cosmo's closed and locked," George told us. "Other offices, too. But you know Charles has the divan where he'll sleep if he works late. He hasn't been out."

Gladys home, then. Safe with her aunt lived just north of the river, which is why my friend could buy the newest fashions from the big stores, at least some of the time. I never met the aunt welcomed Gladys to Chicago when her folks sent her down from some farm up north where her only friends were cows, she'd said. Gladys would invite me, then something would barge into our plans. Her aunt had tickets for a show, or some other relative was after visiting. Always something. So, I never did get to see the comfortable apartment where Gladys had her own room, where her aunt gave piano lessons and regularly entertained up-and-coming politicians and even artists, according to my friend, because after that week unforgettable, everything changed.

Not an hour after George arrived, Mr. R stepped into the back room, his hair smooth again, his jacket buttoned, and him carrying cold drinks he must a brought up from the café off the lobby. We all three aimed ourselves to our work.

"That's right. Keep busy. We'll not declare it a holiday today, for if people ever needed their magic it's here, this week in Chicago. The banks may try to stop me, the churches may think we're the devil, but those who deny us also deny our power to better the city, because, as you are aware, and as I am accustomed to saying, it's the magician who creates the magic. Not the tricks, but the magician and his power to open his audience to the range of the possible. If we believe, they believe. Our customers are like seeds we cultivate with instructions that let them transform an unhappy face to one smiling. In truth, ladies and gentleman," he continued, as if he were holding forth in front of a crowd, and not just we three, "we pass on the power of belief to those with nothing much left to believe in."

I wrote them words out, best I could remember, at home that night, and when I still had my book I would open it and read them again, because he was powerful, Mr. R, when he wanted to be. I didn't think of it at the time or I might a been brave enough to ask if the bank'd turned down his request for a loan to manage the expansion he wanted. But the churches? Was he after thinking it a competition, magic or religion? He never said more about it, only stared at us like he wanted to fix us to himself, his will the paste to do it. He handed around the Dr. Peppers and told us to finish our work that day and we'd see about the next, despite what he'd just said about not declaring a holiday. If the cars were still on strike, maybe we'd keep the office closed for a day. He spoke as if thinking aloud.

"It wouldn't affect the magic, really, because the strike won't last long. I've seen it in my ball."

~

CHICAGO IN GRIP OF CAR STRIKE
AUTOS JAM LOOP

TROOPS MOVING ON CHICAGO
AS NEGROES SHOOT INTO CROWDS

COLORED EX-SOLDIERS
BACKED BY MOB OF 500
TERRORIZE SOUTH SIDE DISTRICT

TOLL OF FIGHTING REACHES 34

Walking my way back to West Monroe in a stream more listless, work finished and the novelty of the morning given way to exhaustion, eyes down or glaring into other eyes, wondering. Young men, the ruffians from some club, Ragen's Colts maybe—them gangsters got up to much of the trouble and proud of it so—those lads taunted the Negroes walking together, not mixing in among the rest like you normally saw with we Micks, the Greeks, and the Hunkies, the Polacks, the Italians, and the Krauts, and the true-born Americans.

The odd person yelling his frustration, generally young, with the energy to holler after such a day. Someone pointing out the smoke rising in the already hazy sky, fires over there, towards the south, where the riots continued for days. Could it be him down there, really, and how would I know without going to Provident Hospital myself to take a look? Even if the strike continued tomorrow, I would have the day to myself and I would say nothing to Margaret about my plans but let her think Mr. R wanted us at our desks, because, as he'd said, Mr. R—the magic business had to continue if any did.

Parched, despite the Dr. Pepper our boss'd given us, my third Dr. Pepper that week, and the breeze from the lake, I bought myself a lemonade and rested. You saw anything that day. Women like me planting themselves right on the curb from there to watch the pant legs, the skirts, the short-pants-wearing runners, the soiled legs of clopping horses, and rolling wheels of motor cars and trucks. Didn't my vision go funny on me, so I saw it all as a river, the Fergus again, streaming and streaming.

When I could, I stood up and continued and, spying the peak of St. Patrick's, I asked God, *Please, please let Desmond live*—even if He might not want to hear from me no more, considering—and hobbled on my way to Bridey's, where they all made a fuss because I was the only one'd been downtown and had the news from there, not to mention the scraps of late editions I'd picked up along the way.

"You won't be goin' back tomorrow, Maeve," said Margaret. "Look at your feet."

I knew the condition without looking, the stockings worn through to the heel, the blister from Sunday broke, and the pus from it gluing the cotton to my skin.

"We'll find you new shoes, at least, and let your feet repair." She brought me a basin of water, and while my feet soaked she fetched me a ham sandwich from the Greek store and generally treated me kind, as a way of softening me, perhaps, before she spilled the news that her union'd be stepping out, too.

"Then I'll have to go tomorrow, won't I, sister? Bridey's goin' to want her money and we have to eat."

Margaret broke down then, sad as I'd seen her since the old days, really. Try as we might, wasn't it hard to keep looking up, when the world and all kept beating us down? First Harry out, then the car men, now the garment workers, and all of them with their point to make, sure. It was more about fairness than being Red, but me, wasn't I glad Mr. R ran the kind of shop he did. If we didn't earn the most, at least I knew we'd have enough to keep a roof over our heads and our stomachs quiet.

She didn't want me walking to the Loop again, but she could hardly stop me, Margaret. It'd always been me who'd led us. She knew my determination from the day I pulled her onto the ship and told her to stop her sniveling, lest the Sisters of Perpetual Grace think her sick and make her stay behind, instead of coming with me on our grand adventure. We would be the brides of Christ and serve in a mission school in a place called Florida, where frosts never whitened the land and sweet soft fruit grew on trees.

Oranges came in our stockings at Christmas one year in Ennis, small and wrinkled, but still that fascinating color. How Mammy'd found them we never learned, but we did know they grew on trees, in Florida, for the sisters'd told us. I said to Margaret, "There won't be no oranges for them not brave enough to go where you can pluck them off the trees, like little suns they are." And so she came. But here she was slumped on the side of the bed, her straw hair fallen out of its pins, her head hanging like that fruit we did eventually pick.

It'd gone dark by that hour. We could smell the conflagration and imagined every sharp noise we heard a shot. Some claimed they could see flames snaking up through the smoke. Bridey feared the city would burn again like it did in the day when Mrs. O'Leary's cow knocked that lantern clear over. I took the rest of the pins out of Meggsie's hair and she fetched the hairbrush and I brushed and brushed until she calmed so and lay back and eventually fell off sleeping.

Not me. It was back to the sill of the window. Gazing out at the ghosts made of clothes ruffling on the lines strung from here to there and back, looking for the good people—though if you looked, often enough you wouldn't see. More commonly they'd surprise you, appearing from out of that mysterious *somewhere,* vexed me then and through all the many years followed and does still. That night I caught not a speck of them, unless it'd been them after making the clothes dance like in an actual breeze, not the reluctant spin of air caused by the fumes and heat coming from miles away, terror enlivening the trousers and overalls, the sheets and pillowcases and towels and baby nappies decorated the neighborhood often stank of Bubbly Creek, that part of the river collected all the putrid waste from the Yards.

I had to go find him. Could he be so bad off he'd forgot me? I've never been one for crying, like Margaret. With me, it was doing released me. I started a letter in my head, one I would finish when I next got my hand on a pencil and paper.

Dear Miss Fay,

It is about the man I love, and me wondering if he is all right, if we will marry as seems likely, despite his injuries. The paper didn't say what it costs for an answer, so I'm putting in these postage stamps, one for your letter to me, and one for extra, like to pay for your advice. We saw your show at the Metropolitan, June it was, and you were marvelous.

Your devoted fan,
Maeve Curragh

I would keep it simple, a single question for her, not to take advantage, and I would not share the answer, if it came, unless she could tell me what I wanted to hear, for Margaret, in her teary state, would just be more bereft if I told her my second chance at a man lay in a hospital full of colored people. There had to be whites, too, or they wouldn't a taken him there, not with feelings running as they were and Desmond himself not in love with the race, something I had to admit as my mind returned a picture of the night we'd met on Halsted Street, Desmond and me. The Negro man running for the car, him tripping, Desmond standing right there with his leg extended. Too, that skinny fella on the going home car and the spear was Desmond's voice when he shamed him into giving me his seat. The workers he'd challenged downtown. I'd noticed, and didn't notice, for it was true what the papers said about the Irish wanting to protect their territory and wasn't I one, though I lived on the West Side, not Bridgeport, and poverty was a bigger threat than colored people to the likes of Margaret and me.

I got into bed alongside my sister and let her hug the side of me, stifling as it was in that upstairs room. I was that scared and that lonesome then, not knowing what I'd find on the morrow.

WEDNESDAY, JULY 30, 1919

MAYBE I DID SLEEP for a spell but, if so, it could a been only for a minute before the sun came up on the Wednesday, when I planned to make my way half across the city to see for myself if it was indeed my man Desmond struck down.

Margaret, seeing my resolve, if not knowing its inspiration, inspected my feet again. Puny to have carried me all the places they had, with a lump the size of my thumb on the right one—a bunion I'd developed soon after we started wearing city shoes, Margaret and me, starting with them never fit properly because we'd hauled them out of a bag of mission donations. The toes though—the little fellow at the end, and the longer one in the middle, on the left foot—oh, weren't they rosy, and the heel of my right foot, skin hanging white at the edge of a crater even redder, and wet as the inside of a mouth. The little fellow on the right not red so much, but yellow where a corn spread around its white eye at the center.

"Maeve, you can't go, not like this. You can't. Sure you'd be crucifyin' yourself."

"I have to, Megs."

Them digits not damaged, crooked, and the whole lot better hid in stockings. She insisted on bandaging the worst with gauze and the tape she kept with her sewing. This would make the shoes even tighter, but she had the idea of cutting open a seam.

"Spoil a good shoe when the comin' in money is goin' to shrink to half if your shop stays out long? I'll keep the laces loose and there are people after offerin' rides in cars. *Just smile if you want a ride.* The papers said it yesterday."

"Well, then..."

Little Margaret, her fair hair tangled again after the restless sleep and her shirtwaist wrinkled and her eyes squinty because of her needing specs, them she got the next year. Offered me her hat, because any walks she'd be taking would be short compared to what I faced, and she didn't even know how far I planned to go. Her picture hat with its edge broad enough to screen me, and smelling of Margaret's head and decorated in a lovely way by herself, who was always searching for feathers and bits of ribbon and silk flowers to change the look of it. Roses of pink and yellow wound all round by a satin ribbon she'd added just that week, the rim straightened—as I'd known she would manage to do after it got bent in the crowd the day the *Wingfoot Express* went down.

Seemed a hundred years ago I stood with the crowd on Jackson Boulevard watching the tragedy unfold. Thirteen killed that day. Nearly twenty in the riot so far. Little Janet Wilkinson. Then a judge jumped to his death. If the summer continued along the same route, there'd be more than the soldiers'd been killed and those came home to die. As many dead as living in the city, their corpses piled up and waiting for graves, and it being as sweltry as it was, they'd add to the stink of the Yards and the blazes offending our noses.

I stepped out that morning into streets lively with folks already, all of us thinking to get an advantage, be one of them found room in the back of a truck or a wagon for a few coins. The newsies long out by then. The little wop boy peddled the *Trib*, his curly hair already damp under his cap, voice ringing above the boy opposite.

RIOTS SPREAD, THEN WANE!

DOWNSTATE TROOPS CALLED TO AID CHICAGO!

COOL HEADED MEN ASK NEW STRIKE VOTE!

RIOTERS IGNORE OVERSEAS
NEGRO WOUND STRIPES!

LOOP EMPTIED OF 250,000 IN RECORD SPEED!

Some of them miniature businessmen read the headlines straight out, but not the imaginative Italian child seemed to own the stop where I would board the car on a normal day. He'd yell something make you curious so's you had to buy a paper and he'd thrust one in your hand and grab another from his stack to tempt the next customer. Couldn't a been ten years of age, though maybe it was his size made him seem so.

Some hopeful passengers hung around, wistfully looking up and down the track, but no car clattered toward us. Men without their car men's uniforms carried signs asking for fair pay for their work—and didn't we all want that—but in spite of my feet I didn't think hard thoughts about the fellas out on strike, since mine would be one of them got the benefit of the pay, and wouldn't that mean a more swell life for us both.

If he wasn't too bad, that is. If the head injury didn't mean he'd lost his wits, the broken leg cripple him so he had to give up the job altogether. It crossed my mind to tap one of them sign carriers on the shoulder and ask if he'd heard any news of poor Desmond Malloy, the popular conductor usually worked this line. I stood for a minute staring at the older man there, seemed a serious sort, him frowning under his bowler hat as if it was only him bearing the responsibility of all that'd happened.

Then a wagon halted and a man hollered, "Ten cents to the river!" Taking advantage, as people will. I was near enough to step on the box he put down and climb on with the crowd laughing about how the old days'd been better. You could always count on a horse and horses didn't form unions, and every other such joke. Even I felt lighter, considering, watching a pickle truck pass us, its back open and people waving from it, the whole affair a holiday, in spite of all the grief, and it not long before the towers of downtown soared into view and people started clamoring to get off. Someone yelled, "The cars aren't running but the El is." We could see a train stretched out in the space between the buildings, then not. So moving, sure. People cheered, and a man hollered, "It's a beautiful day in Chicago!"

Hah! He had to be forgetting all was plaguing the city. Yet the air felt cooler and the elevated cars ran south, where I had to go. Had me pondering. To ride the El and get there quicker, but face the mobs of rioters must be crowding the elevated like they'd crowded the streetcars? People pulled off, and what a fall it'd be from up there onto the road, where any order kept before had been lost in the throng of automobiles and hearses carrying the sick, and horses and buggies, and jitney cabs—some of them pulled by horses, too, others motorized—and trucks. No, I would trust my injured, but dependable, feet.

The driver aimed his nag towards the curb just by the post office. "Far's I'm goin," he announced.

Every corner in the Loop had its newsstand, but the downtown newsboys dressed like their gentlemen customers, in suits with waistcoats and ties, fedoras pushed down over their grimy necks, shouting the latest headlines or a version of them, near the truth.

CITY AT WAR!

5,000 TROOPS UNDER ARMS!

The usual rivers of people merged into a flood overflowed the sidewalk and mixed in with the motoring outfits on the road itself—laundry trucks, open cars, and them closed. A different, testy feel in the shadow of the office blocks. Cautious. Listening.

A shot? Sun white as a peppermint lozenge, clouds definite above the lake, the haze sliding into clumps like dirty laundry gathered in piles. So much to look at I forgot my feet, or they were numb with all the wrapping and the tight fit, me walking till I hit Dearborn, where normally I'd a turned left and continued on to the lovely Marquette Building.

But Mr. R'd said maybe he'd keep the door closed. Who'd be there today, anyway? Billy worked only a few hours, so why risk himself? He'd never showed up yesterday and so probably not today, neither, whether or not he knew Mr. R's plans. With Ruth in her downtown building, she could get to work easy. Could be sitting at her desk already, braiding and unbraiding her hair. If she'd got in the door. If Mr. R had meant what he said about magic being the most important thing and opened The Chicago Magic Company same as usual.

But none of us there to move the magic along to them needed it. None save Ruth. For what would she do if she didn't go to work? Drink pot after pot of tea with the other single girls lived there in their small rooms and gathered in a parlor fitted out to look homey, but never managing to fool those missed home. She'd write to her brother, no doubt, describing all went on that week. Or study something. But what could it be? All I'd ever seen her read was her "True Life Love Stories." She claimed to have a scrapbook full of them at home.

Melancholy George, the artist, was ashamed of his shyness where danger came into it, didn't have the stuff. Them two, same as yesterday, using the office to hide in their ways, like Mr. R'd hid in his bottle. I was glad Eveline'd got out of town for she would a stood up to anybody and hold them off with some smart remark. Given the tempers running hot, those against her choice of man would a been ready to put their fists behind their opinions that week.

Funny, the magic, all of it lying there in books, in cases, in Mr. R himself, yet him as if dead, that powerless. *'Tis the magician makes the magic,* he'd said, and with Anna Eva somewhere I didn't know, and all those others, the Blackstones, the Thurstons, the Oriental man did the card tricks nowhere to be found—all them wanting to avoid the troubles no doubt—it had to be me did whatever needed doing. And if a cape or a hat or a wand or a crystal ball could transform a calamity into a celebration, well, I had none of those with me and I would not stop into the Marquette and ask for the loan of them.

TROUBLE SPREADS TO WEST SIDE!

MAN RIDDLES NEGRO'S BODY WITH 16 BULLETS COVERS IT WITH GASOLINE, AND SETS IT AFIRE!

I stepped over the horse droppings and straw, pages flown out of the newspapers, shopping bags empty, wrappers from candy. Over the steel rails, where we would see cars again before the end of the week, and from Dearborn proceeded one block east to State Street, which led me directly south into the troubles, even shooting.

~

500 WHITES STORM PALMER HOUSE! NEGRO WAITER ESCAPES

The Palmer House itself? That grand place, and white men chasing a Negro worked there? Never mind South State, 'twas just as perilous there in the heart of the city, despite police standing guard at each corner.

The big stores opened, counting on their telephone lines for sales more than shoppers usually arrived on the streetcars. I glanced in the doorway of The Fair to see if the mulatto doorman'd had the courage to stand his post. There was no sign of him. Then came Mandel's and The Boston Store, a soda shop, the Bijou Dream, where Margaret and me'd seen a show. More stores, cafés, hotels down the ladder of elegance from Potter Palmer's place, sure, with signs out front declared the price for a bed. Then a mission, and further along, where the buildings rose to less lofty heights—squatting at the edge of the broad street—lots empty and scraggly with weeds and garbage and two children throwing a ball made you wonder if their mother knew all was transpiring around us.

Then the Fashion Theater, where we'd seen another show, not as fancy as the Bijou, but a place I remembered because there'd been a woman trying to present herself as the next Anna Eva, seemed. A kind of seer. A girl not much older than me, dressed swell, but hadn't the wit to recover herself with something funny when she fumbled the answer to the question asked. She might a made a show of the mistake, tell the public something would trick us into believing she'd given that answer to purposely mislead us. But, no, she only let herself be saved by a man with a monkey and an organ, same as you saw on the street. Trying as she was to make magic, in the end the poor girl, for all her beauty, made nothing but a fool of herself, and the audience hard as audiences could be, threw not pennies, as people did when they liked a show, but crumpled up paper and even the burning butt ends of cigars.

TROUBLES CONTINUE
THROUGHOUT DAY AND NIGHT
HEAVY CASUALTIES!

Rooming house after rooming house, maybe one of them where Eveline lived, and stores sold liquor, cafés, peddlers on this route, too, ringing their bells, offering spuds and tomatoes, corn from farms on the edge of town. More vacant lots made me think of the gap left when you lose a tooth. But even here you found a newsie on a street corner, not every one, like in the Loop, but you could get your paper if you wanted it, or hear the news yelled out.

Beneath the corset, my skin'd gone wet as if I were in the bath, and not just because of the effort of walking those many blocks, or even the heat, because the temperature did not rise so high that day. My hair also damp beneath the band of Margaret's hat and my stomach folding over on itself and roaring, though I had a chunk of bread in my pocketbook and a bit of cheese would go greasy if I left it. The color of the people began to shift in a noticeable manner. More of the storeowners peering out their shuttered shop doors, those staring out the windows of the three-flats, and the rooming houses, too—not all, but many—dark skinned.

Chicago was bigger than Margaret and me'd experienced. We'd been to some parts, and they became the city we knew, the Loop most common, and our neighborhood on the Near West Side. South of the Loop we knew only as the place to ride through on our way to White City and Prairie Avenue. White City, the amusement park, was the furthest south we ever went. Prairie Avenue was closer, where the grand mansions stood. I veered off State, over to Prairie because I'd walked that street plenty of times, first when we arrived and Margaret was looking for a job, then later, to meet her at the house where she assisted the older lady did the laundry for one of them stately households, the one she finally quit on account of the husband and his slick ways.

It was shady there and quiet at the north end of Prairie, another world, sure, than the one existed a couple of blocks west, and in the spot I chose to rest no one but me sat on the curb. No matter it looked odd, odder here without the same crowd filled the Loop. But then wasn't everything odd that week in Chicago? I'm a small woman, I have always been small, and I knew how to make my way, but I was also a woman with tormented feet and I didn't dare loosen the laces any more, because a hurt contained was more manageable than when it spilled out for me and all the world to see.

Laughter sparkled the air, but me not the target of it. No, only a young couple, both dressed in white, and him carrying a basket to the car waiting in front of the big house nearest to where I sat. In a ribbon of sun unrolled through the leaves on the big tree, I saw the girl's blonde curls bounce, and I heard someone calling from the door, "Missy, Missy, you don' forget this here lemonade I fixed you." This somehow made them laugh again, the golden ones, and I was after thinking two things—there could be as many colored as Paddy maids, and the golden couple, they must be off for a picnic in their motor car, a picnic somewhere trouble couldn't sneak up on them.

If they found themselves alone, and her no doubt in a fetching bathing costume, with all the proper accessories, and them secluded—because most Chicagoans would be staying in if they could—what would they do? Thought got me uncomfortable and wound me back to Desmond on top of me, pushing into my deepest parts, probing with that part of him I'd not yet touched. The tender gate to the insides I'd not known before. And then didn't I remember the bruise on my bottom I'd dared not complain about to Margaret?

How might it have gone for my sister and me if Margaret'd looked for another big house wanted a Bridget after she quit the first? Somewhere she'd have a nicer room and all the food she wanted, and wouldn't have to risk her eyes sewing. Them splendid houses, rising three to four stories high, with windows set right in the roofs of some of them, and decorative chimneys and curtains every bit as plush as those we'd seen at the theaters. Plaster work inside, like the Palmer House itself, and marvelous chandeliers. One of these would a been a better place for Margaret I thought then, but she might not a met Harry, who pleased her, if not always me.

No, never good to reconsider, for all things change. What seemed sensible, even wise, can seem foolish in retrospect, and a foolish choice can turn out to have been the wise one. If every piece of a life could be put alongside all the other pieces, to see how one fits into the other, neat as a jigsaw puzzle, but no. We are not given that view from above, only the one we get as if from the back of a train, watching all we've been through get further away.

Not that any such ruminations took up all my thoughts. No, not them, but the bread in my pocketbook and that bit of cheese, both of which I nibbled at daintily as if I'd been sitting inside one of them fancy houses and not on the lip of the street outside. Just as, when I arrived in the city, no one noticed me. I might a been invisible there beneath the green arms of that lovely tree, where birds perched and a breeze stirred and a single leaf drifted down into my lap. Funny that, a leaf curled and brown at the edges in mid-summer, as if to remind that time is just something we imagine. Sometimes a train speeded up past all we want to hang on to, sometimes stalled on the tracks in the suffering heat.

Could be yesterday I sat there fiddling with the crisp spine of that fallen leaf. When I got up to continue on my way, I did not think of Desmond every step either, no, but every other, and devoted the struggle with my feet for the sake of his recovery. It is easier to bear pain, said the Sisters of Perpetual Grace, if you offer it to Our Lord who hung on the cross for three hours, his head bleeding from the crown of thorns, and nails pounded right through the holy flesh of his hands and feet.

Imagination necessarily filled out all I didn't know. First, what'd happened. Could be my man talking rough to one of the Negroes and being attacked, them young coloreds bolder because of the trouble already started on Sunday. Sunday. Or maybe a scene made him look like the kind of man'd win a medal. Defending a body on his car, maybe a child, one like I'd tended in Florida, but older so, to be on the car by herself.

Maybe even his mates from the old neighborhood—boys from some of those wild clans came together for sport, they claimed. Young Micks fired up by drink, some of them. Not Packy, him not a drinker, or much of one, though he liked his beer, Packy did. Those young boys from the clubs, with the eyes burned, they'd be men. Could a joshed him. *Come on, let us have her, Dessie.* Of course, I liked the picture made him look the best and it could a been true, or he might have been torn at the moment, not being fond of Negroes himself, but still and all the man in charge of the car, obliged to defend his passengers.

The recollection of my dawdling there on Prairie Avenue surprises me, I have to confess. Yet it is true I enjoyed the tweet of birds hidden in the branches above me. The rhythm of a hammer pounding not far off gave a kind of comforting order to the hour. Music, too, a piano, maybe a girl practicing the same over and over, scales. I dreamed then that when we married we would buy a piano for our children, and on a summer day I would step outside and listen to them playing simple melodies rivaled the songs of the thrush for their beauty. This got me going again, and once up, the vague image of those piano-playing children quickened my pace, for there'd be no wedding if no man to marry. And if I favored one foot the further I went, it was not the foot preoccupying me.

~

Used to be brick, and some of the yellow limestone mansions, one after another all along Prairie Avenue, the grandest set into lawns surrounded by iron fences, others closer together and nearer the sidewalk. Them houses used to be just for one family and all their hired help. But less than two years since Margaret ran off, a passel of them'd been turned into hotels and rooming houses. One with a sign, *Risk Hotel,* would a raised a smile if it'd been that kind of day. The risk of what? Bugs maybe or something worse, but to advertise it, as if proud, made you wonder what kind of body would ever want to rest there.

The neighborhood changed from block to block. Soon came the stink of wax and dead animal hides from a boot maker, while across the street, people shouted from what had to be a gambling den, given the pair of dice painted on the blacked out window, smoke from cigarettes ribboning out the open door, someone in there bellowing as if there's nothing to worry about as long as the dice rolled his way. Music from a storefront tavern. "I'm Forever Blowing Bubbles," the tune, and didn't it remind me of my first date with Desmond and the upstairs ballroom from where the same song drifted down. A box factory, too, still running. I could hear the thwack of machines from a door didn't need a sign, them boxes stacked outside saying all was needed to be said about the purpose of the industry inside.

On a corner, further south on Prairie Avenue, two buxom ladies wearing the bright colors and lower necklines, the piled high hair and gaudy necklaces you see in stories of girls gone bad. These ladies were coffee skinned and when they called out to me, I understood the tone, fun-making, but the words were buried in deep-south accents I could barely understand, though I'd heard similar, in Florida. I did make out the word roses, though, pink roses, and I knew they were remarking my hat, actually Margaret's hat. I paid them no mind, for in the distance—not so far along I couldn't see it—Mercy Hospital, famous because hadn't the authorities installed President Teddy Roosevelt there after someone tried to assassinate him? A hospital for white people, Mercy, and had Desmond been driven there, instead of the hospital known to be for coloreds, still ten blocks ahead, I would be where I wanted to be and the next would not have been so trying.

The sun climbed to its highest, its hottest. Dazed, stomping on dogs might as well a been dead they were that numb. Words on signs entered my eyes naturally as light—apron factory, lamp shade maker, steam laundry, taxi yard, stables with an arrow pointing down an alley and the predictable stench of piss-soaked straw. Auto cushions, a little grocery with boxes and cans of foods in the window. Not much, nobody wanted to make deliveries to the Black Belt, said the papers, and not surprising so since a white peddler on his cart'd been shot somewhere not far from here. Didn't I hope I would see no blood on the street. A child scrambling out the door of the little shop crossed my path, a colored child, barefoot, in short pants but with no shirt to cover shoulders round and burnished as oft-turned brass doorknobs. He ran, then disappeared into one of the skinny buildings with paper signs in the window advertising rooms for rent.

Mercy Hospital next with its peaked gables and arched windows and shade trees along the walk in front. Policemen in groups of two or three at each side of Prairie, checking motor and horse traffic, and at the main door of the hospital, a doughboy with a rifle standing guard meant Mayor Thompson'd given in to the governor, and the newsies had it right about the troops helping out. If this'd been my destination, I would a had no fear of entering, not with that solider at the door. But, no, I had to leave the less magnificent here, but still quieter Prairie Avenue for Wabash, then State Street, to get to that corner of Dearborn where he lay.

The shouts of two white boys on opposite corners, one with the *Trib*, one with the *Examiner*, comforted me for the familiarity of the sound of young voices bellowing, though the news had got no better, or much newer, in the hours had passed.

WHOLE POLICE FORCE IS ON RIOT DUTY!

AUTHORITIES SAY SITUATION IS IN HAND!

BATTLES START UP AT NIGHT!

I had not gained more than a couple of blocks past Mercy when I heard a sharp noise, could a been an automobile—they were always after blowing up back then—but that day, in that week, it was more certainly a gunshot. Not that I'd heard gunshots often. Cannons, yes, for celebration, and once, in Florida, someone firing a rifle at some wild animal. Too, the sad sound of a report back of Uncle Thomas's house the day he had to shoot his only horse on account of her having gone lame, too lame to get herself out to the grass. Me inside the house, biting my lip because I knew he had to do it, but she was the only horse I'd ever climbed onto the back of, and though she'd only walked around a bit, it never took much of my healthy imagination to think myself Maeve of the faeries and us riding through the sky. Just a wee one I was then.

It may be only because I am looking back I think it was a gunshot I heard on Prairie Avenue, the way you do when knowledge and experience work on memory. But whatever I thought it was stopped me. Stock still I stood there on Prairie Avenue. There were others on the street, a few, and they started running and someone hollered at me, "Better get out of here, miss."

Across Prairie, hand on my head, to steady the hat, I trotted down a street to the side, where I heard more gunshots—no mistaking them a second time—and the clanging bells of police cars driving as fast as they could. Yet closer, and strange, considering, the ragtime music would make you want to tap your feet some on some other occasion. Did the player not realize all going on outside his tavern or the bawdy house, whatever it might be? With the danger around me I had to find some kind of shelter, and picked out what looked like the entry of a store. From there, crouching in the shadow of an overhang, I saw a crowd of boys—they were boys with skin pale as mine, whipped by too fast for me to count, suspenders flying off the backs of some of them, many with their cloth caps, others in the fedoras men wore. Yelling, most of them, a terrible ruckus coming from their crowd. One throwing rocks I believe he must have taken from his pockets, aiming at whatever target seemed likely, maybe chasing someone, and then didn't I want to turn around and go back to the Marquette Building or Bridey's, somewhere safe? But how, how? And if I went back, would I ever find out about Desmond? More noticeable, too, were the grisly billows from fires rioters'd set. My nose stung and my face needed mopping. I opened the door of whatever enterprise I stood outside of and stepped inside. No store, though, only stairs leading up, and looking down, fright on her face, same as fright must've been on mine, a colored lady in a flowered yellow wrapper, as startled to see me, as me to see her.

"Watch'all doin' here? You getch yerself out 'fore you cause some trouble, white girl."

A rustling came from behind her then and another lady, bigger in size, also dressed in a wrapper, but a red one with black lace around the throat, and her hair straightened to twirl into an arrangement made her appear an Amazon queen like any you would a seen on the cover of a Tarzan book—though it's true I was looking up and maybe she only seemed tall from my angle. Her lips full, rouged with something made them shiny, and that smaller woman in yellow moving behind her, letting her take over. While the lady in red did not invite me in, her voice had more kindness in it, so.

"Y'all be careful, honey. You keep yourself hid under your big ol' garden hat and nobody'll bother you. But you stay away from Walgreens, hear? Where those big mobs get together? Just stick to the side streets you gonna be all right. I don' know where you belong but it ain't here. You better get yourself on."

That voice of hers, lazy, even in the circumstances. Creamy like the cocoa the sisters would fix us at Christmas, when we got as many oranges as we could eat and sometimes a letter'd traveled from Ennis all the way to Florida and we'd read it again and again. That's how I remember that lady, kind in her way, despite who she was, should a scandalized me. I should a been outraged to a stumbled into such a house, or maybe they were ordinary women wearing wrappers because they'd slept late, and the tall one'd started the day by putting on her makeup. She was a woman, anyhow, and had enough softness in her I wanted to shelter there until the trouble ended, or forever, and have her bathe my feet and offer me something cool to drink. But I didn't say anything nor put so much as a toe on the stair leading up.

"Go on," she said, shooing me. "Git!" and I saw why when a man wearing no more than a soiled undershirt over his bare brown chest, and a hat, a straw fedora, raced past me, taking the stairs two, even three at a time, and the light streaming in with the open door flashed on something silver—a razor, a knife? She shooed me away for my own protection. But where to go?

~

Sign full of holes said Thirtieth Street, meaning six blocks more to walk before I reached Provident Hospital. Side streets not like the Chicago I knew at all, with buildings so important they had names, like a person—Marquette Building, Monadnock Building—and rose higher than a normal person's eyes could reach. No, here stood narrow bungalows of wood or brick set on small lots, some nicer than others, painted, and with fences matched the railings 'round the porch. That's the best of what this poor road offered. The worst consisted of simple bare boards, flimsy doors shut up despite the heat. In front of one had its parlor windows broken out, household belongings tumbled together on that patch of dirt and yellow weeds passed for a garden. Mixed in with the bushes against the house foundation, shirts and briefs spilling out an enamel basin, a simple chair on three legs, a pair of men's shoes held together by the laces, a washboard. Down the block some front porches sagging, and a couple of children on one, others empty.

Except for them two small heads I saw above the porch rail, there was no one out on this street, but people had to be inside the broken houses, and I feared someone watched me from behind them whole, and also shattered, windows and I walked faster. If I could a shut my eyes and still walk I would a done it, for hadn't I gone and got myself into a situation bad as I'd ever been in and there was nothing for it but to continue, and I thought of praying and did pray, the way you do when it's the first thing surfaces in your mind, before you think about the good of it or if you even believe. It's that natural to some of us, and so I acknowledged my sins and promised penance—if this was not it arriving uninvited.

Then I was there, at Wabash, and hurried over without looking left or right to find the source of the yelling, came from how far off I wouldn't know. I was not the only innocent out, but one of few, and no one else dared raise their heads to see what color face would greet them, for if there were others like me, and there were, sure—those light-skinned people from other countries, got to Chicago first, and resented the Negroes moving into the neighborhood—there were not many, and there I was about to head further south, where the blend of brown and white would begin to favor the darker of the two.

I just had to slip across State, under the El track, and continue along to Dearborn. I had to do it same as crossing the endless ocean of water on the *Mauretania*. To get to where you wanted to be, you had to make the crossing and, so, waiting only for the now and again traffic braved South State—not even letting myself enjoy the bit of cool beneath the elevated—I hobbled over with my eyes down on the bricks made the street. One glance was enough to see the way was clear, but that one glance also showed me the big crowd a few blocks down on State, had to be gangs of Negro men, and policemen keeping them from getting out of hand, soldiers, too, in their brown uniforms, carrying rifles and standing firm along the edge of the street blocks down near the Walgreens drug store the big lady warned me about.

I did not let myself enjoy the fact that I'd made it to the other side, but turned left once I'd got to Dearborn and passed houses so poor the three-flat Margaret and me called home looked like a Prairie Avenue mansion by comparison. Wasn't everyone in the city got rich, but I'd never thought myself among the well off till I spied those clapboard excuses for dwellings, near bad as the poorest parts of Ennis. Pools of water in vacant lots, though it hadn't rained for days or even weeks, and maybe sewage'd seeped there, smelled bad enough. Garbage, cats nosing after rats. Clothes hanging limp and dirty from lines strung across the distance between one porch and another, same as back of Bridey's, but the nappies gray as if they'd never been washed at all.

I'd not walked all this way to gawk and, in the smoke, dense as autumn fog, I could not see clear anyway. Throat burning it was, air worse than it ever got downtown and Lord help us if the wind changed direction and came from the west, gathering the stench of Bubbly Creek. Not that much wind blew, if I recall, and I do trust my recollections, because, for a while, I had the book where I wrote my notes—all of what came before that week in Chicago, then the airship crash to the Sunday and what transpired after. I skirted the actual event of the Sunday just as the pictures would skirt it with billowy clouds and lush music.

I can see it now, my writing good as the nuns'd taught us. "He kissed me and then it happened, the thing that ensured we would be, were already, man and wife." More than I needed to write, and all the gushing, too, about Anna Eva Fay. Came the time I didn't want to be reminded of Anna Eva and of my sightings of the good people, because them, or magic or God, whatever it was, had forsaken me at the hour when I was most in need. Must have been the lying did it. All I'd invented and excused, on account of necessity, guaranteed I'd suffer in this world if not the next, and I'll soon enough find out about that, having reached the age I have.

Writing the week on paper firmed the memories in my brain, like photographs do. I had few of those, even if more in the years followed when the family took pictures for every occasion and I was always included in the one snapped when a new baby came home. Looking over those pictures I could tell which child it was only by the changes in my mug, a hair no one told me about growing out of my chin, or I would have plucked it, for it brought back an image of Bridey. I kept a magnifying glass to use with the paper and it would have worked just as well with the mirror, had I thought to use it with the tweezers. That hair, the fleshy sags beneath the corners of my mouth. The book then, what few photographs there were, and of course her, too, reminds me of everything without saying a word. These things support my recollections.

~

As grand as Mercy, Provident was not. Blockier so, with none of the peaked gables and arched windows of the bigger hospital well behind me, but a covered entrance all the same and it nearly as high, and as many armed men guarded it as the other, for, as I would find out when time and the quieting of my heart let me concentrate on the papers again, there'd been more of the storming going on, same as the Palmer House, a white mob looking for whites inside. Black mobs, too, but why they should siege their own hospital I never did learn. Did explain, though, why the doughboys in their brown, flat-brimmed hats and their long rifles stood in front, for the policemen in Chicago were none too popular with the coloreds and those didn't know why found out later in news of the injustices done.

Trouble'd been simmering since the month before when they never arrested any of the gang'd murdered two Negro men, right on the street, even though a white woman had witnessed the crime and told the papers as much. Nobody official ever paid the price for their wrongs, but so went Chicago then, and so it may go now. It has been years and all since I visited Margaret on the Bluebird bus, and even if I could a made the trip and sat down with my sister and her husband—when Harry was alive—wouldn't a been them set the record straight, for Harry in particular never thought much of the coloreds to begin with, and after the riot summer, things only got worse in his eyes.

But, then, the second Wednesday of them ten days unforgettable, there I finally stood, near him who'd drawn me across the city, half on feet would never be the same—not that I could a bragged about their previous condition. I needed to catch my breath and freshen myself, hope for a washroom, or water from somewhere to drink and splash on my face felt red as a poker straight out of the fire.

Here at last, and I let it flood, all the feeling the pictures and stories call love, warm and terrifying at once. Every bit I'd been holding back for the man inside. The hair rich in color as the most beautiful bay horse, them eyebrows made me smile with all they said, joking. The eyes themselves, including the one tended to wander, not such a deficit after all, for it'd kept him from the worst of the war. Them beautiful hands, long fingered, and the feel of his mouth so close to my cheek and the weight of him on me pressing down. *Desmond,* I'd whispered, and I whispered it again on the front step of Provident Hospital. Minutes away from seeing him, and I prayed—though God must have thought me a fickle one—prayed he'd be awake, the head injury maybe knocked him out eased enough by this day he could recognize her who'd made her way through the chaos to lay a loving hand on his cheek. Desmond.

A hospital for Negroes, especially for Negroes, so what would I be doing there? 'Twas the first question asked me by the soldier at the entrance.

"Can I help you, miss?"

"I came to see my..." What to call him stopped me, for husband had not yet become legally true. "The man I am promised to. I read it in the papers."

"You know this is a Negro hospital."

A fellow younger than me, though taller, like most, and a very narrow face, tanned, and teeth could use some fixing, but not so harsh voiced he frightened me.

"I do, but he was hurt near here, the paper said it, and I checked."

I didn't say what I checked, but all the same, with my oft-practiced skills, I convinced the fellow and he stepped aside to let me enter that place smelled of sick and rubbing alcohol, that rusty blood odor I knew from my monthlies, and the accidents I'd seen on the street involved more horse blood than human, but it smells the same, blood. Fans above, spreading out those perfumes to any of us dared enter, as if warning us, and women, various hues of colored women in their long dresses and their long white aprons atop and their white caps striped with black.

Right away one of them came up to me, Maeve Curragh, whose best shirtwaist was near-ruined from the great circles of perspiration her elbows aimed to hide, her face flushed, her big hat tilted maybe crazily, and she said to me, "Do you have permission to be here? Can I help you?"

Behind her the bustling of people in their hospital uniforms, and someone rolling past on a stretcher, a blanket pulled over the face, had to be dead, sure, and I could only swallow and then the tears came, and though it was Margaret who was the crier, not me, they poured as if from an overturned jug and I couldn't stop, for what if it was Desmond lying under that sheet and rolling down the corridor barely lit? What if I was too late? I couldn't help thinking the worst even though the arm outside the blanket was brown.

"Are you hurt, ma'am?"

Her voice kinder then, her hand at my back steering me to a bench where people waited, one boy whose bleeding forehead his mammy blotted carefully with a towel. Another, older, near my age, with his leg stretched out and misery on his face, and he moaned from time to time while I was there, which was not long. Still, long enough to register people standing, sitting, some children with their mothers, others young men—one of them scowling in the instant my eye met his—some blood dropping right onto the floor. It was no place for a white woman and a prevaricating one at that.

"It's not me," I started to explain, but the kind nurse only offered me a cloth, more nappy-size than a handkerchief, same

as the mother was using on her injured son, and just as useful
for wiping my face.

Before she hurried into the room across from the bench
she said, "It's all right. The doctor will see you when it's your
turn. Could be some time."

For those few minutes I waited, I entertained the notion
something *had* gone wrong with me and 'twas only myself
couldn't see it, being the fool I was. If I'd continued to wait,
maybe the tall doctor I'd spied when the door across opened—
his white coat stained, his specs slipped down his nose, sprigs
of ivory through tufts of hair sprung from a scalp dark as any
of the patients here, save for me—maybe that man would
examine me and find a cause for everything and come up
with a cure to rid me of it all. So coursed my wild hope, half-
acknowledged, for at the same time I had no intention, really,
of sitting there waiting for anyone, not in this company, people
who must've hated or at least resented me. Not in any other
company neither. I'd yet to accomplish my mission.

When the double entrance doors opened wide and a
couple a policeman carried in someone on a pallet, someone
stabbed—a tailor they said, near death—the doctor bustled
out of his examining room and listened to the man's heart, and
shooed away anyone in the path leading to the operating theater
down the hall. With everyone's attention focused there, 'twas
my chance to leave the bench for the stairway in the center of
the building. More humble those steps than the ones where I'd
perched with Ruth at the Marquette—felt like a year before,
though it'd been only a day. Wood for this banister, and it well
worn above the iron railings supported it. No marble, no, but
the portal leading to the second floor worth more to me than
any marble or brass or beautiful mosaic pictures.

Where I would find him, I did not know. I would have to
put on my most assured manner, aim to be casual. Be someone
who not only belonged here, but was accustomed to the place

despite her appearance, this small white-skinned woman with a hobble in her step and a hat hid her true looks. I would search every room until I found him. I never thought I would not find him. It would be only a matter of method, peering into a room, all more or less like the first, walls painted white, ceiling fans turning high up, iron bedsteads, men resting, some groaning, some old, the stink of their uncontrolled bowels. No Desmond there. Nor in the room across, more beds, these for women, must a been. A long-aproned nurse, back turned to me, tending to a very large lady, bulk almost too great for that narrow iron bed. I slipped in and slipped out.

Unless I was mistaken, there'd been a light face on one of them pillows, the face of a white woman. The clock on the wall said one o'clock.

The image of that clock returns as if it is ticking right here in front of my eyes as I lay on this bed and stare at the fellow in the picture framed on the wall across. Professor Einstein himself, but with his wild hair and the drooping mustache colored a bright turquoise blue against a field of yellow, and words in the same screaming blue as his hair: "The only reason for time is so everything doesn't happen at once."

They could a put a holy card there, or a calendar or something, but they left the room as it was when the oldest ran off, them maybe thinking she'd return soon, or I wouldn't be here for long. No doubt they are right, at least about me. I know what stands near, big, quiet, waiting for me. When does not matter. With me here living a week transpired half a century ago, it more alive than the sounds from down below, I can't help but consider what my companion on the picture across from me says, the man everyone called a genius. Yet despite all the clocks, the calendars, the day and the month and the year printed at the top of each edition of all the many papers so's everyone could keep track of what went on when, everything did happen at once that week in Chicago, and the sorting out has taken a lifetime.

I was torn between continuing along them hospital corridors until I found Desmond, or finding a place to tidy myself first, for with the crying, and the sweating, and the exhaustion, I had to look a fright. Some cold water on my face would help, and a minute to smooth my hair and adjust my hat smelled of my dear sister, the oil came from her hair, and didn't she seem that far away.

I found cleaning closets, cabinets for storing medicines, another room with a glass window for patients with infectious diseases, a sign above the window forbidding entry. As I continued down the hall I never nodded to any who passed, but carried on as if I knew exactly where I was going and what I planned to do when I reached my destination.

That confidence, or the good people, or St. Brigid, or magic, or just dumb luck, ensured I did see a lav. I slipped in, and while it was only a toilet with a small sink, mirror above, it gave me a chance to breathe and cool my face and flap my arms like the addled birds rising up from the frying pan in George's drawing of "The Wizard's Omelette." This I did in an effort to dry the ponds beneath. Of course, I could not wait there long enough for any kind of breeze to spring up, no, and so only let myself drift a second as if I'd actually sprouted wings and I could raise him, like we saw in the books at the mission when angels gathered someone up to heaven, but this time it would be a heaven of our own making, us together, and my love for him would speed his healing. He would walk again, and work the cars, and we would have our four children who would not only swim but also play the piano. If you believe something, it has to be so, just on the power of conviction. Mr. R'd said it and the books said it, too. I closed my eyes, and if something slipped inside my heart, like grains of soil at the edge of a ditch, could it a meant my faith was wanting? Was it me, then, the one at fault?

At the end of the hallway, another stairway, and the first room at the top of it small, and sad so, for instead of the usual iron beds were cribs made of the same stuff, children, babies in them, like the little ones I cared for in Florida and came to love. Like the little sisters we'd left behind in Ennis, the youngest, Kathleen, whose face we'd never see. One of the children was standing, his head afire with a full head of frizzy hair, like a halo created by the light behind it, and bawling in a heartbreaking way, but futilely, with no one to comfort. Between his wails, he caught sight of me and he cried even harder, maybe hoping I'd pick him up and didn't I long to, but from there in the corner, fussing over another, came the shh-shh of someone too busy to do all there was to do. While the child continued to mourn his unhappy state, his face wet with tears glistened on his clear brown skin, and two thick trails of white snot escaping his nose, I moved along before the busy one could see me.

Still, it stayed with me, that scene, and it caused me to wonder what satisfaction I might find in nursing. This was later, when it came up again, that wanting to help feeling led me to the job took me out of the city. At that moment, though, it was not nursing I aimed for, not a profession, no, but marriage, and a family, and a life in Chicago maybe not as swell as the folks at the north end of Prairie Avenue, but comfortable all the same. A man with a steady job and a house somewhere in the city, further west on Monroe maybe, or one of the nicer neighborhoods across the river.

Yes, chaos in the ward for children, but no less outside on the ground where bells clanged and loud shouts pierced the open windows three floors up. I could hear feet tramping and hollering. Later it came out that most of them, five hundred or so, injured in the riot'd been colored people. Many injured would a been taken to Provident and could a been dying right around me, suffering anyway, but there had to be one white man here, if the papers were right, and sometimes they were not, I knew, because you saw a box regular, on page two, for corrections. When the governor put out his report about the riot, turned out the papers'd had most of it wrong really, most of them days. Wouldn't you know they downplayed that part, seeing how it was their news being criticized. Just because it'd been there for us all to read, plain as day in black and white, didn't mean it'd been true, those stories. Seems a good part'd come from the imagination of reporters as frightened as the rest of us.

I heard another child also wailing in another small room across the hall, but another ward for children? Could there be so many little ones sick? The door was half shut, but I opened it a bit and stared in and saw the source of the misery, another baby perhaps not sick, but upset for a reason only he knew. Flaxen-haired and cradled by a woman with hair the same, her standing and jiggling and blocking from my sight the person lying in the bed.

Maybe this was the room saved for white folks needed it, so my heart sped again and I licked my lips, and blinked my eyes clear, for if he should be conscious I wanted him to take pleasure from looking at me, and didn't I wish I'd stopped at one of the candy stores downtown and brought a box of fudge to treat him, or something comforting, or a cold drink. But I could run down after I'd stayed awhile, run down to the street when it was safe and find something with the bit of money in the pocketbook I'd clutched tightly through all the city.

It was him. Though a white cotton bandage swathed his head, though his bruised lids covered that memorable green, and his long leg was lifted in a device for holding it steady till it healed, and the bottom of the big foot exposed, though he was not the same charming car man with a grin could liven your day and a patter could boost a smile to a laugh, it was him. The nose a little big, those hands with the long fingers beautiful so, even then, lying on the white sheet, and I was about to rush forward to pick up one of them hands and hold it to my lips when the mother of the crying child turned and saw me.

"Thank goodness," said she. "I thought he was the only one. Why they didn't just take him to Mercy I don't know. It's dangerous. I didn't even feel safe getting here—had to take a cab—let alone walking in. I heard talk of holding some whites hostage, but I couldn't keep away. Where is your husband? Is there a special room for us?"

She moved close to the bed then and took the hand I meant to kiss, and patted it, and said there, there, or some such, and in my ears a tornado was howling, funneling right into my bowels. She's talking about how he got mixed up with a group of thugs on the cars, late on Sunday. Sunday! Didn't do a thing himself, wouldn't, she said, even if he had no great love for all the Negroes moving into all the white neighborhoods and taking over the city. Attacked. Right in his own neighborhood, not six blocks from Wentworth Avenue. Attacked!

"Are you all right?"

"Me?" I whispered it.

"Is he bad, then? Your husband? Are they operating?"

I wanted to tell her he's the same one lying there, still handsome, if powerless, unconscious. But it was never her put him up to his flirting, never her who made him choose me. The child of theirs quiet, curious about the small woman in the big hat like a trembling statue at the foot of his father's bed. Something cold, the deepest violet inside pushing to burst out of me. The tornado that'd tunneled in my ears passed through quickly enough but, instead of clear sky, bruised clouds and a ringing like the after-chime of a struck bell.

"He's gone," I said. And my eyes flooded like they'd done downstairs when I came in so exhausted and someone said a kind word. For sure, he was gone, just as certain as if he died of his wounds, which he did not. I looked in the list of the thirty-eight dead published later in the week and saw no Desmond Malloy. While all the air went out of my hopes there in Provident Hospital, as I stood at the end of the bed where he lay, unconscious still, or perhaps only sleeping to avoid the trouble could rise should he recognize me, people were breathing their last in some other part of the building, and in the other hospitals, too, most at the biggest, Cook County Hospital, which I had not stepped foot in yet, but would, and not for dying.

EPILOGUE

I NEVER MORE SAW the man I'd thought my own on the Madison line when the cars started up again, not on that first Saturday, not any other day. Nor on Halsted where I continued to wander that summer after work, sometimes going into a show by myself, rather than back to Bridey's room and Margaret's talk. She did not pester me long, Margaret. I told her I'd had news about him being hurt in the riot and I didn't know if I'd see him again. When I said the same to Eveline, she assured me I'd find another. "Plenty of fish in the sea," she added, not knowing it would take an act of Congress to get me anywhere near water again, which fear I passed on to my daughter. Sadly. For all she ended up near to his height, with that peak pointed down her lovely forehead, Irene Janet never took to swimming.

I am a small woman, I was always small, and maybe my size made it obvious sooner. Come Thanksgiving I could no longer disguise my condition. I wished Mr. R could wave his wand and reverse time, so instead of the unfortunate woman who apologized with words and the whole beat down position of her body and told him she would be leaving at the end of the week, so instead of that wretched creature it would be the earlier version of Maeve Curragh there standing before him, trembling at the prospect of working in such a grand building where she expected to see all the famous magicians she knew from the vaudeville stages.

Even before that moment Eveline guessed and said to me, not unkindly, "I wish you would a talked to me, like I said. You can do things to stop babies coming. You bog trotters. You never have enough of them. Criminy!"

Mr. R'd seen it all before, and Florence, and Ruth maybe, too. Florence never said much and Ruth only cried and hugged me. Not too close, though, not so she came in contact with my rounding middle. "And you thought he was the one! Poor Maeve." Torn she was between scolding and comforting, because I told them all he'd died—same as I told Margaret, and my Irene, who later told the same to her children. In the eyes of my workmates, that news took the edge off my sin or my recklessness, whatever it was they called it in their minds. Foolish, no matter how you looked at it.

Oh, but I'd wanted him so!

My last day at The Chicago Magic Company, as I got off the car that already dark November evening, knowing the next hurdle to face was going to be Bridey, the newsies were hollering the way that they did.

LIGHTS ALL ASKEW IN THE HEAVENS!

And didn't I look up to see if my predicament'd affected even the stars, but no. It was the first I heard of that Professor Einstein was to become so famous on account of twisting our sense of time. The same Professor Einstein now stares at me from the wall across as I stew here in the juices of the past bubbled up, about to dissolve me.

I was a marked woman. Gladys did not give me up entirely, but I never saw her much. Sure she was busy with Florence, the two of them out looking for clothes, and maybe attending them parties at the aunt's house. Gladys's aunt. I wouldn't a had the outfit for those parties myself, so it was just as well I never went. I didn't blame Gladys for anything, nor Margaret when Harry made her choose between me and him. She pleaded with me to understand. They'd found the flat they wanted and would be married before my child came into the world. So far along I was by then, there'd be no way to disguise my condition. Harry's family would think bad of her, Margaret said, to be the sister of someone did what she was supposed to wait to be married to do. Of course I understood, it being me in the wrong, and all. We suspected Harry would come round after making his stand.

And so it was Eveline saved me. When my time came 'twas Eveline and Mr. Jordan took me to Cook County Hospital and went and fetched Margaret who eventually found Gladys and they were all there to greet us with flowers and a cake, me and little Irene Janet—who was born at midday and better for her, so, because the good people might not meddle with her. When Cook County let me go with her, my daughter, back to my room, Mr. Jordan brought me more of the typing supported us that first year, Irene's first.

Yet, didn't I miss the magic company, and in those hours I sat with my own child at my breast, a proper womanly breast, didn't I daydream of getting back into that business teased your powers of belief, though in my case even Mr. R couldn't bring back what'd been there and then gone again so quickly. Couldn't make what appeared disappear, or the other way round, no matter how elegantly he might flourish his cape and say "Presto!"

I was already practiced in the art of illusion, as hadn't himself been so? The magician of magicians with his power to inspire belief. You can call it lying or dress it up and call it illusion. Irene's never heard of the fellow. She knows her late father, and the children their late grandfather, by the name of Patrick Dwyer, the poor fellow died of influenza, and I made Margaret promise to never say different. Of course the timing's off, but with time itself different than we thought, what does it matter? It may turn out that it's not only time we invent, but people, things. It may be that life itself is an illusion, we almost dead ones at the threshold between two rooms is all, two rooms different only on account of the angle of light pouring in. I will know before long, sure.

Whenever the Bluebird bus took me and Irene to visit Margaret and Harry and their two boys, her cousins, in the city, I always looked in the directory, under M. There were many D. Malloys, and a wild thought occurred to me sometimes. Maybe I'd acted too quick. Accustomed to disappointment, hadn't I somehow looked for every opportunity to find it? Could a been another D. Malloy, after all, and it just the blazing bandage around his head confused me. The woman at the bed'd never said his name—Desmond—the same I'd whispered so breathless the Sunday the riot broke out. Desmond. The first and last time I was in a position to breathe like that at all into a man's ear. Desmond.

AFTERWORD

WHILE EXAMINING OLD newspapers at the Newberry Library in Chicago a number of years ago, I came across a time period—July 21 to July 30, 1919—that astounded me for the size of the headlines on consecutive days. During those ten days in Chicago, a blimp crash in the Loop, a major race riot, a streetcar strike, and a child abduction all competed for top story status. These big events played out against a post-WWI backdrop that mixed the return of soldiers and sailors with the Great Migration of African Americans from southern to northern states, and the urban influx of self-supporting single women living apart from their families.

The Nineteenth Amendment—which gave women the right to vote—had been passed by Congress the previous month, and the Wartime Prohibition Act—which banned the sale of beverages containing more than 2.75% alcohol—took effect on June 30th. Class warfare became deadly when so-called "Bolsheviks" sent bombs to prominent politicians and those investigating "the Red Scare." To round out an incredible summer, the Black Sox Scandal erupted during the World Series—with Chicago White Sox players accused of intentionally losing games.

1919 was also the year when, during a total solar eclipse in May, Sir Arthur Eddington put Einstein's theory of relativity to the test and altered our concept of time.

Just as immigration continues to create tension in Europe and the United States today, the Great Migration of African

Americans from the south to the north caused tensions that erupted in what was called the "Red Summer of 1919"—due to the blood spilled on the streets of twenty-five American cities. Chicago's African American population had increased from 44,000 in 1909, to almost 110,000 in 1919, an increase of about 148 percent. Competition for jobs in the city's stockyards was particularly intense, pitting African Americans against whites (both native born and immigrants). Tensions ran highest on the city's South Side, where the majority of black residents lived, many of them in old, dilapidated housing and without adequate services.

On July 27, 1919, an African American teenager drowned in Lake Michigan after he violated the unofficial segregation of Chicago's beaches, and was stoned by a group of white youths. His death, and the police's refusal to arrest the white man whom eyewitnesses identified as causing it, instigated a week of rioting between gangs of black and white Chicagoans. When the riots finally ended on August 3rd, fifteen whites and twenty-three blacks had been killed, and more than five hundred people injured. One thousand African American families lost their homes when they were torched by rioters. It was the worst of the riots in the United States that year, and the worst in Chicago's history. Much of the mayhem was blamed on white "athletic" clubs, such as the Hamburg Club, of which Chicago's future mayor, Richard J. Daley—then seventeen years old—was a member.

The final death toll for the crash of the *Wingfoot Air Express* was one crew member, two passengers, and ten bank employees. Twenty-seven members of the bank's staff were injured. The bank reopened for business the day after the crash. While seventeen Goodyear Tire & Rubber Company employees—including the blimp's pilot—were arrested after the crash, there were no charges filed and no trial. However, within hours of the crash the Chicago City Council passed a resolution urging the adoption of regulations to control air traffic above the city.

Thomas Fitzgerald, the man who abducted and murdered six-year-old Janet Wilkinson, was convicted and sentenced to death by hanging. He was executed on October 17, 1919 at the Cook County Jail.

The strike by employees of Chicago's elevated and surface lines—which began a day after the race riots had, and involved 15,000 workers—ended after only four days, on August 2nd. Workers in other Chicago industries—stock yards, steel mills, clothing, agricultural equipment, etc.—as well as actors, also went on strike that year.

~

As a former journalist, I was intrigued by the coverage of these events in Chicago's nine general circulation newspapers of the time. My primary newspaper sources were the *Chicago Tribune* and the *Chicago Daily News*, including the latter's fantastic photo collection, held by the Chicago History Museum. I also consulted back issues of the *Chicago Defender*, the *Herald Examiner*, and popular magazines and dime novels of the time, when reading was a major leisure activity, and—just before radio became popular in the 1920's—how people got their news.

As a novelist, I wanted to imagine the lives of people historians rarely bother with. *The Reason for Time* presents the life of an ordinary person who lived through those extraordinary days in Chicago. While Maeve Curragh is a fictional character, she is typical of the young women wage earners who were living on their own in American cities during the first decades of the twentieth century. An Irish immigrant, she works as a clerk at a job that pays poorly, she lives in a boarding house, she takes many of her meals at cheap lunchrooms, and enjoys the city's plethora of theaters—for the then-declining vaudeville shows, and for films. She hopes marriage and children are in her future.

~

The most useful source I found for information about race relations in Chicago in 1919 is the exhaustive study by The Chicago Commission on Race Relations, *The Negro in Chicago; A Study of Race Relations and a Race Riot* (University of Chicago Press, 1922) [https://archive.org/details/negroinchicagost00chic].

Carl Sandburg wrote about the race riots as a reporter for the Chicago Daily News. His articles were later published as a collection, *The Chicago Race Riots, July 1919* [https://archive.org/details/chicagoraceriots00sand].

Readers interested in the condition of single women should consider Joanne J. Meyerowitz's excellent book *Women Adrift: Independent Wage Earners in Chicago, 1880-1930* (University of Chicago Press, 1991).

Those and other non-fiction books, as well as novels of the time—including Studs Lonigan, by James T. Farrell—helped me to fill out my imagined July in Chicago, the year when the notion of time and many other things changed forever...not only for Maeve Curragh.

∼

EDITOR'S NOTE

Gary Krist's non-fiction book *City of Scoundrels: The 12 Days of Disaster That Gave Birth to Modern Chicago* (Crown, 2012) covers the tumultuous days of late July 1919 from a political perspective.

To learn more about Carl Sandburg, please visit: http://www.nps.gov/carl

Acknowledgments

The Reason for Time began as an idea that occurred to me while browsing newspaper microfilm at the Newberry Library in Chicago. The staff of that institution, of the Chicago History Museum, and of the Harold Washington Library always courteously, and sometimes even enthusiastically, answered questions, searched for materials, and showed me the way around equipment. Thanks to all of them. My niece Amanda Brady put me up during the research phase, and I am grateful for her hospitality and her interest in the project. Also to Gwyneth Campbell, for helping me access newspaper files at Northwestern University. Finally, I must most sincerely thank Emily Victorson for her enthusiasm, and her tireless attention to detail.

ALSO PUBLISHED BY ALLIUM PRESS OF CHICAGO

Visit our website for more information:
www.alliumpress.com

Shall We Not Revenge
D. M. Pirrone

In the harsh early winter months of 1872, while Chicago is still smoldering from the Great Fire, Irish Catholic detective Frank Hanley is assigned the case of a murdered Orthodox Jewish rabbi. His investigation proves difficult when the neighborhood's Yiddish-speaking residents are reluctant to talk. But when the rabbi's headstrong daughter, Rivka, offers to help Hanley find her father's killer, the detective receives much more than the break he was looking for. Their pursuit of the truth draws Rivka and Hanley closer together and leads them to a relief organization run by the city's wealthy movers and shakers. Along the way, they uncover a web of political corruption, crooked cops, and well-buried ties to two Irish thugs from Hanley's checkered past. Even after he is kicked off the case Hanley refuses to quit. With a personal vendetta to settle for an innocent life lost, he is determined to expose a complicated criminal scheme, not only for his own sake, but for Rivka's as well.

◆

For You Were Strangers
D. M. Pirrone

On a spring morning in 1872, former Civil War officer Ben Champion is discovered dead in his Chicago bedroom—a bayonet protruding from his back. What starts as a routine case for Detective Frank Hanley soon becomes anything but, as his investigation into Champion's life turns up hidden truths best left buried. Meanwhile, Rivka Kelmansky's long-lost brother, Aaron, arrives on her doorstep, along with his mulatto wife and son. Fugitives from an attack by night riders, Aaron and his family know too much about past actions that still threaten powerful men—defective guns provided to Union soldiers, and an 1864 conspiracy to establish Chicago as the capital of a Northwest Confederacy. Champion had his own connection to that conspiracy, along with ties to a former slave now passing as white and an escaped Confederate guerrilla bent on vengeance, any of which might have led to his death. Hanley and Rivka must untangle this web of circumstances, amid simmering hostilities still present seven years after the end of the Civil War, as they race against time to solve the murder, before the secrets of bygone days claim more victims.

Honor Above All
J. Bard-Collins

Pinkerton agent Garrett Lyons arrives in Chicago in 1882, close on the trail of the person who murdered his partner. He encounters a vibrant city that is striving ever upwards, full of plans to construct new buildings that will "scrape the sky." In his quest for the truth Garrett stumbles across a complex plot involving counterfeit government bonds, fierce architectural competition, and painful reminders of his military past. Along the way he seeks the support and companionship of his friends—elegant Charlotte, who runs an upscale poker game for the city's elite, and up-and-coming architect Louis Sullivan. Rich with historical details that bring early 1880s Chicago to life, this novel will appeal equally to mystery fans, history buffs, and architecture enthusiasts.

◆

Beautiful Dreamer
Joan Naper

Chicago in 1900 is bursting with opportunity, and Kitty Coakley is determined to make the most of it. The youngest of seven children born to Irish immigrants, she has little interest in becoming simply a housewife. Inspired by her entrepreneurial Aunt Mabel, who runs a millinery boutique at Marshall Field's, Kitty aspires to become an independent, modern woman. After her music teacher dashes her hopes of becoming a professional singer, she refuses to give up her dreams of a career. But when she is courted by not one, but two young men, her resolve is tested. Irish-Catholic Brian is familiar and has the approval of her traditional, working-class family. But wealthy, Protestant Henry, who is a young architect in Daniel Burnham's office, provides an entrée for Kitty into another, more exciting world. Will she sacrifice her ambitions and choose a life with one of these men?

Company Orders
David J. Walker

Even a good man may feel driven to sign on with the devil. Paul Clark is a Catholic priest who's been on the fast track to becoming a bishop. But he suddenly faces a heart-wrenching problem, when choices he made as a young man come roaring back into his life. A mysterious woman, who claims to be with "an agency of the federal government," offers to solve his problem. But there's a price to pay—Father Clark must undertake some very un-priestly actions. An attack in a Chicago alley…a daring escape from a Mexican jail…and a fight to the death in a Guyanese jungle…all these, and more, must be survived in order to protect someone he loves. This priest is about to learn how much easier it is to preach love than to live it.

◆

Her Mother's Secret
Barbara Garland Polikoff

Fifteen-year-old Sarah, the daughter of Jewish immigrants, wants nothing more than to become an artist. But as she spreads her wings she must come to terms with the secrets that her family is only beginning to share with her. Replete with historical details that vividly evoke the Chicago of the 1890s, this moving coming-of-age story is set against the backdrop of a vibrant, turbulent city. Sarah moves between two very different worlds—the colorful immigrant neighborhood surrounding Hull House and the sophisticated, elegant World's Columbian Exposition. This novel eloquently captures the struggles of a young girl as she experiences the timeless emotions of friendship, family turmoil, loss…and first love.

A companion guide to *Her Mother's Secret*
is available at www.alliumpress.com. In the guide you will find photographs of places mentioned in the novel, along with discussion questions, a list of read-alikes, and resources for further exploration of Sarah's time and place.

Set the Night on Fire
Libby Fischer Hellmann

Someone is trying to kill Lila Hilliard. During the Christmas holidays she returns from running errands to find her family home in flames, her father and brother trapped inside. Later, she is attacked by a mysterious man on a motorcycle. . . and the threats don't end there. As Lila desperately tries to piece together who is after her and why, she uncovers information about her father's past in Chicago during the volatile days of the late 1960s . . . information he never shared with her, but now threatens to destroy her. Part thriller, part historical novel, and part love story, *Set the Night on Fire* paints an unforgettable portrait of Chicago during a turbulent time: the riots at the Democratic Convention . . . the struggle for power between the Black Panthers and SDS . . . and a group of young idealists who tried to change the world.

◆

A Bitter Veil
Libby Fischer Hellmann

It all began with a line of Persian poetry . . . Anna and Nouri, both studying in Chicago, fall in love despite their very different backgrounds. Anna, who has never been close to her parents, is more than happy to return with Nouri to his native Iran, to be embraced by his wealthy family. Beginning their married life together in 1978, their world is abruptly turned upside down by the overthrow of the Shah and the rise of the Islamic Republic. Under the Ayatollah Khomeini and the Republican Guard, life becomes increasingly restricted and Anna must learn to exist in a transformed world, where none of the familiar Western rules apply. Random arrests and torture become the norm, women are required to wear hijab, and Anna discovers that she is no longer free to leave the country. As events reach a fevered pitch, Anna realizes that nothing is as she thought, and no one can be trusted... not even her husband.

THE EMILY CABOT MYSTERIES
Frances McNamara

Death at the Fair

The 1893 World's Columbian Exposition provides a vibrant backdrop for the first book in the series. Emily Cabot, one of the first women graduate students at the University of Chicago, is eager to prove herself in the emerging field of sociology. While she is busy exploring the Exposition with her family and friends, her colleague, Dr. Stephen Chapman, is accused of murder. Emily sets out to search for the truth behind the crime, but is thwarted by the gamblers, thieves, and corrupt politicians who are ever-present in Chicago. A lynching that occurred in the dead man's past leads Emily to seek the assistance of the black activist Ida B. Wells.

◆

Death at Hull House

After Emily Cabot is expelled from the University of Chicago, she finds work at Hull House, the famous settlement established by Jane Addams. There she quickly becomes involved in the political and social problems of the immigrant community. But, when a man who works for a sweatshop owner is murdered in the Hull House parlor, Emily must determine whether one of her colleagues is responsible, or whether the real reason for the murder is revenge for a past tragedy in her own family. As a smallpox epidemic spreads through the impoverished west side of Chicago, the very existence of the settlement is threatened and Emily finds herself in jeopardy from both the deadly disease and a killer.

Death at Pullman

A model town at war with itself . . . George Pullman created an ideal community for his railroad car workers, complete with every amenity they could want or need. But when hard economic times hit in 1894, lay-offs follow and the workers can no longer pay their rent or buy food at the company store. Starving and desperate, they turn against their once benevolent employer. Emily Cabot and her friend Dr. Stephen Chapman bring much needed food and medical supplies to the town, hoping they can meet the immediate needs of the workers and keep them from resorting to violence. But when one young worker—suspected of being a spy—is murdered, and a bomb plot comes to light, Emily must race to discover the truth behind a tangled web of family and company alliances.

◆

Death at Woods Hole

Exhausted after the tumult of the Pullman Strike of 1894, Emily Cabot is looking forward to a restful summer visit to Cape Cod. She has plans to collect "beasties" for the Marine Biological Laboratory, alongside other visiting scientists from the University of Chicago. She also hopes to enjoy romantic clambakes with Dr. Stephen Chapman, although they must keep an important secret from their friends. But her summer takes a dramatic turn when she finds a dead man floating in a fish tank. In order to solve his murder she must first deal with dueling scientists, a testy local sheriff, the theft of a fortune, and uncooperative weather.

◆

Death at Chinatown

In the summer of 1896, amateur sleuth Emily Cabot meets two young Chinese women who have recently received medical degrees. She is inspired to make an important decision about her own life when she learns about the difficult choices they have made in order to pursue their careers. When one of the women is accused of poisoning a Chinese herbalist, Emily once again finds herself in the midst of a murder investigation. But, before the case can be solved, she must first settle a serious quarrel with her husband, help quell a political uprising, and overcome threats against her family. Timeless issues, such as restrictions on immigration, the conflict between Western and Eastern medicine, and women's struggle to balance family and work, are woven seamlessly throughout this mystery set in Chicago's original Chinatown.

Bright and Yellow, Hard and Cold
Tim Chapman

The search for elusive goals consumes three men...

McKinney, a forensic scientist, struggles with his deep, personal need to find the truth behind the evidence he investigates, even while the system shuts him out. Can he get justice for a wrongfully accused man while juggling life with a new girlfriend and a precocious teenage daughter?

Delroy gives up the hard-scrabble life on his family's Kentucky farm and ventures to the rough-and-tumble world of 1930s Chicago. Unable to find work, he reluctantly throws his hat in with the bank-robbing gangsters Alvin Karpis and Freddie Barker. Can he provide for his fiery young wife without risking his own life?

Gilbert is obsessed with the search for a cache of gold, hidden for nearly eighty years. As his hunt escalates he finds himself willing to use ever more extreme measures to attain his goal...including kidnapping, torture, and murder. Can he find the one person still left who will lead him to the glittering treasure? And will the trail of corpses he leaves behind include McKinney?

Part contemporary thriller, part historical novel, and part love story, *Bright and Yellow, Hard and Cold* masterfully weaves a tale of conflicted scientific ethics, economic hardship, and criminal frenzy, tempered with the redemption of family love.